PENGUIN CANADA

THE WORD FOR HOME

Joan Clark is the author of many other books for children, including *Wild Man of the Woods*, *The Hand of Robin Squires* and *The Moons of Madeleine*. Her last novel for children, *The Dream Carvers*, won the 1995 Geoffrey Bilson Award for Historical Fiction for Young People, the 1995 Mr. Christie's Book Award and the 1996 Hibernia Book Award, and was shortlisted for the Ann Connor Brimer Award. In 1999 she was the recipient of the Vicky Metcalf Award for Children's Literature. Her fiction for adults includes *The Victory of Geraldine Gull*, *Eiriksdottir* and *Latitudes of Melt*. Born and raised in the Maritimes, she lived in western Canada before settling seventeen years ago in St. John's, Newfoundland, the setting of this novel.

The
Word for
Home

For Joy
a story of sisters
in downtown
St. Johns.

Joan Clark

Joan C.

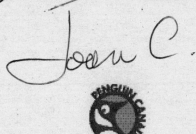

PENGUIN CANADA

Published by the Penguin Group

Penguin Books, a division of Pearson Canada, 10 Alcorn Avenue, Toronto, Ontario,
Canada M4V 3B2

Penguin Books Ltd, 80 Strand, London WC2R 0RL, England

Penguin Putnam Inc., 375 Hudson Street, New York, New York 10014, U.S.A.

Penguin Books Australia Ltd, 250 Camberwell Road, Camberwell, Victoria 3124, Australia

Penguin Books India (P) Ltd, 11, Community Centre, Panchsheel Park,
New Delhi – 110 017, India

Penguin Books (NZ) Ltd, cnr Rosedale and Airborne Roads, Albany, Auckland 1310,
New Zealand

Penguin Books (South Africa) (Pty) Ltd, 24 Sturdee Avenue, Rosebank 2196, South Africa

Penguin Books Ltd, Registered Offices: 80 Strand, London WC2R 0RL, England

First published in Viking by Penguin Books Canada Limited, 2002
Published in Penguin Canada, a division of Pearson Canada, 2003

1 3 5 7 9 10 8 6 4 2

Copyright © Joan Clark , 2002

Manufactured in Canada.

NATIONAL LIBRARY OF CANADA CATALOGUING IN PUBLICATION DATA

Clark, Joan, 1934–
The word for home / Joan Clark.

ISBN 0-14-100502-5

I. Title.

PS8555.L37W67   2003   jC813'.54   C2002-904496-0
PZ7.C5477Wo 2003

Visit Penguin Books' website at **www.penguin.ca**

for
Emma, Hanna & Emily

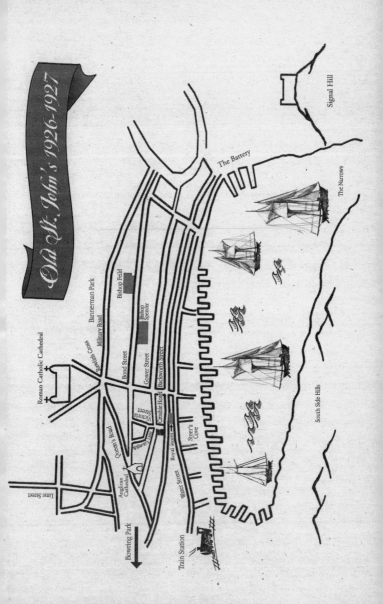

Old St. John's 1926-1927

Signal Hill

The Narrows

The Battery

Roman Catholic Cathedral

Bannerman Park

Bishop Field

Rawlins Cross

Military Road

Bishop Spencer

Bond Street

Gower Street

Buckworth Street

Queen's Road

Victoria Street

Anglican Cathedral

William's Lane

Constable Hotel

Steer's Cove

Royal Stores

Water Street

Lime Street

Bowring Park

Train Station

South Side Hills

The
Word for
Home

*T*HE FIRST TIME SADIE MORIN WAS AWAKENED BY THE SCRAPE of her landlady's key was in early October when she was in bed with her little sister, Flora. The bed had a rickety iron frame with an ancient spring that groaned if either of them moved a fraction of an inch. Sadie felt a mattress button digging into her hip but she didn't dare move. If she moved, her sharp-eared landlady, Mrs. Hatch, would hear and Sadie didn't want to give herself away, to alert her to the possibility that she might be listening. She heard the key turning in the lock of the mystery room door across the hall. Sadie thought of it as the mystery room because a month ago, soon after she and Flora began boarding with Mrs. Hatch, she told them that the room across from theirs was out of bounds and that under no circumstances were they to go inside. As if they could—Sadie had tried the door handle several times but it was always locked.

Now Mrs. Hatch was opening the door and closing it behind her. Odd that she should be going into the room so early in the morning. What time was it anyway? Sadie lifted her head and looked at the clock ticking on the dresser, but it was too dark to read the time. Judging by the greyish light seeping beneath the blind, she thought it might be six o'clock, maybe six-thirty. What was Mrs. Hatch doing inside the room at this time of day? Was there someone inside? If there was, wouldn't Sadie hear the person moving? Wouldn't she hear Mrs. Hatch and the person talking? But she heard nothing, not even the whisper of a voice or the creaking of a floorboard. With the absence of sound, Sadie's alertness waned and soon she felt herself drifting away from wakefulness toward the dozy world of sleep.

1

Willicott's Lane

WHEN SADIE WOKE AGAIN IT WAS TO THE CLUNKY sound of their landlady shovelling coal from the scuttle into the kitchen stove directly below the bedroom. There was a grate on the floor through which air from the stove was supposed to heat the bedroom but it took forever—this was in 1926, before most householders in St. John's could rely on furnaces for heat. If only she could stay in bed for another half hour, the room would be warm enough for her to dress without shivering. Sadie shifted her hip from the mattress button, the springs complaining beneath her weight, and looked at her little sister, who was curled on her side, thumb jammed into her mouth, the other hand clutching the blanket edge—her habit was to hold the blanket against her nose while she sucked her thumb. Though Flora was eight years old, Sadie thought of her as a baby, a sweet-faced baby with round cheeks and rounder eyes. When they were open, Flora's eyes were bright blue, a Dutch blue, their mother used to say. Before their

1

mother died in Ontario a year and a half ago, Sadie and Flora had slept in twin beds, but after her death they had begun sleeping in the same bed, facing each other, their arms entwined until they fell asleep, after which they moved away, into their own dreaming spaces.

Warily Sadie swept a hand across Flora's side of the bed. Good, it was dry. Wetting the bed was another change that had taken place since their mother's death. Not every night, just sometimes. Relieved, Sadie shifted to her other side so she could look at the time—it was now light enough to see the clock face with its mechanical robin marking each second by tugging on a worm. Her mother had given her the clock two years ago on Sadie's twelfth birthday. It was seven-thirty, which meant there was no lying in. In fact Mrs. Hatch was already coming up the stairs. Sadie waited her out, counting the creakings of wood: ten, eleven, twelve . . .

"Girls!" Their landlady's voice was like the screech of chalk being dragged across the blackboard. "Get up, girls!" She'd say it again if Sadie didn't reply, "We're getting up!" One good thing about Mrs. Hatch—and there didn't seem much that was—was that she didn't come into their bedroom if it could be avoided, preferring to shout through the door.

"Time to get up, Flora." Sadie reached over and kissed her sister's forehead, the way their mother used to when she came into their bedroom to wake them for school. Flora mumbled something in the scrambled language of sleep, and Sadie swung her legs off the mattress and, sitting up, groped for her slipper socks, pulling them on before standing on the cold linoleum floor. She put on her plaid flannel bathrobe, picked up her facecloth, towel, soap, toothbrush and powder, none of which, their landlady insisted, could be left in the bathroom as they would in a home, and padded downstairs. Passing through the kitchen on her way to the bathroom beside the back door, she said "good morning" to Mrs. Hatch, who was stirring their breakfast on the stove, her hair still tied in torn cotton rags. There couldn't possibly be anyone inside the mystery room, Sadie thought grumpily, because if there was, their landlady would frighten them to death. "I suppose it is," Mrs. Hatch conceded and continued stirring the potage that Sadie was convinced only a fairytale witch would expect them to eat. Sadie had used the word "potage" in one of her letters to her father. She had hunted up its meaning in the school dictionary after the headmistress at school had used it in class. It meant "mess," which was the right word to use to describe the porridge Mrs. Hatch expected them to eat.

When she and Flora were in their school uniforms: navy blue dresses with detachable white collars and cuffs, and were seated opposite each other at the kitchen table, Mrs. Hatch plunked two bowls of porridge on the mustard-coloured oilcloth.

"Here you are," she said grandly as if she was presenting them with a feast. She took a bottle from the icebox and poured them each a tepid glass of milk. The first week they began boarding with Mrs. Hatch, there had been a pitcher of milk and a bowl of brown sugar on the table in addition to the glasses of milk. The second week the pitcher disappeared, and the third week, the brown sugar. They hadn't had sugar on their potage for two whole weeks. The milk was slightly sour, but stirred into the porridge, it was just possible to force the potage down.

Flora picked up her spoon and poked holes in the porridge before adding the milk, stopping to watch the way it bubbled in the holes. She put her elbows on the table and, holding her head between her hands, said, "If only we could have sugar."

Mrs. Hatch was at the stove pouring herself a cup of tea. She never sat with them at the table the way a normal family would for meals; instead she ate by herself, usually before they did. "There'll be be no more sugar," she said. "Sugar is a luxury you can live without. If I gave you girls whatever you wanted, you would eat me out of house and home."

We wouldn't, Flora mouthed between her hands as Mrs. Hatch picked up her tea and carried it through the doorway separating the kitchen from the front room where the cheap floral curtain had been rolled around the rod to allow the warm kitchen air to pass through. Their landlady's black laced shoes were the last part of her to disappear through the doorway.

Mrs. Hatch had a small pointed head that she swung in front of her as she walked, as if she was testing the air. She reminded Sadie of a ferret she had seen three years ago tied to a lamppost in front of Polanski's General Store in Copper Cliff where Sadie had gone to buy a pound of lard for her mother's pie crust. The ferret had a rope harness tied around its middle that allowed it to raise the upper part of its body. When Sadie passed the ferret, it lifted its head and thrust its nose in her direction, as if it couldn't see very well and had to locate her scent. After she had made her purchase and was outside on the wooden step, she saw the ferret's owner untying it from the post. He was a prospector with a bird's nest beard and a backpack to which he had tied a tin cup, frying pan, pot and plate that clinked together when he moved. He gave Sadie a foolish scarecrow grin and, lifting his hat, wandered down the dusty street holding his pet on its rope leash, the ferret swinging its head back and forth as it moved.

After Sadie finished eating, she carried her bowl and glass to the sink and washed them in the basin of soapy water left for that purpose. The porridge felt like a gluey lump stuck partway down her stomach, which was not the way her father would describe it. "It sticks to your ribs," he would likely say, meaning that by eating porridge she wouldn't feel hungry until noon.

"Sadie," Flora said in a small, plaintive voice. She was still playing with her spoon. Sadie knew what was coming. Her little sister wanted her to throw her porridge into the garbage but that wasn't a smart thing to do because their landlady would find it and a lecture would follow. Sadie leaned toward her sister's ear and hissed, "Eat it!" Then in a louder voice intended to reach Mrs. Hatch's ears, she said, "I'll go upstairs and make the bed. We have ten minutes before we leave for school."

By the time Flora finished eating, Sadie was waiting for her at the back door with their bookbags. "We're leaving," she called to Mrs. Hatch as she and Flora stepped onto Willicott's Lane, a wide path that ran at right angles between Gower Street and Victoria Street and was flanked on one side by the back brick wall of the Masonic Temple, and on the remaining sides by tiny back gardens, most of them overgrown. Sadie waited for Flora to run through the Collinses' garden and knock on their back door, a signal that they were waiting for Peggy. Within minutes a small dark-haired girl Flora's age appeared. Peggy was in Flora's class in school and though they had met only after the Morins had moved to Willicott's Lane, they had already pledged themselves friends forever.

Sadie's friend Teddy Dodge was waiting for her at the bottom of the lane on Victoria Street. They had met a month ago when she, Flora and their father were staying at the Crosbie Hotel where Teddy's parents worked, his father as assistant manager and his mother as the supervisor of the housekeeping staff. The Morins had stayed at the hotel until a boardinghouse and school could be found for Sadie and Flora. The sisters attended Bishop Spencer College, a girls' school; Teddy attended Bishop Feild, a boys' school that was a stone's throw away from Spencer. As usual Teddy's books were balanced against his hip and his glasses were partway down his nose. Two years older than Sadie, he had adopted a custodial manner toward her, as if she needed looking after, when it seemed to her that he was the one in need of being looked after, at least in the manner of his uniform, which was usually rumpled and not always clean. This morning, for example, there was a yellow spot, possibly egg, on his tie and his jacket looked as if it had been slept in. Though he had only been living in St. John's for four years, Teddy knew the city well and was friendly with most of the people he and Sadie regularly saw on their way to school. Whenever the milk wagon passed them on Gower Street, as it did the same time every morning, Teddy waved to the driver and shouted, "Good Morning, Mr. Walsh!" and Mr. Walsh doffed his cloth cap and returned the greeting.

And just now when they passed the ice man standing at the rear of his wagon wiping sawdust from a block of ice before carrying it into the house where a woman waited in the doorway, Teddy shouted, "Good morning, Sir Dicky!"

Immediately the elfin man in the knitted cap and sweater shot back, "Good morning, Sir Teddy!"

Sadie heard the Irish lilt in his voice and smiled, pleased at the reminder of Ireland.

Sir Dicky didn't look big or sturdy enough to carry a huge block of ice, but as they watched, he slid a canvas sack over a glistening chunk and hoisted it onto his shoulder, holding it steady with his hands as he staggered toward the doorway and on into the house, one of a row that ran the length of the street. In this part of St. John's all the houses were joined together, but each was different in some way: a few had dormer windows or bell-shaped roofs and no two were painted exactly the same. Whatever the colour: dark grey, green, blue or wine, the trim was always dusted with black from coal fires whose acrid smell hung in the damp morning air.

"I hope Sir Dicky stops in Willicott's Lane," Sadie said. "The ice box is empty and the milk has gone off." She stood to one side while a woman in a black skirt and shawl hurried past, her gaze preoccupied, downcast. Except for the delivery wagons and children making their way to school, the street was empty, most people having left for work half an hour ago.

"Heard anything more from your father?" Teddy asked.

"Only the letter from Badger." Badger was the place where Sadie's father had got off the train; from there he and another geologist, Gutsy Pike, had to hike to Buchans, a mining camp in the interior of Newfoundland.

"I'm sure you will one of these days," Teddy said kindly.

Sadie said nothing. She didn't want to start the day worrying about her father—once she started worrying, it was hard to stop. In any case, a letter from him would surely arrive this week.

She and Teddy parted company at the corner of Gower and Prescott streets because Teddy's school was on the opposite side of the street from Sadie's, not far from the Bull's Eye Shop, which sold candy, taffy apples and bread. Teddy crossed the street and Sadie walked toward her little sister who was waiting on the school steps—they usually entered the school together.

"Hello, Sadie."

Sadie turned and saw Nelly Goodyear smiling at her. Beside her was Eunice Baird, a tall rangy girl with dark brooding eyes. Both girls were in Sadie's grade-ten class.

"Hello," Sadie said. As soon as she stopped to talk to Nelly, Eunice moved away. She did this every time Sadie came within

arm's reach of her. Did she think Sadie had something conta-
gious like lice? She'd had lice once in Copper Cliff. To get rid of
them, her mother had cut her hair and, after smearing her head
with a vile-smelling tarry substance, banished her outdoors.

Nelly pretended not to notice Eunice's rudeness and Sadie was
too proud to ask her to explain it. Nelly might not tell her
anyway—she was someone who wanted to be on the good side
of everybody. Sadie knew this from watching her at school. A
blonde pudgy girl with a dimpled smile, during recess she went
from one person to another, laughing and talking, never stopping
for long, spreading her friendship as far as it could go. Eunice, on
the other hand, stalked around the classroom and the corridors
alone; even when she was with other girls, she walked ahead or off
to one side as if she couldn't be hemmed in. She was a tiger inside
a cage, not really seeing people on the other side of the bars.

A grade-eleven school prefect came outside and began
ringing a bell twice the size of a cow bell, swinging it back and
forth in a wide arc. Sadie herded Flora and Peggy inside and
downstairs, where they hung their coats in the corridor, each of
them having been assigned a hook with a wooden box directly
below, on the floor. Millie, Sadie's best friend—so far her only
friend at school—was waiting for her. Millie's real name was
Jane Miller but no one except the teachers called her that.
Millie had already hung up her jacket and was holding her
books close to her chest—she didn't own a bookbag. Sadie
straightened her collar and cuffs, which always went askew
when she took off her jacket. Before she could pick up her
bookbag, Eunice came out of the washroom and strode along
the corridor at a furious clip, her shoulder jolting Sadie aside.
Eunice must have known she had bumped her—she might
even have done it on purpose because she didn't say, "Oops!"
or "I'm sorry." She said nothing at all.

"Townies!" Millie spat out. "They thinks they's better than the rest of us. They don't need manners."

"Is that because they live in St. John's?" Sadie knew townies lived in the city and bay girls lived in fishing outports. Millie herself was from an outport called Heart's Content.

'Yes, and Eunice is the worst of the crowd because her father's a fish merchant."

"Oh," Sadie said.

"They owns everything," Millie explained.

"I guess that means they can do whatever they want," Sadie said, and picking up her bookbag looked around for Flora, but her little sister had already gone upstairs.

2

Bishop Spencer

A FEW MINUTES LATER, SADIE WAS UPSTAIRS HERSELF, standing beside Millie for morning assembly in the high-ceilinged gym. The girls had finished singing "To Him That Overcometh" and were now listening to Spoony's announcements—although Sadie was a new girl at Bishop Spencer, she already thought of the headmistress as Spoony. Commanding the centre of the stage, Miss Witherspoon warned the girls that they could expect a fire drill at any time during the week and reminded them that all contributions for the school sale on Wednesday were to be brought to the school by Tuesday afternoon for ticketing. Spoony then held up a white cuff, dangling it at the end of a majestic arm so that the girls could see what it was.

"Unless I am mistaken," she said, "this cuff belongs to one of our elementary students."

It was Flora's cuff, Sadie was sure of it.

"I am issuing a stern warning to all you girls that from now on any deviation from the Spencer dress code will result in a conduct mark. School has been underway a month. Even those of you unaccustomed to wearing a school uniform have had ample time to adjust to wearing ours. We must honour our traditions."

Spoony shook the cuff distastefully, as if it were contaminated by disease. "Let this be a warning to you all," she said and left the stage. A giant of a woman whose cane might have been a sceptre, she moved like a queen followed by her handmaidens—six school mistresses who had been sitting in a row behind her as she spoke.

As the elementary girls left the assembly in pairs, Sadie looked at her sister's uniform to see if she was the one with the missing cuff. Sure enough, Flora was holding one hand over the wrist where the cuff should have been. Sadie chided herself for not remembering to check Flora's uniform before she came upstairs.

Sadie and Millie left the gym and went straight to their grade-ten room for their first class, which was poetry with Spoony.

"Here goes nothing!" Millie muttered, slouching into the seat behind Sadie. Millie hated poetry and claimed that she wouldn't understand it if God himself was the teacher.

Spoony limped into the classroom carrying a book. Though the headmistress seemed not to care what she wore—today it was a tweed skirt, plain white blouse and scuffed oxfords—her dowdy appearance did not diminish her presence. Size gave her authority. The headmistress was not only taller than most women but broad in shoulder and hip. She had a man's way of seeming to occupy most of the available space. That is, most men except Sadie's father. Russ Morin was a spindly-legged, narrow-chested man who moved like a dancer, never occupying a solid block of space for long, instead searching for openings he could easily duck through.

In September, when the Morins visited the school, Sadie's father had been uncertain, even timid in the presence of Miss Witherspoon, whom he later described as a daunting, formidable woman, as if he meant to explain why he hadn't stood up to her when she'd insisted that Sadie and Flora repeat their grades. During their meeting in the headmistress's second-floor office, Miss Witherspoon had sat behind her desk, a circle of sunlit dust motes crowning her sandy-coloured hair while Sadie, Flora and their father sat on the shadowed side of the room.

"Judging from their report cards, your daughters appear to be good students," she had said in her clipped British voice. "Nevertheless, if they wish to attend Bishop Spencer they will be required to repeat their grades."

Sadie remembered her father sitting with his hat on his knee, one hand cupping an elbow, the other fingering his mustache, which he did when he was ill at ease, "Why should that be? As you say, my daughters are good students."

Miss Witherspoon leaned back in her chair and said, "Ah but you see, they did not attend a British school."

Her father ran his fingers through his wren-coloured hair and shook his head disbelievingly. "That may be but except for the province of Quebec, all Canadian schools are British in their way."

"May I remind you, Mr. Morin, that you are not in Canada but in Newfoundland."

"I am aware of that." Sadie's father spoke sharply, which was unusual for him.

Sadie remembered Miss Witherspoon's chest rising, like a large bird puffing itself up. "Mr. Morin, Bishop Spencer is unquestionably the best school in Newfoundland for Protestant girls and there is no possibility of your daughters attending it unless they repeat their grades. If you cannot agree to that, might I suggest that you look for another school."

Russ Morin looked at Sadie. "Are you prepared to repeat a grade?"

"I have never failed a grade," Sadie said.

"It is not a question of failure," Miss Witherspoon said imperiously. "It is the sorry state of Canadian educational standards that is found wanting, not anything you girls have failed to do. You are now living in another country and must adjust accordingly. In Newfoundland we do things the British way." The headmistress pinned Sadie with one of her intense, probing stares. "Will you accede to our conditions?"

Sadie looked at Miss Witherspoon, and then at her father, knowing that he was leaving the decision entirely up to her. She was angry at him for abandoning her when she most needed his support. But it was typical of him—ever since her mother's death, he had been leaving more of the difficult decisions to her.

She sat there trying to decide, but how could she when she'd only arrived in St. John's a few days ago and knew nothing of the schools? Though there were other Church of England schools in the city that she and Flora might be able to attend, there was no time to consider them, because within the week their father would be leaving the city to work in Buchans. He needed to have Flora and her settled before he left. Why had he dragged them to a place that didn't recognize the schooling they had already accomplished? Sadie sat in the corner biting her lip, knowing that as the older sister she had to give in to something that was unfair. Neither Flora nor her father looked at her—Flora was looking at her feet and her father was looking at his hat. The only one looking at Sadie was the headmistress, who sat with her head cocked, fingers interlaced beneath her chest, her eyes appraising Sadie. When she couldn't bear one more second of appraisal, Sadie reluctantly agreed to repeat a grade.

Creases appeared on either side of the headmistress's mouth, which might have meant she was smiling.

Sadie's father patted her arm and said, "You've made the right decision. Your mother would want you and Flora to have the best education possible."

"I am sure she would," the headmistress said. "This is a well-run school. Our rules are strict but every rule has a reason. Although we demand decorum and respect from our girls, Bishop Spencer is a happy school." She looked at Sadie and Flora. "I am confident that in due course each of you will find her proper place."

Now the headmistress opened her book and advised the grade-ten girls to prepare themselves for a reading of Part 3 of "The Rime of the Ancient Mariner." They were to sit quietly with their hands clasped on their desks in order to avoid the temptation of picking up paper and pencil, which, Spoony said, would impede their ability to listen. They were to concentrate on the poem, remembering that in Parts 1 and 2, which they had been studying the past few weeks, an old, seafaring man was telling a long tale about his ship being driven to the South Pole, a place of ice and snow where nothing lived except an albatross, a large bird believed to be an omen of good. Inexplicably, the mariner had slain the albatross, after which it became a weight of grief and guilt upon his shoulders. Thus burdened, Spoony explained, the mariner's ship was driven into the Pacific Ocean where the sea was becalmed and the ship was "as idle as a painted ship upon a painted ocean." Sadie remembered the line from their previous reading. She could see the ship stuck where it was, motionless, of no more use than a scrap of paper stuck to a floor.

> There passed an early time. Each throat
> Was parched, and glazed each eye.
> A weary time! a weary time!
> How glazed each weary eye,
> When, looking westward, I beheld
> A something in the sky.

Spoony's voice boomed toward Sadie, pulling her into the riptide of words. The "something in the sky" was a fearsome phantom ship aboard which was a Spector-Woman and her deathmate.

> Her lips were red, her looks were free,
> Her locks were yellow as gold:
> Her skin was as white as leprosy,
> The Nightmare Life-in-Death was she,
> Who thicks man's blood with cold.

Sadie's concentration left the poem and veered backwards, toward her mother.

～

When Mary Morin died, her face had been white, her eyelids purple. But her lips hadn't been red or her hair gold. In death her mother's lips had been a mottled blue and her hair a coppery red. Sadie's breath stopped as it always did when she saw the picture of her mother stretched out on the bed. Breathe, she told herself. Breathe. She took a deep breath and reminded herself that she had not actually seen her mother's dead face. She had been in school when her mother died, and by the time she got home a sheet had been drawn over the body. Sadie hadn't had the courage to ask that it be pulled back; her mother had been buried inside a closed coffin without her ever asking. Now she thought she should have asked. If she had seen her mother's face, maybe she wouldn't be imagining it now. Please God, may she not lose her breath now, not in a classroom of strange girls, beneath Spoony's searchlight stare.

> The Sun's rim dips; the stars rush out;
> At one stride comes the dark;
> With far-heard whisper, o'er the sea,
> Off shot the specter-bark.

Spoony's words rolled over Sadie like a wave, flattening, calming. The moment of panic passed and she concentrated on the poem. She was caught up in pictures of a star-dogged moon, dew dripping from sails, the souls of sailors whizzing by.

Abruptly Spoony stopped her recitation and directed Millie to explain the meaning of "specter-bark." Sadie knew that during the reading her friend had been hiding behind her, hoping to avoid one of Spoony's questions. She heard Millie lurch to her feet and clear her throat.

"I don't know, Miss."

"Miss Witherspoon."

"I don't know, Miss Witherspoon."

"Do you know the meaning of bark?"

"Bark grows on a tree, Miss Witherspoon. I has a small canoe my brother made from me birchbark. I uses it to store my pencils." For Millie this was a brave speech.

The surface of class decorum was broken by nervous titters and giggles, and from Eunice, a derisive snort. If Millie had been sitting in front instead of behind her, Sadie might have been able to whisper the answer to Spoony's question without being detected. As it was, all she could do was wait for the inevitable, humiliating dressing-down.

"I would have thought that a fisherman's daughter would have known the meaning of bark. One of the reasons I chose to study "The Ancient Mariner" was because it is in its way a seafaring poem. Furthermore, Jane, you *have* a birchbark canoe that you *use* for storing your pencils." Spoony looked around the room. "Can someone explain the meaning of bark as it is used in the poem?"

Eunice's hand shot up.

"Yes?"

Eunice stood beside her desk. "A bark is a boat, Miss Witherspoon. A 'specter-bark' is an imaginary boat."

Creases bracketed the headmistress's mouth as she said, "Strictly speaking, a bark is a small sailing ship, but a boat will suffice as a definition. Thank you, Eunice, you may sit down." Without so much as a glance toward Millie, the headmistress told her to sit down.

At dinner time, after the bell rang and the canon boomed the noon hour from Signal Hill, Sadie collected Flora, the negligent cuff restored to her wrist, and the sisters walked Millie as far as Rawlin's Cross. The route was out of their way but after Spoony's going over, Sadie didn't want her friend walking alone. Sometimes Millie walked with Gert, another bay girl who boarded at Spencer Lodge, but today there was no sign of Gert. The detour added ten minutes to Sadie and Flora's usual walk to Willicott's Lane but neither of them minded. They were in no hurry to see their landlady or to eat one of her awful dinners.

"You're late," Mrs. Hatch said after they had left their shoes on the mat at the back door. The sisters had not only expected to be greeted in this way but had defiantly willed it, knowing that their walk to Rawlin's Cross would bring out their landlady's finickiness about them being late. Neither of them offered an explanation but went to the sink and dipped their hands into a basin of warm water—Mrs. Hatch discouraged washing hands under the tap, claiming that running water was wasteful.

"Your dinners are in the oven," she said and went into the sitting room, leaving Sadie to put the food on the table. Today's dinner was boiled potatoes, mashed turnip, fried sausage and a glass of water. They ate their dinner in silence, listening to the sound of Mrs. Hatch's knitting needles, knowing that there was no point in talking since every word was overheard. Even a whisper brought a "Speak up girls! Speak up!" from the front room.

Flora swung her legs back and forth as she ate, while Sadie stared out the window. This was her favourite view in the house. Now that the giant oak tree had lost some of its leaves, the window allowed her a glimpse of Signal Hill and the Narrows where the harbour opened to the sea. From this window she could look down the sloping grass of what their landlady claimed had long ago been part of the Gill Estate. Sadie saw the crow with an injured wing in an upper crotch of the oak. It had been there for a week and was seldom alone. Usually one or two crows kept it company and brought it food. One of them was there now, hopping sideways along the branch until it was close enough to empty something from its beak into the injured crow's mouth.

When the sisters finished eating, they carried their dishes to the sink, washed them in the basin of water, wiped them dry and returned them to the cupboard. While Flora went upstairs to the bathroom, Sadie went into the sitting room to tell Mrs. Hatch about Wednesday's sale, and to ask if she could use the kitchen to make chocolate fudge.

"If you clean up afterwards, I have no objection."

"I'll have to make the fudge today because Miss Witherspoon says the items must be ticketed tomorrow. Could I wash the floor on Wednesday instead of today?"

Their father had agreed that Sadie and Flora would do light housework every day after school as well as on Saturday morning.

Mrs. Hatch continued knitting.

"I suppose it is possible this once, but you must not make a habit of it. Also, you must wait until I am finished at the cathedral before making fudge. I must be here when you are using the stove."

Mrs. Hatch belonged to the Church of England Altar Guild and Tuesday was the day she brushed down the vestments and choir gowns.

Sadie fidgeted with her belt as she always did whenever she had to ask Mrs. Hatch for something. She didn't know why she was so nervous around their landlady. Why should she be? After all, their father had given Olive Hatch a tidy sum of money to ensure that Sadie and Flora would be well taken care of and she had every right to ask for some of it. Her nervousness had to do with not knowing what their landlady was really like. Sadie had seen the way Mrs. Hatch had acted with her father and the Reverend Mr. Eagles. With them she had been

eager to please, dipping her head like an anxious pet wanting
to be noticed, hiding her sharp, protruding teeth when she
smiled. With Sadie and Flora she did not bother concealing her
teeth but bared them like fangs when she was displeased—and
she was often displeased. Also with them she frequently jerked
her head sideways as if she expected to catch them doing something that was disallowed. She did this now, holding her knitting aloft, waiting for Sadie to continue.

"I will need money to buy chocolate and sugar," Sadie said
in a rush and though it was her father's money, she added,
"please."

"I don't think your father would approve of you wasting his
money in that way."

"I think he would agree that making fudge for the Spencer
sale is a worthy cause. After all, the funds are to be used to help
the school."

The knitting needles continued clicking and sounded, Sadie
thought, like the clashing beaks of angry birds.

"The school should deduct its expenses from students' fees,
which are high enough without expecting students to pay
more. I suggest you find something else to contribute to the
sale."

Sadie turned away quickly so she wouldn't be tempted to
retort, knowing that a saucy retort would only make things
worse. She went through the kitchen to the bathroom and
tapped on the door. Flora let her in.

"Sour Olive won't let us make fudge for the Spencer sale,"
Sadie whispered. "I hate her!"

Flora spat in the sink and turned on the water.

"I hate her too," she said companionably. Then she looked at
Sadie in the mirror. "Cross my heart I do." She turned the tap
on full blast so that Sour Olive could hear water gurgling down

the pipe and be even more cross than she already was. The sisters giggled and snorted. Tears rolled down Sadie's cheeks— it wouldn't take much to change from laughter to despair. If her mother were here, there would be no difficulty making fudge; in fact, her mother would want to make it herself. Sadie bit her lip to stop the fatal words about missing their mother from which, once said, there would be no turning back. She leaned over the sink and splashed water on her eyelids.

That evening Sadie opened the box of handkerchiefs Mrs. Leeson had given her mother one Christmas and took out two of them and put them at either end of the dresser, one for Flora and one for herself. The handkerchiefs, of pure Irish linen, were as white as doves and shaped like bird wings, having been folded triangularly inside a green box decorated with shamrocks.

Norah Leeson and their mother had been close friends in Ireland. She and Mary had attended the same school in Mallow, trained as nurses in the same hospital in Dublin and crossed the Atlantic together. In Halifax, Nova Scotia, Norah met an engineer, Brian Leeson, and moved to Corner Brook on the west coast of Newfoundland. Mary met a geologist, Russ Morin, and moved to Copper Cliff, Ontario, where Sadie and Flora were born. Mary and Norah had not seen each other since but had kept in touch with birthday and Christmas cards. The Leesons' address was inside a small leather book that had belonged to Sadie's mother and was now in the dresser drawer where Sadie kept her underclothes.

When Sadie went downstairs for breakfast in the morning, she noticed that a small cardboard box had been placed on the table beside her spoon. Mrs. Hatch saw her looking at it.

"The box contains a Christmas ornament I'm donating to the Spencer sale," she said and began digging their porridge out of the pot.

Was the ornament meant to make up for the fudge? Well, it didn't and Sadie wasn't about to thank her, if that's what their landlady expected. Instead, she looked out the window and noticed that the crow was alone on the branch, its head bent forward as if it was sleeping.

She didn't open the box until she, Flora and Peggy were at the corner of Gower and Victoria streets on their way to school. Inside the box on a flat square of yellow cotton was a tin owl, no more than four inches long. The fawn-coloured tin was coming apart at the seams where the two halves of the owl had been joined together. There was nothing the least bit ornamental about the owl. When it was new it might have been attractive, but since then most of its painted feathers, as well as its yellow eyes, had been scratched off.

"What have you there?"

Teddy Dodge had come up the street behind them without their being aware. "It's supposed to a Christmas ornament." Sadie held up the owl. "Would you hang this on a tree?"

"It's too ugly to hang on a tree," Flora said and ran ahead with Peggy.

A head taller than Sadie, Teddy loomed over her, a puzzled expression on his face.

"Our landlady is donating this to the Spencer sale," she said.

"She expects someone to pay for it?" he said as he and Sadie began walking along Gower Street. "If it was me I'd pitch the thing in the trash."

"I couldn't do that. Mrs. Hatch might find out. I've seen her talking to some of my teachers after church."

"Are you afraid of her then?"

"Oh no!" Sadie felt herself blushing, which always happened when she lied. "I guess," she paused, hating to admit it, "I am a little bit afraid."

"Intimidated," Teddy said quietly. He was a reader who used big words. He also liked to talk and had already changed the subject and begun telling her about a history project he was working on. "I'm writing an essay about my forebear Tristam Dodge, who came to Ferryland in the 1600s." Teddy explained that Ferryland was really the Colony of Avalon and talked about the place all the way to the corner of Bond Street, where he and Sadie parted company.

At recess Sadie took the owl and the handkerchief to the teacher in charge of sale contributions, Miss Bugle, who thanked her profusely. Mild-mannered and dithery, Miss Bugle was enthusiastic and encouraging with everyone. Sadie knew that she would appreciate the handkerchief because she had already explained in class that she had a collection of handkerchiefs from various countries. "Your handkerchief is a welcome addition to our sale," Miss Bugle said, "especially since, as you know, Irish linen is the best money can buy." Having seen the boxes filled with teddy bears and dolls, puzzles and games, bread, cookies and cakes being carried down the corridor earlier this morning, Sadie knew that Miss Bugle was probably trying to make her small contribution more significant than it was.

"The ornament inside the box isn't my contribution but my landlady's," she said.

"Please thank her for me," Miss Bugle replied, but she didn't open the box.

That evening after Flora was asleep, Sadie put a quarter at either end of the dresser for the morning's sale. That left fifteen cents change in the dresser drawer. The remainder of the spending money her father had given her was tucked inside Madeleine, the cloth doll the Irish aunts had given her when she was a child. Nineteen bills were well concealed beneath Madeleine's pantaloons—her father had given her a twenty-dollar bill but Sadie had broken it in order to buy stamps to mail letters to her father in Buchans. Because Flora was a snoop who would find the money, Sadie told her where it was and made her promise never to mention it to Mrs. Hatch. She wouldn't either; for a little girl, Flora was good at keeping promises. It had not once crossed Sadie's mind that she could have bought sugar and chocolate with the money inside Madeleine. Making fudge for the school sale didn't qualify as an emergency but as an unforeseen expense. Now that their father was gone and she was responsible for looking after Flora and herself, she had no intention of paying for something Mrs. Hatch should be providing.

In the morning when Sadie went downstairs for breakfast, she saw a nickel beside her glass of milk, and another beside Flora's.

"The nickels are for you girls to buy yourselves a treat," Mrs. Hatch said magnanimously, as if by dispensing their father's money, she was being generous and kind.

When she and Flora got to school, Sadie noticed that Mrs. Hatch's owl had been placed on the white elephant table between a crystal candy dish and a miniature silver bell. The table was a browser's delight and among the assortment of sale items was a tortoise-shell comb, a Chinese fan, a snake paperweight, a large mouth organ, ten monarch butterflies arranged inside a picture frame, wooden bookends on which dwarves had been carved, a jewellery box containing necklaces, bangles and rings, and on the floor beneath the table, a basket of blue-eyed Siamese kittens. Flora wanted one of the kittens but knew that was out of the question—Mrs. Hatch would never allow a kitten. She disliked both cats and dogs. Not only were they a nuisance, she said, but they ate food that could be given to the poor.

All the sale tables had been set up in the gym. There was a fancy-work table for knitting and crocheting, a bake stall, a homemade-candy table, a toy stall, a handkerchief stall and a fruit and vegetable stall. The last was Spoony's idea—she wanted to highlight foods grown in Newfoundland. Laid out on a white tablecloth were bunches of turnips, parsnips and carrots and hills of potatoes. There were jars of partridgeberry and bakeapple jam; raspberry and cranberry jelly. It was only after every table and stall had been twice surveyed that Flora bought a mechanical monkey she thought was cute in its red trousers and blue jacket, its winding key made to look like a belt buckle. Sadie bought two bangles, a green one for Millie, who had no money and a blue one for herself. There was enough money left over to buy taffy apples at the Bull's Eye Shop for Millie, Flora and herself.

On the way home after early dismissal, Sadie warned her sister not to mention their purchases to their landlady because she would want to know how they had paid for them. It was bad enough that they were returning with the owl. At the end of the sale, when the students were asked to collect the unsold items, Sadie had noticed that the owl had been marked down from ten cents to five cents, and although it had crossed her mind that Mrs. Hatch would be displeased to see this, she didn't remove the stickers. As soon as she entered the kitchen, she put the box containing the owl on the table which was set for dinner.

"Did you enjoy the sale?" Mrs. Hatch called from the front room.

"It was fun," Flora said.

The sale had been fun. There had been a festive air at Spencer. Sadie had felt it the moment she entered the door. There was no marching in twos, no lines filing into morning assembly, no whispered exchanges. Instead girls sauntered through corridors and around the gym, laughing and talking, making no effort to keep their voices down. All this under the benign gaze of Spoony and her teachers, who had taken on the role of tolerant benefactors overseeing the tables and stalls, smiling and chatting among themselves, leaving the responsibility for a relaxed kind of order to the prefects, who were busy dispensing ice-cream cones from a table downstairs.

"Thank you for the nickels," Sadie said politely—having enjoyed herself, she was willing to set Sour Olive's meanness temporarily aside. "We spent them on ice cream."

"Vanilla," Flora added.

Putting a finger to her lips, Sadie pointed to the box on the table and she and Flora began to giggle. It was the kind of giggling that had to run its course and couldn't be easily stopped or explained. For them giggling was a way of releasing the unsaid and at the same time enjoying each other. Hearing Mrs. Hatch get up and come toward the kitchen, the sisters ducked into the bathroom, flushing the toilet twice and turning the water full blast to mask the giggling. When they came out of the bathroom, their mouths turned down in the effort of keeping their faces straight, Mrs. Hatch was back in the rocker, ordering them into the front room.

Chastened, they stood before her as she peered up at them with her weak eyes.

"I have something to say to you before you eat your dinner." She pointed to the sofa covered with one of her knitted afghans and the girls sat side by side facing her. Sadie felt so giddy from the morning's pleasure and from the fit of giggling, which was in danger of erupting again, that she forced herself to concentrate on the framed photographs of a boy and a girl on top of the piano, bracing herself for the scolding she knew was coming.

Baring her teeth in a fake smile, Mrs. Hatch said, her voice low as if she was determined to placate them, "I must remind you again about the way you girls waste water. I have no doubt that before you moved to St. John's you were in the habit of wasting both water and electricity. As I mentioned, it is only recently that a sewer was installed in Willicott's Lane."

Sadie held her breath. Knowing words like "sewer," "poop" and "pee" usually made her sister giggle, she slid her gaze sideways and was relieved to see that Flora was behaving herself, sitting with her legs straight out, her back against the sofa, doing her best to look like a solemn, obedient child.

"And," Mrs. Hatch continued, "it was only last year that our lane got the electricity, and that we now have the benefit of electric lights. There are still homes at the west end of the city without electricity or running water." She paused, mindful perhaps, that her voice had become strident. When she began speaking again, it was low and coaxing. "It is easy for young-sters like yourselves to take these luxuries for granted, but I see no reason why they should be wasted and squandered. From now on I want you girls to remember to use the basin to wash your hands. I also want the chamber pot emptied in the shed before breakfast."

"Why not empty it down the toilet?" Sadie asked.

Mrs. Hatch looked shocked and somewhat repelled, as if the answer to Sadie's question was too delicate to address. "If you must know, it's to avoid clogging the pipes and having the toilet back up, which recently happened to Mrs. Porter on Victoria Street. When the pipes are clogged, it's very costly to free them up. Mrs. Porter told me what she paid the plumber and I cannot afford that expense."

Sadie had no answer for this. It was true that she took elec-tricity for granted, and that if the pipes became clogged, they would probably be expensive to repair. But it was also true that Mrs. Hatch wanted to get back at her for returning with the unsold owl and that having the chamber pot emptied every morning was the way to do it. "I'll empty it," she said, though it was Flora who used it.

"That's decided then," Mrs. Hatch said, a whiff of triumph in her voice. "You girls had better eat before the food gets cold."

Neither of them was hungry but they ate their dinners, knowing that unless they cleaned their plates they would receive a lecture about starving children in Africa and India, as if their uneaten food could somehow be whisked halfway around the world. They would be told that they were fortunate children when they did not feel fortunate, especially now that they were living with Mrs. Hatch.

3

Letter from Buchans

EVERY SATURDAY AFTERNOON SINCE THEIR FATHER HAD left for Buchans, Sadie and Flora went upstairs after their chores were done and wrote him a letter about what they were learning in school. Sadie wrote most of the letter, while Flora drew a picture of someone. Though she drew quickly, almost carelessly, her pictures always conveyed something quirky or whimsical about their subject. Mr. Buckle, the white-haired school janitor, was drawn as a gnome with an elvish cap, Miss Witherspoon was drawn as a ship's captain looking through a telescope, and Mrs. Hatch was drawn as a large green olive with twiggy arms and nose. At first Sadie worked eagerly on the letters because it made her feel closer to her father, but as the weeks passed without any letters arriving from him, she began to worry about how he was and if her letters were reaching him.

As the weeks of October passed and no letters arrived, the worry alternated with anger. Sadie was angry at her father for leaving Flora and herself with a woman they detested and going to a place where he couldn't be reached—the camp in Buchans didn't have a telephone and neither did Mrs. Hatch. According to her father, Buchans was less than five hundred miles away, but as far as Sadie was concerned, it could have been on the moon. If either she or Flora found themselves in an emergency, he couldn't be reached, and if something awful happened to him, she wouldn't know about it until long after-wards. Her father should never have left them in this situation, especially so soon after their mother died. This shift between anger and helplessness happened mostly on the weekends when Sadie had time on her hands. By Monday she would have cheered herself up by thinking *this week a letter will come* and by reminding herself *again* that no train ran to Buchans to deliver or pick up mail. Her father had told her that to reach Buchans, supplies had to travel by land and water from the train stop in Badger. Sadie had seen this for herself when she'd studied the map on the grade-ten classroom wall. She'd seen that her father was working in the middle of the island in a place completely cut off from anywhere else. As a prospecting geologist, her father's work discovering valuable metals and minerals had always taken him to places in the middle of nowhere, but it seemed that Buchans was more nowhere than other places he had been.

Finally, the last Friday in October, the sisters returned to Willicott's Lane after school to find a letter from him on the kitchen table. Before Mrs. Hatch could put them to work (she was out but would doubtless walk in at any moment), the sisters dashed upstairs with the letter. Kicking off their shoes, they curled up side by side on the bed while Sadie read the letter, both she and Flora squirming with pleasure at the words "My darling daughters."

Buchans, October 1, 1926

My darling daughters,

I am writing this letter, not on anything as civilized as a desk or a table, but on a board balanced on my knees. I am leaning against a bunkhouse wall so poorly built that daylight can be seen through the cracks. Around my shoulders is a blanket I wear inside to block out the wind blowing through the cracks. Such wind! But I must not complain, for I was warned beforehand about the wind, and the black flies which, I am relieved to say, have recently succumbed to the frost and no longer regard me as a tasty meal.

Eight of us share this bunkhouse which is one of a half-dozen built in forest scrub. If the expectation of finding extensive seams of gold bears out, a town will be built here with proper houses, a school and churches as well as a railway line from Badger. To reach Buchans, our party had to boat down the Exploits River, along Red Indian Lake and up the Buchans River, a journey requiring several portages and complicated by a persistent mother bear and her cubs who scattered our food supplies so that we arrived in Buchans not only weary, but very hungry indeed.

It pleases me greatly to know that my girls are warm and safe in St. John's. I hope that you are being as helpful and polite to Mrs. Hatch as your mother and I would wish, and that you are keeping up with your schooling under the watchful eye of Miss Witherspoon.

   As for my work, I am assaying the main ore body which
is called Lucky Strike. Any day now I expect to be working
underground analyzing the ore drilled at hole number
fifteen. If the ore continues to be of a consistently high
grade, I am sure that plans to establish a town here will go
ahead. A mill is to be built near the Lucky Strike. A mining
engineer will be arriving in early December to take over the
planning and development of the mill and the town.
Perhaps when he arrives, we will have a telephone. After I
have met with him about future prospects, I will make my
way to St. John's, for I am determined to spend Christmas
with my girls. Until then you may be assured that I am well.

                          Your loving father

P.S. So far I have received only two letters from you. I have
nailed Flora's pictures of Captain Witherspoon, "Olive"
Hatch and the elf Mr. Buckle to the cabin wall beside my
bunk. Please keep the letters and pictures coming.

Sadie read the letter once more before Mrs. Hatch called
them downstairs to sweep up the dirt they had tracked in. (At
the sight of the letter, they had neglected to leave their shoes on
the mat.) For the time being, Sadie forgot how much she hated
sweeping and swept not only the dirt tracked in but the front-
room floor and the stairs. Buoyant with relief that her father
was safe and sound, she hummed as she worked. What made
her feel especially glad was the news that her father was willing
to work underground again. Sadie took this as a good sign. He
had been working in the Copper Cliff mine when the news
came that her mother had died, and after the funeral he had
refused to work underground again. He had never explained

why, but Sadie thought it must be because he feared that he wouldn't be able to work underground without thinking about her mother's death. Eventually his supervisor warned him that a continued refusal would cost him his job. Last summer, when the offer came to work in Newfoundland, he had jumped at the chance to leave Copper Cliff, claiming that a change of scenery would enable him to do a better job. Sadie had also been eager to leave Copper Cliff, which, especially after her mother died, she had come to think of as a bleak, dreary place. Though she had never spoken about this to Flora, Sadie thought her little sister had become more cheerful since moving to St. John's.

St. John's was a more cheerful-looking place than Copper Cliff. It was cozy-looking too with steps between hilly streets and tucked-away lanes and gardens, and there were trees, green grass and parks. The city had none of the buoyant greenery of Cork, where the Irish aunts used to live, but it was far prettier than Copper Cliff with its landscape of charred stumps and blackened rocks that Sadie's mother used to call a wasteland. The air stank of sulphur from the roasting pits, and there were days when the choking smoke from the smelters was as thick as fog. There was fog in St. John's but it wasn't vile-smelling. It was sea mist that moved in and out depending on the weather, clinging in tiny globules to Sadie's skin. She had not yet been down to the harbour. Mrs. Hatch had forbidden Flora and her to go down to the waterfront, which she called a den of iniquity, home to drunkards, thieves and hangashores, which Mrs. Hatch said were lazy people. She claimed youngsters who went down to the waterfront were in danger of being kidnapped by wicked men and carried away to a foreign land where they would be traded as slaves. Why, only last year a girl was snatched from the wharf by wicked men after she had delivered her father's dinner. Carried away she was, probably bound hand and foot, a rag stuffed in her mouth to keep her from screaming for her father.

At least in Willicott's Lane Sadie could smell the sharp, salty air that came from the harbour. Because the lane was on a hill, depending on where she was inside the house, she could sometimes see the fog rolling in and could hear the bleat of the Fort Amherst horn.

Even with the kitchen window closed, she could hear the foghorn. Whenever she heard its lost-sheep voice, she found it comforting, probably because it echoed how lost she so often felt. It was hard living in a strange city without her mother and her father working far away. Though she liked St. John's, it still wasn't home. As ugly as Copper Cliff had been, the familiarity of the people and the town had helped make it home. And not everything had been ugly: there had been the forsythia bush by the back door that in spite of the poisonous air yielded yellow blossoms every spring; there had been the blanket-sized bit of grass where as a baby Flora used to play, and the Samulskis' tabby cat who liked to curl up on the back doormat. But all that was past. She had left Ontario behind and must now try to make Newfoundland home.

Sadie stopped sweeping the kitchen floor to look out the window at a swath of fog floating through the city like a mantle of gentle mist. She found it soothing to watch the fog easing itself across the Southside Hills, slowly engulfing the houses. She would have stood there transfixed until the hills themselves disappeared if Mrs. Hatch hadn't spoken, startling her into dropping the broom. "No more dilly-dallying. The upstairs hall and your bedroom are to be thoroughly swept if you expect any supper. You can sweep the kitchen after you eat."

Sweeping the kitchen floor was a routine chore that Sadie was required to do every day after she and Flora had washed and dried the supper dishes. The bigger chores were done on Saturday, and the next morning the sisters were busy wiping their bedroom furniture as well as the front-room furniture and the kitchen cupboards, inside and out. There was also the carpet to be carried outside to the clothesline where Sadie and Flora took turns whacking it with a broom until it gave out tiny puffs of dust. This was a chore they undertook energetically, giggling whenever one of them sent up a larger puff than the other.

After their chores were finished and they had eaten their dinner, Mrs. Hatch went to the cathedral to polish silver for next day's communion service and Flora went out to play with Peggy. Sadie could hear their voices through the upstairs window she had opened for this purpose, wanting to keep an ear out for her little sister.

Sadie was sitting at the table in their bedroom basting Flora's donkey costume. She was clumsy at sewing and would have preferred to be doing almost anything else, but had grimly set her mind to finish the basting today. Sewing costumes was something her mother had done with flair, and Sadie remembered her with a tape measure around her neck, humming as she knelt to pin up the bottom of Sadie's pumpkin costume. She could hear her mother saying, "If I put a drawstring inside the hem, I could stuff the costume with crumpled newspapers to make you look pumpkinish. How would you like that?" Sadie had liked it. She could still hear the rustle of newspapers as she had waddled from door to door collecting Halloween treats. The memory of her mother's girlish enthusiasm brought on a fit of weeping and Sadie put down the basting, took a handkerchief from the dresser drawer and blew her nose.

To cheer herself up, she read her father's letter for a third time, but this only made her feel worse, because she began remembering Saturday afternoons in Copper Cliff after her mother died. Her father used to take Flora and her to Sudbury by streetcar to watch the *Perils of Pauline* matinee. When they got home, they would sprawl on the floral carpet of their small sitting room, reading the weekend funnies, *Jane Arden* and *Mutt and Jeff,* and shelling peanuts while their father sat in his leather chair, reading the newspaper and smoking his pipe. The letter increased her nostalgia for those Saturday afternoons because it reminded her that her father had been cut loose in the wilderness just as she and Flora had been cut off from the familiar world they had known in Copper Cliff.

Taking out paper, she dipped her pen into a bottle of Waterman's ink and began a letter to her father. Because she was feeling gloomy, she wanted to write him a letter of complaint. She wanted to tell him about their landlady not allowing them sugar with their porridge and only giving them one glass of milk a day. She wanted to tell him about the amount of housework they were expected to do in order, Sour Olive said, for them to earn their keep. But why tell him these things when he wasn't here to change them? When he came back for Christmas, she would tell him what Sour Olive was really like and they would move to another place. Until then it was probably better to say nothing about their landlady's meanness. Instead she would write him about Christmas.

St. John's, November 2, 1926

Dear Dad,

Flora has been assigned the part of a donkey in a play in the Christmas concert and I am making her costume. Last week she was given an envelope containing a pattern and instructions and a list of the materials we would need: grey flannel, black wool (for the ears and tail), buttons (for the eyes) and thread. I don't know much about sewing but I decided I should try to make the costume and I did get it cut out (it wasn't hard) and I'm now basting it together. It's supposed to be finished by December 15th so there's lots of time.

I'll be in the concert too, but I won't be wearing a costume. I'll be singing in Miss Marsh's choir. The concert will be on December 21st and I hope with all my heart that you will be there.

That's about all the news I have for now. Flora is outside playing with her friend Peggy. When she comes in, she'll draw you another picture for your wall.

Love,
Sadie

Later, after Flora had drawn a stick picture of Peggy with her arms outstretched as she ran to catch a ball, the sisters walked along the lane and down the Victoria Street steps and posted the letter at the Crosbie Hotel. There was a mailbox further along Duckworth Street but the hotel was closer. Also the hotel brought back memories of being with her father in early September when she and Flora lived in his suite, two adjoining rooms with a bathroom attached. When he was bundled inside his blanket in the bunkhouse trying to keep warm, did her father think about those carefree hours? He didn't talk about his troubles or feelings the way her mother had. He didn't seem to know how. What she most liked about his letter was that, without perhaps meaning to, he had told her how he felt and that, like her, he was trying to make the best of the situation.

4

Wanda

BECAUSE IT WAS SUNDAY, MRS. HATCH LEFT THE HOUSE early the next morning carrying the altar cloth she had laundered the day before. Although Sadie did Mrs. Hatch's ironing, she was not allowed to iron the altar cloth or the Reverend Mr. Eagle's surplice, both of which her landlady made a show of ironing, holding them up to the light to make certain they were without a scorch mark or crease, afterwards draping them over a chair back in the sitting room with strict instructions that they not be touched.

It was the Reverend Mr. Eagles who had brought Mrs. Hatch and the Morins together. As they were leaving the cathedral after a morning service last August, Sadie's father had introduced himself to the reverend and asked if he could recommend a boardinghouse for his daughters. "I could indeed," the reverend said, hooking his hands onto his surplice like claws. "Among my flock is an honest, Christian woman who is the owner of a clean, respectable boardinghouse. If you step aside until I have finished greeting the congregation, I will introduce her to you." And so the Morins had waited patiently until the reverend was finished and had fetched Mrs. Hatch from the nether regions behind the altar where she had no doubt been hanging up choir gowns or straightening hymnals. Mrs. Hatch had been eager and timid that morning, the reverend jovial and persuasive. Between them they convinced Sadie and her father that the house on Willicott's Lane was the right combination of comfort and convenience for the sisters as well as being within a reasonable walking distance from the school. "What more could you ask?" the reverend said, lifting himself to a height greater than his own. He was a squat, full-bellied man who had a habit of rising on the balls of his feet where he rocked back and forth as he spoke. Sadie knew that he would rock back and forth through most of this morning's sermon, especially during those parts when he was urging the congregation to become more Christian, as he put it, "in thought and deed."

Before their landlady left for church, she insisted that the sisters be dressed in their Sunday clothes—woollen jumpers which were last year's Christmas presents from the Irish aunts. She was taking no chances that they might decide not to go. Half an hour after Mrs. Hatch left for church, Flora was still at the kitchen table, trying to force down the last of her bread. On Sundays Mrs. Hatch made a big show of making them fried bread, which she expected them to eat without syrup or jam. Only by sprinkling it with salt had Sadie managed to finish hers, and she was now carrying the chamber pot outside. It occurred to her that she could flush the contents down the toilet and their landlady would never know, but as tempting as it was, she dismissed the thought because of having to be an example to Flora. If her little sister saw her defying Mrs. Hatch's orders, she might become balky and rebellious, which would only make Sour Olive worse. Until their father returned at Christmastime, it was better for both of them to cooperate with their landlady and to do what was expected of them.

Sadie walked down the slight incline to the shed, which contained an old privy, and carefully placed the pot on the ground. She opened the shed door and immediately clamped her hand over her mouth to stifle an involuntary "Oh!"

Inside the shed, a big woman wearing a mangy fur coat was slumped over the hole. Her face was red and puffy and there was a slit in her lower lip as if someone had sliced it with a knife. The woman lifted her head and looked at Sadie.

"It's all right, girl. It's only me, Wanda Hatch."

"Wanda Hatch," Sadie said.

"That's right, I'm the old biddy's daughter." She looked at Sadie through a half-closed eye and smiled crookedly. "Didn't know she had a daughter, did you?"

"No." Sadie remembered the wooden-framed photo of a girl about Flora's age dressed in a summer frock that she studied each time she dusted the top of the piano in Mrs. Hatch's front room. She couldn't see much resemblance between the little girl and this woman.

Wanda looked at the pot. "I see she's still getting her boarders to do her work. You are a boarder, aren't you?"

"Yes. Me and my sister."

"It beats me why she don't empty the pot down the toilet."

"She says it plugs the pipes."

"Don't you believe it. I knows her. She's being pure mean. Well, I better shift me arse so you can empty that pot. Do you need a pee?" Wanda said, using a word Sadie couldn't bring herself to say.

"I already went inside."

Wanda looked at her appraisingly. "You're not from here, are you?"

"No. I'm from Ontario. Canada."

"So how come you and your sister are boarding with Ma?"

"Our mother's dead and my father works at the mine in Buchans."

"So you're stuck with Ma." Wanda Hatch tried to stand up and fell back, groaning. She reached out for Sadie. "Give me a hand, will you? That bastard worked me over so bad I can hardly move."

"That's terrible," Sadie said. "Bastard" was another word Sadie couldn't say. Did Wanda mean she had been set upon by a wicked man down by the harbour?

"I'll survive." Wanda said. For someone who had been beaten up, she seemed amazingly calm. "A few hours' rest upstairs will put me to rights."

Was she planning to rest on her mother's bed or on Sadie's and Flora's?

"You needn't worry," Wanda said. "I won't take your bed. I'll use my brother's." She gave Sadie another shrewd look. "You don't know about him either?"

"No."

"He's dead, killed in the Great War. The odd time I gets in a jam I uses his bed." Holding on to Sadie's arm, Wanda lurched to her feet and leaned against the shed wall. Her coat smelled of alcohol and stale tobacco. "I've been waiting until Ma left for church."

"My sister and I are going to church."

"Would you mind helping me upstairs before you go?" Wanda said.

"I wouldn't mind at all," Sadie said. Her ambition was to become a nurse and Wanda Hatch was definitely someone who needed nursing. And there was something about Mrs. Hatch's daughter that Sadie liked. Now that Wanda was standing, she looked small. It must have been the bunched-up coat that had made her look big. Sadie took her by the elbow and together they made their way up the incline to the house.

"If he's dead, why does your brother have a bed?"

"Good question," Wanda said grimly. "One I often asks myself."

"Where is the room?"

"Upstairs," Wanda said and gave her a strange look that said, "Where else would it be?"

The mystery room. Sadie wondered if Wanda's brother could be inside the room, as a corpse or something, but she didn't know how to ask if this could be true without sounding silly.

Flora was at the kitchen table playing with the last bits of her bread. Sadie had never known anyone who could play with food like her sister, talking to peas and carrots as if they were pretend people. Flora stopped playing the moment Wanda stepped onto the mat.

"This is my sister, Flora."

"Hello, Flora. I'm Wanda, Mrs. Hatch's daughter. Can I ask you a favour?"

Flora nodded solemnly.

"I'm going to go upstairs for a rest. I'll slip away later on. Don't tell Ma I was here." Wanda grimaced and Sadie thought she was probably trying to wink but couldn't because of the welt over her eye.

"All right," Flora said.

"She won't tell," Sadie said. "She's good at keeping a secret." Then she added. "You can trust us."

Up the narrow stairs she and Wanda went, Wanda grasping the rail for support. When they had gained the upstairs hall,

Wanda opened the door to her mother's room, reached behind the bureau and withdrew a ring with two keys on it. Using the larger key, she opened the door of her brother's bedroom. One glimpse assured Sadie that there was no corpse in the room and that except for the furnishings, it was empty. The same glimpse told her that the room was far more luxurious than Flora's and hers. On the table in front of the window was a gold-framed photograph of a young man in a soldier's uniform.

Wanda saw her looking at it. "That's him, Corporal Thomas Hatch, who died a hero's death at Beaumont Hamel." Her voice was bitter. Was she not proud of him? She patted Sadie's arm.

"Thanks for your help. You're a good girl." She closed the door before Sadie could get a closer look at the room. She heard the key click. The sound was both final and disappointing, because Sadie now knew the answer to what was inside the room and it was nothing interesting or mysterious. The only mystery was why Mrs. Hatch bothered to lock the door.

Sadie returned to the shed, emptied the chamber pot, rinsed it out and put it beneath the bed. She then went downstairs to the sitting room and picked up the photograph of a boy from the top of the piano, a piano whose top was also locked. As far as she knew, the piano was never played. Flora came into the living room and Sadie showed her the picture. "This must be Mrs. Hatch's son." She pointed to the photo of Wanda. "And this is the woman upstairs."

Flora studied the photographs. Then she looked at the piano top and asked, "Where is Mr. Hatch?" For a little girl she could ask penetrating questions.

The next morning on the way to school, Sadie asked Teddy the same question, but he didn't know anything about Mr. or Mrs. Hatch. He didn't think his parents would know either,

having moved from Carbonear to St. John's only four years
ago. In any case, he said, the Carbonear crowd was different
from the St. John's crowd.

But Teddy knew a lot about Beaumont Hamel.

"Beaumont Hamel was part of the Battle of the Somme.
Only 68 of the 778 Newfoundlanders who went over the top
survived intact. The Irish sustained heavy losses too but no
regiment lost more than Newfoundland's. A generation of
young men wiped out." Teddy's voice trembled. Sadie stole a
glance at him but he didn't see the glance because his head was
bowed. "Our boys didn't have a chance. The German guns were
dug in all along the ridge. The attack should never have been
ordered."

Flora, who had been skipping ahead with Peggy, rushed
back and thrust two bookbags at Sadie. "Hold these. Peggy and
me want to play leap frog."

"No!" Leap frog wasn't a game to play on the street, especially when you were wearing a school uniform—but Flora
paid no attention.

"My mother's youngest brother was killed," Teddy said. "He
was only a boy."

"I'm sorry," Sadie said, sorry partly on Teddy's account and
partly because people killing each other made her feel sad. It
was bad enough that people got sick and died without them
deliberately killing each other.

"A memorial to those who died at Beaumont Hamel was
erected in France and an identical memorial is going to be
erected in Bowring Park. If you like, I'll take you there some
day and show you where it will be," Teddy said, then added, "in
the summer."

"Thank you," Sadie said for want of anything better to say.
She could hardly say that she looked forward to seeing the

place where a war memorial would be. It wasn't as if it would be "going out" with Teddy. In any case, she had already seen the Sergeants' Memorial to the men who had died in the Great War at the end of Bond Street.

"The park is beautiful in summer. We could take a picnic and make a day of it."

Maybe he *was* thinking of it as "going out." The thought of "going out" with Teddy made Sadie blush. It was infuriating how the least little thing made her blush. Did every single thought and feeling need to be written on her face?

Sadie went into Thomas Hatch's room after school on Wednesday when Flora and Peggy were playing outside and Mrs. Hatch was at her sewing circle, a carry-over from the Women's Patriotic League which, she said in her smug self-satisfied way, was making a quilt in order to raise funds for the Church of England Orphanage for Girls. Sadie went upstairs and, groping behind the landlady's dresser, found the ring of keys. From watching Wanda, she knew the larger key opened the mystery room door. Because she was in a hurry, she didn't give a second thought to the smaller key but opened the door and stepped inside. Again she saw how much grander this room was compared to Flora's and hers. Not only did the window provide a better view of the harbour but there was a fireplace, and the bedspread, which Wanda had left smooth and unwrinkled, was gold brocade with a tasselled trim, instead of faded chenille. The lampshade beside the bed was also trimmed in gold. In front of a window hung with gold brocade drapes was a polished wooden table with a long narrow drawer. On the table was a Bible opened, Sadie noticed, to "Matthew, Chapter 5" where a sentence was underlined in pencil: "Blessed are the meek for they shall inherit the earth." Beside the Bible was the framed photograph of Thomas Hatch she had glimpsed earlier. The frame was made of golden leaves twined together into an oval shape. Sadie picked up the photograph. Unlike the photograph on top of the piano, in this picture Thomas Hatch looked a bit like his mother. He had the same shape face, the same colour hair. But his cheeks were full, which made it seem that he had not yet lost his baby fat. He looked boyish and hopeful, not at all the way Sadie would have expected a soldier to look. *He was only a boy,* Teddy had said of his uncle. Did Mrs. Hatch come in here to look at the photo and read the Bible? She certainly kept the room clean, because it was spotless, the furniture so well polished that it gleamed.

Sadie heard a door slam downstairs. *Mrs. Hatch,* she thought, *She's back! What if she finds me here?* She put the picture back on the table, tiptoed out the door and locked it. She was returning the key ring to the nail behind her landlady's dresser when to her enormous relief, Flora appeared on the stairs. She glanced up at Sadie and said, "What were you doing in that room?" She had seen Sadie locking the door.

"Nothing much."

Flora looked at her quizzically, waiting perhaps for an explanation.

"I just looked around while I was waiting for you to come in and help me clean the bathroom," Sadie said. This was partly true and seemed to satisfy her sister.

They went downstairs and got to work, Sadie thinking about the room upstairs, Flora grumbling about not being allowed to join Brownies. Mrs. Hatch had refused to allow them to join Brownies or Guides, pointing out that they must choose between these clubs or the Christmas concert. They were already required to stay after school twice a week to practise for the Christmas concert instead of doing chores for their landlady. Whenever her sister grumbled about Sour Olive,

Sadie usually joined in, but not today. Today she was thinking about Thomas Hatch and Teddy's uncle, about the boys killed in the war. It wasn't something she had given a lot of thought to before. At school in Copper Cliff, they had celebrated Armistice Day in November but it had seemed little more than a lesson; nothing really connected to her. But now that she was living in Newfoundland, she felt more connected to the Great War, partly because Teddy's uncle and Thomas Hatch were killed at Beaumont Hamel and also because she was closer to Europe where the war was fought.

The following Friday, during the Armistice Day ceremony at school, Sadie kept thinking of Thomas Hatch. The day before, every girl in Spencer had made a crepe-paper poppy and now they filed into assembly holding them. Eunice Baird, whose uncle was another casualty of Beaumont Hamel, recited "In Flanders Fields." After her recitation, which was sombre and respectful, the students sang "Ode to Newfoundland" and carried their poppies to the front of the gym, where they placed them on a wreath that would be placed on the war memorial on Sunday after church. After the service at the cathedral, Sadie and Flora followed the congregation to the Sergeants' Memorial, where they stood in the mizzling rain listening to a trumpeter play the last post, after which there was an interval of silence. When the wreath bearers began laying their wreaths on the memorial, Sadie and Flora returned to Willicott's Lane. Mrs. Hatch wasn't there but had put Saturday's leftovers, fish and potatoes, on plates in the icebox. After they finished dinner and did the dishes, Flora went to Peggy's house and Sadie went upstairs and let herself into Thomas Hatch's room. She had heard her landlady in here early this morning and wasn't surprised to see a poppy lying on the open Bible whose pages had been turned to "Matthew, Chapter 5" where another passage was underlined: "That thine alms may be in secret: and thy father which seeth in secret himself shall reward thee openly." Did their landlady turn a page each morning? Did she hold a memorial service every single day? Sadie sat on the bed and thought about her mother. If there was a memorial room to her mother, would she visit it every day? For months after her mother had been buried in Copper Cliff, a plain grey stone to mark the place, she had thought of little else except her mother. Even asleep she had thought of her and woken up panic stricken because she had seen her lying cold and lifeless beneath a mound of rain-soaked earth. But gradually, Sadie stopped seeing her mother lying beneath the mound. This didn't mean that she had stopped thinking about her but that she had begun thinking of her in another way, not as a body buried in the earth but as a comforting and reassuring presence. Sometimes her presence was so real that Sadie could hear her mother's voice inside her head. Usually she said something Sadie remembered hearing her say, but sometimes she made a comment or observation that was new to Sadie. Not today. Today her mother said nothing—inside this memorial to Thomas Hatch, she was as silent as a grave.

5

The Soiled Sheet

BY LATE NOVEMBER SADIE HAD BECOME SO ACCUSTOMED to the door across the hall being opened in early mornings that she either slept through the sound or, if wakened, immediately went back to sleep. On the last Saturday of the month she was awakened early, not by Mrs. Hatch but by the distressing awareness that her leg, which had trespassed onto her sister's side of the bed, was damp and cold. Flora had wet the bed. She must have forgotten to use the chamber pot during the night. Sadie sighed and tears of frustration pricked her eyes. Just when it seemed that Flora's bedwetting was over and done with, here it was starting again. *I might as well get up and wash the sheet,* she thought, *I certainly won't get back to sleep.*

She sat up and pulled on her slipper socks and plaid bathrobe. Throwing back the covers, she yanked the undersheet off the bed. Too bad if Flora minded. Her little sister whimpered and rearranged herself on the mattress, a gesture of innocence that reminded Sadie that it wasn't Flora's fault that she had wet the bed. It wasn't as if she had done it on purpose. *Let her sleep,* she thought tucking the blanket around her sister. *It won't take two of us to wash the sheet.* Sadie opened the bedroom door, the sheet bunched in her arm, and tiptoed down the creaking stairs to the kitchen, which was cold because the stove had not yet been lit. The air was still a murky grey and Sadie switched on the overhead light, plunging the world outside the window into black. She went into the bathroom for the tin bucket and, filling it half full with water, put the sheet in to soak. Then she busied herself starting the fire in the stove, crumpling up old newspaper and adding kindling, as she had done under her landlady's instructions several times before.

She was shovelling coal into the stove when she heard Mrs. Hatch behind her. "And what's got you up so early on a Saturday morning?" Standing in the doorway in her bathrobe and slippers, her hair tied in rags, she sounded more curious than cross.

"I'm washing a sheet."

"Somebody wet the bed."

"Yes."

"Was it your sister?"

Sadie wanted to say, "Who do you think?" but instead banged the stove cover down hard.

"If it was your sister, then she should be the one washing the sheet."

"She's only eight years old."

"Eight years old is old enough to wash a sheet."

"If you say so." Sadie knew she was being flippant but, really, what did it matter who washed the sheet?

Mrs. Hatch left the doorway and coming close to Sadie, poked her head close to hers. "Don't you get saucy with me, my girl."

Sadie looked down at the squinting eyes—she was slightly taller—and said, "I am not your girl."

Mrs. Hatch bared her teeth. "Go up and bring your sister down here!"

Flora had been awakened by the voices coming through the heat register and by the time Sadie reached their bedroom, she was sitting on the edge of the bed, her feet dangling over the side. "I wet the bed, didn't I?"

"Get dressed," Sadie said.

The sisters dressed slowly and Sadie took her time braiding Flora's hair, wanting to make it clear to Sour Olive that she was in no hurry to follow her orders. By the time they went downstairs, the kettle was steaming and the sun had cleared the Southside Hills. There was a ribbon of bent sunlight—one-fifth of a rainbow—shimmering on the kitchen wall. Mrs. Hatch was waiting at the kitchen table.

"You took long enough," she said, "But of course girls make a habit of dawdling."

Sadie bit her lip to keep herself from saying anything saucy.

Sour Olive looked at Flora, "Since you're in the habit of wetting the bed, it's time you learned to wash your sheet."

"All right," Flora said.

Without moving from her chair, Mrs. Hatch began issuing orders.

"First, you pour boiling water into the bucket and soak the sheet for an hour. The kettle is on the stove." Mrs. Hatch had already drained the cold water from the bucket.

Flora went to the stove, Sadie following close behind. For a moment it looked as if Flora would try to lift the kettle with her bare hands.

"Use hot pads," Mrs. Hatch said.

Sadie gave Flora the hot pads. "Be careful," she said.

Flora tried to lift the kettle, but it was too heavy for her and Sadie reached out to help.

"Let her do it herself," Sour Olive screeched. "If you interfere, she'll never learn."

Shut your mouth, you hateful woman, Sadie thought. *Just shut your mouth.*

Because she couldn't lift the kettle, Flora kept tipping it forward so that the water would pour into the bucket. Instead, the boiling water dribbled down her leg. She let go of the handle with a shriek, and the kettle slammed flat on the stove, the water bubbling from the spout sizzling on the hot iron.

Flora was hopping around on one foot and wailing, "I'm hurt, Sadie. I'm hurt!"

"Shush!" Mrs. Hatch said. She was now on her feet. "A burn's no cause for carrying on!"

Sadie glared at her. "This is your fault. You filled the kettle too full." She didn't wait to hear what Sour Olive had to say to this accusation but turned her attention to Flora, who was still hopping about and wailing. Sadie put a hand on her shoulder and said, "Sit in a chair and let me look at your leg."

"Such carryings-on," Mrs. Hatch muttered.

Mrs. Hatch scuttled from the room and Sadie knelt down and told Flora that she was going to take off her stocking—the burn was below the knee.

"But it will hurt worse if you take it off!"

"No it won't. It will help. You'll see."

Though anger and fear made her throat feel as if it was stuffed with a piece of dry cloth, she managed to speak calmly. "I'll just roll down this stocking, very slowly, like this. There. Now, that didn't make it worse, did it?"

Flora stopped wailing and shook her head.

Sadie peeled the sock down past her ankle. There was an angry-looking six-inch scald mark below the knee.

"I'm going to fill the bucket with cold water. I want you to put your leg it in and keep it there for a while." Sadie had once seen her mother tend a scalded thumb in this way. "You stay here while I get the water, all right?"

"All right." Flora was making an effort not to cry but her chest was heaving.

Sadie emptied the bucket into the sink and filled it with cold water. Then she went to the ice box, chipped away ice with a knife and added it to the water. Flora winced when Sadie lowered her leg into the water but she didn't make a sound. Sadie rubbed the ice gently against the scald.

When Mrs. Hatch came downstairs half an hour later, Flora was resting the leg on a chair, with a tea towel warming her foot, and Sadie was sitting beside her, holding her hand.

Mrs. Hatch peered at the scald and said, "Some butter would help."

"I won't put butter on it until she's seen a doctor."

"Seen a doctor!" Mrs. Hatch said. "You don't think a kitchen burn requires a doctor! A doctor costs money."

Sadie stood up and faced her. "My sister is going to see a doctor," she said. "If my father were here he would insist on her seeing one."

Sour Olive blinked rapidly and for a moment looked confused. But she recovered quickly. "I doubt you'll find a doctor's office open on a Saturday. You may have to wait until Monday. I'm sure it won't matter if you wait. It's not as if Flora's leg is broke."

"She's seeing a doctor today." Sadie was standing her ground, whether their landlady liked it or not.

"Have it your way," Sour Olive said. "I'm going out." She put on her jacket and stood at the door, holding her purse. "If you must see a doctor, it should be Dr. MacDonald. Sometimes he won't charge. If he does, tell him your father will pay at Christmas. His office is on Duckworth Street at the foot of the Victoria Street steps." The door had barely closed behind her when Sadie muttered, "Good riddance," using the same tone of voice her mother used when she was riled.

Sadie said, "Do you think you can walk to Duckworth Street?"

"Of course I can," Flora said. She was returning to her spunky self. "But I don't want my stocking on."

"It's probably better for you to keep it off." Sadie gave one of Flora's pigtails a tug. "You wait here while I get our jackets."

Upstairs, Sadie took two one-dollar bills from Madeleine's pantaloons and put them in her pocket. Then she carried their jackets downstairs.

Flora had no difficulty walking and soon they were at the bottom of the Victoria Street steps. The doctor's office, which was to the right of the steps, was open. Inside, more than a dozen old people sat in chairs against the panelled wainscotting. Sadie gave the nurse their names, and she and Flora took the last two chairs, Flora sitting beside a woman and Sadie at the end. The woman, who had a face as ruddy and creased as a shrunken apple, looked at Flora's leg and said, "What happened to you, love?"

"I scalded it trying to lift a kettle of boiling water," Flora said mournfully.

"My, my. You're too little to be lifting a kettle of boiling water."

"I know."

The woman was called into the examining room soon after and Sadie and Flora were left to themselves. They occupied themselves playing I Spy using old calendar pictures of country scenes tacked to the walls. The waiting room was nearly empty when they were finally called in. By then it was past noon and the nurse had gone to dinner.

Dr. MacDonald was a huge bearish man wearing a starched white coat. He came into the examining room and immediately his gaze went to Flora's scalded leg. She was sitting on the one chair, Sadie standing beside her. He knelt down for a closer look at the scald. "It looks to me like you've been near boiling water," he said.

"She has." Sadie explained how Mrs. Hatch had insisted that Flora lift the kettle.

The doctor said nothing but stood up and left the room, leaving the door ajar. They heard him rummaging in a room across the hall and moments later he returned with a roll of bandage and a tin of salve. He knelt again and asked Flora to tell him how she happened to be lifting Mrs. Hatch's kettle. As he applied the salve, Flora told him everything—about their mother dying in Copper Cliff and their move to St. John's and their father working in Buchans. She had a dramatic way of speaking and was so caught up in the telling that the doctor bandaged her leg without her seeming to notice. Sadie thought Flora was telling the doctor more than he wanted to know but he didn't seem to mind. When he had finished bandaging, he leaned over and gave Flora's pigtail a gentle tug. The gesture bothered Sadie. How dare he be affectionate with her little sister! She immediately regretted the thought. Her sister was amusing in the way of little children and it was to be expected that he would be fond of her.

Dr. MacDonald handed Sadie the bandage roll and salve. "Apply the salve and rebandage the leg once a day for a week. After that you can leave it unbandaged. It's better if she doesn't wear a stocking for the next two or three weeks."

Sadie got right to the point. "How much do I owe you?"

"There will be no charge."

"But . . ." She looked at the bandage roll and salve.

The doctor waved a hand. "No buts."

Sadie's cheeks flamed. "But I have money and I expect to pay."

"Later," he said gruffly and, holding the door open, swept them out of the room with his hand.

This time, as they were walking through the waiting room, Sadie noticed the broken floor tiles and the peeling chairs, which rescued her pride because the shabbiness told her that the doctor must have quite a few patients who didn't pay. When they were on the street, Sadie asked Flora if she would like a chocolate ice-cream soda.

"We'll spoil our dinner," Flora said, mimicking Sour Olive's scolding voice.

"It's past dinner time," Sadie said. "Besides if we stay away long enough, it will be too late to do Sour Olive's stupid chores."

The sisters walked along Duckworth Street as far as Caines, which had a real ice-cream parlour where they could have a table to themselves. They sat at a marble-topped table, drinking their sodas slowly, intermittently blowing bubbles through their straws. Sadie would have preferred to have ordered a strawberry soda but chose chocolate so that she and Flora would have the same thing. Because of what had happened this morning, she felt that she and Flora had never been closer and she didn't want to do anything to change the feeling between them. She wanted to hold on to the closeness for as long as she could.

When they were back inside Mrs. Hatch's kitchen, Sadie noticed the sheet on the drying rack beside the stove, but the sight of it gave her little satisfaction; after being so mean, washing the sheet was the least Sour Olive could do. There was no sign of either their landlady or dinner.

"Let's go upstairs and read," Sadie said. *If there was no dinner*, she thought, hoisting her defiance like a flag, *they would do no chores*.

Instead of reading, Sadie wrote to their father about the scalding, leaving out the part about Sour Olive's meanness—this was another thing he would hear about at Christmas. She told him that everything was all right and that the doctor had taken good care of Flora. "Mrs. Hatch didn't think she needed a doctor," Sadie wrote, "but I insisted."

Later, when Sour Olive called them down to supper, she said nothing about the chores and did not ask about their visit to Dr. MacDonald, but she made of big show of having made them chocolate pudding for dessert. Knowing Flora's sweet tooth, she was either trying to get on her good side or make up for being mean. It occurred to Sadie that their landlady had opposed their going to the doctor, not so much because of the expense but because she didn't want him to learn the circumstances of the scalding. She didn't want it to get out that she had mistreated Flora. It mattered to her that other people, particularly people of importance like the doctor and the reverend, had a good opinion of her.

6

Gaiters

Before moving to St. John's, Sadie's father had been warned about the terrible weather in Newfoundland. The winters, he had been told, were nothing but freezing rain, ice and snow; the weather was so bad that Newfoundlanders had special words to describe it, words like mauzy and misky. But so far this winter, the weather was better in St. John's than Sadie remembered it being in Copper Cliff. If she was in Copper Cliff now, she'd have been wearing galoshes since November, maybe even October. But here it was the first week in December and it was only last night that enough snow had fallen to prompt her to dig out her winter boots. This was what she was thinking while she was eating her gluey porridge, watching the snow accumulate on the empty branch of the oak tree where the sick crow had taken refuge. One morning last week when Sadie looked out the window and noticed the empty branch, she knew that the crow's wing must have healed enough for it to have flown away to whatever place it called home.

While Flora was finishing breakfast, Sadie went upstairs and dragged the suitcase containing last winter's boots from beneath the bed. Sitting on the one chair in the room, she tried to pull on her old galoshes over her new shoes, but as hard as she tugged they wouldn't go on. She tossed them into the suitcase, regretting the fact that when she, Flora and her father had been shopping for school clothes in September, they hadn't thought about winter boots. Knowing she would have to walk through the snow in her shoes, she added an extra pair of stockings to her school bag to put on after she got to Spencer. Flora came upstairs and tried on her last year's galoshes. Luckily they fit.

Downstairs, when they were at the door, leaving for school, Mrs. Hatch directed her critical gaze toward Sadie's feet.

"You can't walk to school like that. You'll catch your death of cold."

"My boots don't fit."

Mrs. Hatch opened a drawer beneath the counter and pulled out two waxed-paper bread bags and a roll of string. "You'd better wear these bags over your shoes. Cut two lengths of string and tie them on."

"I won't wear them," Sadie said. "I'll be laughed at." She didn't expect Mrs. Hatch to insist because since the scalding she'd become slightly more inclined to give way.

"I expect Bishop Spencer girls would think themselves above wearing bread bags," Mrs. Hatch said and put them and the string back in the drawer. She was right. No Bishop Spencer girl would be caught dead wearing bread bags on her feet, not when a missing cuff or a sagging hem was enough to bring ridicule from girls like Eunice Baird, who seemed to delight in other's shortcomings and mistakes.

Quite apart from Eunice, Sadie's instincts were to avoid

drawing attention to herself. Reserve came naturally to her. She was much less outgoing than Flora, more inclined to watch and wait. During choir practice at school, for instance, she naturally sought the back row, not because she was especially tall but because she preferred not to be noticed. She didn't want anyone to notice her body, which was an ongoing source of unreliability and unease. At Flora's age she hadn't paid much attention to it, but now that she was fourteen, she was aware of it all of the time. The problem was that her body was constantly changing and was like a weed that couldn't be tamed. When she awoke in the morning, there was a cold sore beneath her lip that hadn't been there the day before; when she tried to comb her hair, it no longer did what she wanted; blonde waves sprang up all over her head, making her look as if she was wearing a wig; when she looked in the dresser mirror, which was spotted with black as if mildew was trapped inside, her breasts looked swollen and she thought she could feel them straining against the cloth of her uniform. There was always something to shock and dismay—no part of her body could be depended upon to be the same from one day to the next.

This morning, all through music, which Miss Marsh had substituted for the grammar normally taught first class in the morning in order to accommodate the Christmas concert, Sadie was obliged to stand in cold sodden shoes. There had been no time to change into the dry stockings. Even though Sadie was behind the other girls on the stage, in her usual place in the back row of the choir, Tina Wareham noticed her feet. While Miss Marsh was busy sorting pages of sheet music, Tina pointed to the wet imprints on the floor, setting off a series of nudges and glances at Sadie's feet that continued until the teacher demanded and received immediate silence.

"Today I am assigning each of you a position which you are to keep for the duration of our practices. These are the positions you will be in for the Christmas concert. Is that understood?"

"Yes, Miss Marsh."

"Very well, Sadie, you are to stand here beside Eunice." Miss Marsh indicated the front row.

Not Eunice, Sadie wanted to say but couldn't because no one argued with Miss Marsh. Wet shoes squishing with every step, Sadie moved beside Eunice and stood with her hands straight at her sides to avoid accidentally grazing Eunice's shoulder or arm.

"Jane, you might as well stand here too. At the end, next to Sadie."

At least Sadie had Millie on the other side.

The moving and shifting continued until Miss Marsh was satisfied, and the practice began. The two songs she had chosen for the concert were new to Sadie, but during the past two weeks she had memorized both tunes and now knew the words. They began singing an old English folksong called "Golden Slumber." Beside her, Sadie heard Millie singing loudly off key. She enjoyed singing so much that she didn't seem to realize that she couldn't carry a tune. Trish couldn't either, but it didn't matter because her voice was soft and she had been left in the back row. Why had Miss Marsh put Millie in the first row, knowing that she was an enthusiatic singer? They had sung only six bars when Miss Marsh clapped her hands, a signal that the singing was to stop.

"Jane Miller, I shall have to insist that you sing with less exuberance. This is a lullaby, not a vaudeville tune. It wants to be muted, hushed."

"Yes, Miss Marsh."

When they began again, Sadie couldn't hear as much as a whisper coming from her friend and she knew that Millie had stopped singing and was mouthing the words. Miss Witherspoon came into the gym to listen and seemed pleased with what she heard. At the end of "Hope Carol" she applauded enthusiastically and told the girls they were coming along nicely. Afterwards, when Sadie was squelching past her on the way to her next class, she saw the headmistress eyeing her wet shoes. Sure enough, at the end of the geography class Sadie was told to report to the headmistress's office. There she stood behind a student about Flora's age who was mortified to have "RL-Returned Lesson" written in red ink across the top. When the little girl went into the office, Sadie heard the headmistress going through the assignment, explaining what she had done wrong, speaking with more tolerance than she had done with Millie.

When it was Sadie's turn to enter the office (now there were two girls behind her with returned lessons), the headmistress asked her if she had winter boots.

"Yes, Miss Witherspoon, but I found out this morning that my galoshes no longer fit."

"Then you will have to replace them, won't you?"

"Yes, Miss Witherspoon." Sadie fidgeted with her belt, already worrying about how she would approach Mrs. Hatch for money to buy new boots.

"Very good. We can't have wet shoes ruining out new hardwood floors, now can we?"

"No, Miss Witherspoon."

"Well then, you may go." She picked up a pen and made a notation. Sadie was at the door when the headmistress spoke again. "You should know that in Newfoundland, we refer to them as gaiters, not galoshes."

How was I to know that? Sadie thought crossly. *Nobody told me!* By the time she had reached the classroom, she was laughing at herself, for hadn't she just been told?

At noon, when Sadie sat down opposite her sister to a dinner of fried bologna, boiled cabbage and buttered bread, there were three one-dollar bills beside her plate. Mrs. Hatch was at the stove making tea—now that it was winter she thought the sisters should drink something warm at noon.

"The money is for a pair of winter boots. Only yesterday I saw a pair of gaiters advertised for two and a half dollars at Knowlings," Mrs. Hatch said. "Be sure to bring me the change."

Knowlings was where Sadie's father had taken them to buy new school shoes. The salesman, a stooped greying man, had far too much to say about the size of her seven-and-a-half shoe and made the foolish remark that women's feet were bigger nowadays because women were doing the work of men. Weren't women employed in munitions factories during the war? Weren't they driving trucks in England and France? Weren't they in the thick of action, working in field hospitals and the like? The salesman spoke as though the Great War was still going on although it had ended eight years ago. Sadie made up her mind not to buy the gaiters at Knowlings.

"Thank you, Mrs. Hatch," she said politely, relieved not to have to ask for money or to take more bills from inside Madeleine's pantaloons.

"You're welcome I'm sure," their landlady said. "You and Flora may buy them directly after school. The ironing will have to wait until tomorrow," she added, her voice sagging with reproach. Did she expect Sadie to be two places at once?

Sadie bought a pair of black gaiters in Smallwood's Shoe Store for two dollars and fifty-eight cents. Unlike her old galoshes, the rubber gaiters had broad toes that made her feet

look even bigger. Afterwards she and Flora wandered around
the Royal Stores looking at things Flora liked. There was a
pencil case, a hairbrush and a box of paints she badly wanted.
She tried to coax Sadie into spending the forty-two cents
change on one of these items. "Please, Sadie, couldn't you buy
me this one little thing? I won't ask for anything else." But Sadie
didn't give in to her wide-eyed pleading. She said the change
would be returned to Mrs. Hatch and promised they would
come back later to do their Christmas shopping.

On Wednesday afternoon Spencer girls were given early
dismissal in order to accommodate a staff meeting. Rather
than return to their chores in Willicott's Lane, the sisters
whiled away the time in Spencer Lodge where the out-of-town
girls stayed. It was the best time to visit Millie's room, because
Miss Witherspoon and Miss Marsh, who had rooms at the
Lodge, were occupied at the school.

Millie shared a room with Gert Green and the Aspell twins.
The girls slept in four metal cots lined up against one wall. The
cots were packed so closely together that there was no space for
a table between—the only other furniture in the room were the
two dressers on the opposite wall that the girls shared between
them. The girls were expected to do their homework in the
sitting room downstairs, under the watchful eye of Miss
Witherspoon and Miss Marsh.

Millie kept her valuables in a small wooden box one of her
brothers had made from a board that had washed ashore from
a shipwreck. The wood was pitted and scarred from having
been dashed against the rocks but it had been sanded and
polished until it shone. There was a small padlock on the
chest. Millie took a key she kept, along with a ring, on a string
around her neck and opened the box. She took out several
photographs, which she arranged in a fan clasped to her chest.

"You sit here, Flora," Millie said bossily and patted a place on the cot. "You sit here, Sadie. I'll sit in the middle."

When Sadie sat down, her knees touched the next cot. "You can sit on Gert's bed if you wants," Millie said. "She won't mind."

"I'll stay here," Sadie said. Although Millie was a year older than she was, there was something childlike about her. It was as if they were playing house and she and Flora were Millie's children.

Millie laid a photograph on Gert's cot.

"This here's Nan." She pointed to a white-haired lady sitting in a rocker outside a square clapboard house. Millie laid out a second photograph. "This here's Mom and Dad with my brothers." Millie counted them off. "Harry, Rick, Bert, Winston and Joe."

Sadie saw four men wearing fishermen's overalls lined up like grinning fence posts. In the middle of the line was their smiling, dark-haired mother and their tight-lipped father.

"This picture was taken before Dad got his teeth," Millie explained. "That's why he looks so crooked."

The third photograph Millie placed on the bed showed a young man taller and thinner than Millie's brothers but, like them, dressed in overalls and boots. "This here's my boyfriend, Ray. We're engaged."

"Engaged!" Sadie was shocked. "Aren't you too young to be engaged?"

"All the girls my age at home are either married or engaged," Millie said. She lifted the ring from her chest. "Ray give me this before I left. He said he don't want me marrying a townie. Fat chance of that." She giggled.

Sadie examined the ring, which was a plain gold band.

"See how worn it is," Millie said. "It's old. Ray found it."

"Where?"

"Inside a fish."

"Truly?" Flora was goggle-eyed.

Millie held them in suspense as long as she could. Then she burst out laughing.

"It was his Gran's. But a long time ago, down the shore there was a ring found inside a fish. Cross my heart. 'God Above Continue Our Love' was written on it." Millie sighed. "It was some romantic."

When Sadie asked where had it come from, Millie looked at her as if she was daft. "Like I said, from inside a fish."

"But how did the ring get inside? I mean," Sadie persisted, "why did the fish swallow it?"

"Cod will swallow anything that's shiny. That's why they's easy to jig," Millie said. Then realizing that Sadie was still perplexed, she said, "There must've been a shipwreck on the sea bottom and the ring was in the wreck somewheres."

The three of them were silent, thinking exactly where the ring might have been on the ship.

Flora said, "Do you think the ring was on a woman's finger and the cod pulled it off?"

"Maybe," Millie said, her voice wistful and soft.

"But it had 'God Above *Continue* Our Love,' written on it," Sadie said, "so I think the ring might have been inside a man's pocket and he was taking it to his future wife."

"It could've been that too." Millie sighed. "Either way it was sad."

The next picture Millie showed them was of her Aunt Jane, who was a nurse in Boston. There was one of her aunt wearing a starched white uniform and cap, the kind of uniform Sadie wanted to wear one day. She was standing in front of a large stone building, probably the hospital where she worked. There was another photo of the same woman, this time wearing a flowered dress, standing in front of the house in Heart's Content, her arms linked with Millie's and her mother's— Millie's mother and aunt were sisters.

"It's my auntie who's paying for me schooling," Millie said. "She wants me to get my education. Being the only girl, I'm her favourite. She's all the time sending me presents."

"We have Irish aunts who send us presents," Flora said. "They live in England."

"If they's Irish, why do they live in England?"

"They moved during the Troubles," Sadie explained. "When Protestants weren't wanted in Southern Ireland. Their names are Rachel and Rose. Before they moved to Brighton, England, my mother took us to visit them in Cork. They lived in a mansion grander than this." Sadie waved a hand at the high windows and ceilings of the lodge, the heavy chandelier hanging from a circle of plaster ivy. "We stayed there three months. It was after the Great War."

"I don't remember any of it," Flora declared. "I was a baby."

Sadie had been six, old enough to remember the lily pond and the pony, the servants and the chauffeured car, the motor trips through green countryside, the lush meadows where chestnut-coloured horses grazed, the roads bordered by hedgerows and crumbling stone walls. She remembered Flora sitting on her mother's knee, the breeze riffling her mother's hair, a dreamy expression on her face. Her mother had been happy in Ireland. Before she died, she told Sadie that though she loved Ireland, she loved their father more, perhaps to explain why she had put up with living in Copper Cliff.

"After our mother died, the Irish aunts wanted us to live with them in Brighton, but we wouldn't leave our father." Sadie didn't say that the Irish aunts didn't think much of their father, that they thought their younger sister had married beneath her. Though their father had agreed to be married in a Protestant church, the aunts didn't approve of the fact that he had been born a Catholic. Flora didn't know any of this—there were many things that Sadie thought her sister was too young to know.

Millie asked, "Have you pictures of your parents?"

"Oh yes," Sadie said. There was a photograph of her parents in their bedroom at Willicott's Lane, as well as one of her mother. The picture of her mother was the first thing she had unpacked.

"When can I see them?"

Mrs. Hatch had already made it clear that the sisters weren't to bring girls home.

"I'll ask Mrs. Hatch," Sadie said. "She's been a bit nicer since Flora scalded her leg."

"Show me your scald," Millie said.

Flora obligingly rolled down her stocking and showed off the scabby, red wound as if it was a badge of honour.

Millie whistled, a skill no doubt learned from her brothers. "That's as bad as anything I've seen," she said approvingly. "It's worse than the rope burn Ray got last summer when he was hauling in his father's traps. He made a big fuss and went around whinging until I give him a kiss. That's the way men are." When neither of the sisters replied, Millie went on loftily, "Women are used to pain, but the least little ache and men cry like babies."

"Oh," Sadie said. She had no idea if what Millie said about men being babies was true. Except for her father, she didn't know any men, unless she counted Teddy. It occurred to her that for all Millie's backwardness at school, she knew a lot that had nothing to do with book learning, but had to do with everyday life. This realization made Sadie look at Millie differently. She saw her as someone who was practical and down-to-earth, someone who in many important ways was far more grown up than herself. She also saw something else, which was that Millie's real life wasn't happening in St. John's but in an outport far away with the blissful, homesick name of Heart's Content.

7

A Taste of Christmas

Buchans, November 22, 1926

My Darling Daughters,

We have snow on the ground here and must keep the stove going in the bunkhouse all night. Last night it was my turn to keep it going. With eight of us, each of us has one turn a week. For the most part, my cabin mates are good-natured fellows, which is fortunate since we are required to spend so much time together.

I am now working underground, examining the cores taken from the stopes by a diamond drill. As I anticipated, the ore is of a consistently high grade. The other prospecting geologist, Gutsy Pike, and I share a ten-hour-day shift, which means we each work two hours above ground and three hours below. In the evenings Gutsy and I amuse ourselves by playing cards and studying the geological map of Newfoundland, looking for likely spots of finding gold.

When your letter arrived telling me about Flora's donkey costume and the Christmas concert, I realized that I had forgotten to leave you with money to buy Christmas gifts. Please use the money I gave you to cover unforseen expenses and I will replace the amount when we are together at Christmas.

Every evening before going to sleep, I cross off another day on the calendar. I have made my travel arrangements for coming to St. John's and expect to arrive there December the twentieth. I have written to the Crosbie Hotel for reservations. It makes me happy to think that in a few weeks I will be with my wonderful girls.

Your loving dad

P.S. I have just received your letter telling me about Flora's scalding and am grateful that it wasn't more serious and that her older sister very sensibly insisted on her seeing a doctor. It is a relief to know that she is in my Sadie's capable hands.

Sadie read this last line over and over, so that she could savour "in my Sadie's capable hands." She knew that at the time of the scalding, she had acted capably. She hadn't felt capable but she had been capable enough to look after Flora. Sadie particularly savoured the words, "my Sadie," because they made her feel that there was something about her that her father treasured.

He had left a blue thumbprint on the letter, on the lower right-hand side of the page. It had been left there by accident and was an indication that her father's fountain pen must be leaking. She imagined him getting up from the bunkbed and cleaning his thumb with a damp cloth. He wouldn't use his handkerchief or his towel but would search around for a rag. Her father was fastidious about keeping his belongings and himself clean and though he lived in a bunkhouse, Sadie was sure that he hung up his trousers at night and brushed off his hat. She had never seen him dishevelled or unkempt. Even when he returned from a prospecting trip in Ontario carrying a backpack, his hat tipped at a jaunty angle, he had always looked well groomed. He would come into the house, spread his arms wide and say, "Where are my lovelies?" and Sadie and her mother and Flora would rush into his arms, flushed and laughing, while he grinned at them fondly. Her father had a grin that crooked upwards toward the left, making it seem as though his ear was tugging it up. He knew how to wiggle his ears and would do it on request to amuse Flora. Or he would pull a nickel from behind an ear or out of a sleeve. Quick-fingered and deft, he liked playing the magician and knew how to make cards appear and disappear without seeming to touch the deck. Sadie wondered if he was entertaining his bunkhouse mates with card tricks, and if he would learn new tricks to show Flora and her at Christmas. In less than a week he would be here, and Flora and she would be moving into the Crosbie Hotel, away from Sour Olive and her miserly meals.

At school they were now singing Christmas carols during assembly and every morning Spoony reminded them about Santa Claus Day. For the past week, Spencer girls had been bringing in gifts and putting them on a table decorated with red and green crepe-paper streamers. The gifts were clothes and toys the students had outgrown and would be packed into boxes and distributed among the city's poor on Santa Claus Day. It was important, Spoony said, for Spencer girls to share

the benefits of their advantaged positions with the disadvan-
taged in St. John's. Sadie thought about what she could give.
She supposed she could give her old winter boots, though they
weren't all that old and she had planned to save them for
Flora—most of Flora's clothes were Sadie's hand-me-downs.
Before assembly was over, Sadie had decided that she would
buy toys for Santa Claus Day as well as mugs for Flora and
herself because Spoony had also announced that the school
prefects would be serving hot cocoa during recess to those girls
who brought their own mugs.

By doubling up their weekday chores the sisters earned Mrs.
Hatch's permission to take off the whole of Saturday, and after
breakfast they went downtown to buy Christmas presents,
using six dollars Sadie had taken from inside Madeleine's
pantaloons. Flora was beside herself with excitement at the
prospect of having money to spend. She wanted to buy the first
thing she saw but Sadie insisted that they look everything over
carefully before spending a cent. They browsed through
Bowrings and Ayre's but ended up making most of their
purchases at the Royal Stores, where prices were lower. Flora
picked out a music box for the Santa Claus table and Sadie
picked out a dancing top. Remembering that their mother
always sent her sisters tinned ham for Christmas, they bought
the Irish aunts a tin of ham. Neither of them could think of
anything else the aunts might like—because they were rich,
they probably had everything they wanted. They bought a
wine-coloured fountain pen trimmed with gold for their
father. Flora bought a yo-yo for Peggy and Sadie bought a deck
of cards for Millie, who claimed that most evenings in Heart's
Content were spent playing cards around the kitchen table.
The sisters dithered about what, if anything, to buy Mrs. Hatch
before settling on a nightcap to cover the strips of torn sheet

she wore at breakfast. To them the cap was something of a joke. When they were alone, they often poked fun at Sour Olive's curlers, which Sadie said made her look like she'd had a bad scare. They also bought two mugs bearing a picture of King George and Queen Mary for drinking cocoa at school.

Saturday evening the sisters wrapped the Irish aunts' present, which contained a letter from Sadie and a picture from Flora. On Monday after school while Flora was playing inside the Collinses' house, Sadie walked down to Water Street and mailed the parcel at the main post office where Mrs. Hatch collected the mail. She was walking toward the Royal Stores to buy Flora's Christmas present when she came face to face with Wanda Hatch. Wanda was wearing the same mangy fur coat but her face had lost its puffiness and her lips seemed normal—her mouth was so heavily lipsticked that it was hard to tell.

"Well, I'll be," Wanda said. "Sadie, isn't it?'

"It's good to see you, Wanda," Sadie said. She meant it too.

"How you been keeping, girl? Is the old biddy as cranky as ever?"

"She's been nicer since Flora got scalded." Sadie explained what had happened the day Sour Olive was teaching Flora how to wash the soiled sheet.

"You be careful," Wanda said. "Don't let her fool you. Ma has a way of lying low. Listen, if you ever needs help, you come to me and I'll see you right. Even if you just wants to talk, you come."

"Where do you live?"

"For now I lives on Lime Street but you're more likely to find me at the Anchor and Chain where I works." Wanda pointed to some place behind Sadie. "It's just along here a ways in Steer's Cove. I'm on my way there now." She began moving away, speaking over her shoulder as she went. "I got to go or I'll be late. Don't forget what I said!"

During the next week whenever she had free time, Sadie sewed Flora's donkey costume which, with the help of Miss Forbes, the domestic science teacher, she managed to finish on time. She wrote end-of-term tests and for the umpteenth time reread her father's recent letter. During the week, Mrs. Hatch left a parcel card on the kitchen table and Sadie went down to the post office to fetch a package from the Irish aunts. In the evenings the sisters busied themselves making Christmas wrap from brown paper, decorating it with sequins and stars. They made snowflake cutouts and hung them in the window. They made coloured paper chains and draped them over the mirror. If they were in Copper Cliff, by now they would have cut a tree as well as spruce boughs, which they would have used to decorate the house. Except for their bedroom, there were no decorations inside Number 2, Willicott's Lane and the house remained as dreary and cheerless as ever.

"Are you putting up a Christmas tree?" Flora asked at breakfast one morning.

"I have a small tree I take out on Christmas Eve," Mrs. Hatch said. She was cleaning her eye glasses and without them couldn't see very well. When she turned to look at Flora, she reminded Sadie of a small underground animal blinded by light. "I can't afford to put up a large tree."

Sadie wasn't bothered by the absence of a tree because she knew that when their father arrived, they would put up one of their own. In a few days he would appear and whisk Flora and her to the hotel where they would eat delicious meals and sleep on a mattress that didn't have buttons gouging Sadie's hip. They wouldn't have to scrub, polish or dust, and Sadie wouldn't have to carry a chamber pot outside to the shed on cold mornings. With her father coming, she wasn't even bothered by being an outsider at school. What did she care if Eunice didn't like her? Soon she would be spending all her time at the hotel with her family. Already Sadie felt a lightness in her body, a quickening in her step, a jubilant lift in her heart. Now when she washed the dishes and swept the floor she sang, "Deck the Halls" and "I Saw Three Ships." At supper one night she was emboldened to ask their landlady if she could play the piano. Sadie had taken piano lessons in Copper Cliff and knew how to play "Silent Night."

"Certainly not!" Sour Olive replied. "That piano is never played!"

"Why not?" Sadie said.

"None of your business!" Mrs. Hatch slapped down Sadie's bowl so hard that some of the corn chowder slopped onto the oilcloth. After she ladled out Flora's chowder, their landlady went upstairs, leaving the sisters giggling and snorting with merriment. What did it matter if Sour Olive knew they were laughing at her? A few more days and they would be out of her clutches.

The sisters had planned to meet their father's train but he arrived earlier than expected and was drinking tea with Mrs. Hatch when they walked into the kitchen after school. For a moment they simply stood on the mat, too surprised to move. Their father stood up and spread his arms wide. Shrieking "Dad!" the sisters hurtled themselves into his arms, leaving wet footprints on the linoleum floor—they had forgotten to take off their boots.

"My delicious, delectable, delirious daughters!" This was another of their father's games.

Sadie grinned and said, "My funny, fabulous, fantastic father!"

The sisters began talking at once and didn't stop until their father put up his hands in protest. "Slow down, my lovelies. Now, do you have homework?"

"No."

"It's Christmas, Dad!" Flora said, as if he should know better than to ask.

"Well then, we'll go to the hotel for a while. I've already told Mrs. Hatch we'd be going."

Mrs. Hatch was nowhere in sight, having slipped away during the excitement.

Leaving their school bags by the door, Sadie and Flora went outside and, linking arms with their father's, walked down the lane. Sadie kept stealing sideways glances at him, at his hat pushed to the back of his head, his neat mustache, his crooked grin—he hadn't stopped grinning since they had walked into the kitchen.

"You look the same," she said.

"You mean I'm no handsomer than when I left?"

She giggled. "No."

"Well, you, my daughter, are more beautiful than when I left." Sadie blushed with pleasure. No wonder she adored him.

"Am I more beautiful?" Flora asked.

"Of course," their father said. "That goes without saying."

His suite on the second floor of the hotel overlooking Duckworth Street contained a bedroom for their father and a sitting room where Sadie and Flora would sleep on a pull-out bed their father called a davenport. Besides the davenport, the sitting room was furnished with two plush green chairs, a coffee table, a smoking cabinet, a rolltop desk, two floor lamps and a Persian rug.

Flora wanted to know if they could sleep on the davenport tonight.

"Not while you have school the next day. You need a good sleep."

"It doesn't matter if we get a good sleep," Sadie said. "Flora's finished her schoolwork and I've written my end-of-term tests."

"You can sleep here tomorrow night." Their father sat on the davenport and the sisters sat on either side of their father. "We don't like Mrs. Hatch," Flora said. "We call her Sour Olive."

"Why don't you like her?"

And Flora launched into a litany of complaints about how Sour Olive wouldn't give Sadie money to make fudge for the Spencer sale but had given her a broken owl for the sale table instead. How hard she made them work, Sadie especially, cleaning and ironing and emptying the chamber pot. How stingy her meals were, porridge every morning and only one glass of milk a day. Flora stuck up her finger. "Only one!" She leaned forward and rolled down her stocking. "That's my scald. I got it because Mrs. Hatch is so mean. She made me wash the sheet, and when I tried to lift the kettle, the boiling water went down my leg."

Sadie said that she thought Mrs. Hatch had made Flora wash the sheet to punish her for wetting the bed.

"But I don't wet the bed any more!"

"Good for you." Their father looked thoughtful.

Now was the time for Sadie to ask their father if they could move—she had planned to ask the question, though not this soon. "Couldn't we move, Dad? Couldn't we find a nicer landlady?"

Her father said, "After Christmas I will make inquiries, but from what I was told last summer, it may be difficult to find another boardinghouse within walking distance of the school. We don't want to jump from the frying pan into the fire."

"What do you mean?"

"Does Mrs. Hatch beat you?'"

"No."

"Does she yell and scream and call you names?"

"No."

"Does she refuse to feed you?"

"No, but her food is awful."

"Even so I wouldn't want to move you to a place that was worse, would I?"

"No."

"I'm hungry," Flora said. "Can we eat?"

Downstairs in the dining room, they ordered fried chicken and mashed potatoes. For dessert Flora ordered the most outrageous one on the menu: ice cream covered with gooey chocolate sauce and walnuts—she didn't have to worry about pimples. Sadie and her father ordered apple crumble with custard sauce. While they were waiting for dessert, Sadie noticed Teddy at a table by himself, reading a book propped up against the salt and pepper shakers. He looked lonely eating all by himself. *But it's Dad's first night home,* she said to herself, and didn't look at Teddy again.

8

Russ, the Magician

N<small>EXT MORNING, SADIE WANTED TO RACE DOWN</small> Victoria Street to the Crosbie Hotel for breakfast instead of choking down another of Sour Olive's potages before going off to school, but her father had insisted that she and Flora attend school. He said he had Christmas shopping to do without them and that their teachers must be expecting them to rehearse for tonight's concert, which of course they were. After assembly, everyone in the grade-ten class stayed in the gym for rehearsal, everyone except Millie who was late as usual. An hour later when choir practice was over and there was still no sign of Millie, Sadie asked Miss Marsh if she knew where she was.

"She's gone to Heart's Content and won't be back until after the Christmas holidays," Miss Marsh said briskly. "Outport girls usually have difficulties with transportation and when Gertrude Green's father arrived earlier than expected, Millie had no choice but to make use of the opportunity to return home." Sadie was disappointed. She had brought Millie's Christmas present with her to school and now she wouldn't be able to give it to her until January.

Sadie was following her classmates out of the gym when Miss Marsh called her back. "Sadie, I want you to tell Nelly that the two of you are to help me decorate the theatre. You are to ask Mr. Buckle to fetch the boxes of Christmas decorations from the storage room so that you and Nelly can carry them to the theatre. I'll meet you there."

"Yes, Miss Marsh," Sadie said. Spencer teachers expected every comment or instruction to be met with a respectful reply.

"Very well then." Miss Marsh had bulging eyes and a plump crouching body that reminded Sadie of a toad's, a harmless but busy toad. "You had better be off."

Upstairs in the classroom the grade-ten girls stood about laughing and chatting, Nelly in a cluster with the other class prefects: Eunice Baird, Patricia Munn and Sandra Murray. The prefects were class monitors whose job was to supervise the hallways at recess as well as the procession into assembly, and to ring the large brass bell with its wooden handle. Sadie tapped Nelly on the shoulder and repeated Miss Marsh's instructions under the hostile stare of Eunice. It was a who-do-you-think-you-are-butting-in-where-you're-not-wanted stare.

But Nelly seemed pleased to see Sadie. "Decorating the theatre together will be fun," she said.

Eunice glared at Sadie and said, "Why did Miss Marsh ask *you*? We're the prefects. *We* should be decorating the theatre."

"*I'm* a prefect," Nelly said. "Let's go, Sadie." And taking hold of her arm, she led her away.

"Why did Miss Marsh pick a Canadian?" Eunice grumbled loud enough for Sadie to hear.

As they were walking to the theatre carrying the decorations, Sadie asked Nelly why it mattered to Eunice that she was from Canada. "In Copper Cliff where I lived before coming here," Sadie said, "everyone was from somewhere else, places like Finland, Italy and Poland. I don't see why it matters where you're from."

"I don't either," Nelly agreed. "I think people should try to get along no matter where they're from."

"How do you get along with Eunice?" Except for Millie, Nelly was the only classmate Sadie would dare ask this question. She thought it was safe asking her because Nelly was always friendly with Sadie and was herself from out of town.

Nelly laughed. "I put up with her, like everyone else."

At the theatre, Miss Marsh assigned Sadie and Nelly the duty—it hardly seemed a duty—of tacking tinsel streamers in swoops across the stage skirting and fitting tinsel branches together to make a tree. When this was done, they arranged the greenery and fake poinsettias above the footlights. It was fun working with Nelly, who was an easy-come, easy-go kind of person, willing to get down on all fours with Sadie when they were trying to find lost tacks dropped on the floor.

By noon they were finished and Nelly went home to her aunt's house on Circular Road, while Sadie fetched Flora from school and they returned to Willicott's Lane and the dismal prospect of another one of Sour Olive's dinners. They were surprised to find a meal of creamed peas on toast and, wonder of wonders, a second glass of milk. Mrs. Hatch seemed almost pleasant, and when they had finished the dishes, hurried them upstairs to pack with only a passing reminder to leave their room tidy. Their father arrived soon after, and he, Sadie and

Flora carried their clothes and belongings down to the hotel and settled in. At five, they put on their woollen jumpers and went downstairs with their father for an early supper in order to be ready for the concert at seven. Before leaving Willicott's Lane, Sadie's father had asked Mrs. Hatch if she'd like to accompany them to tonight's concert and to Sadie's enormous relief, their landlady declined. "I'm much obliged for the invitation," she said piously, "but I'm expected at a meeting of the Women's Christian Temperance Union."

The Christmas Concert and Bishop Spencer Prize Giving was a splendid affair. Teachers, students, parents and friends were all wearing their best clothes and every seat in the Casino Theatre was taken—the closest their father could sit to the front was the twenty-third row. The concert began with Miss Marsh's choir. Sadie was nervous about being in the front row where floodlights shone in her face and there was no place to hide, but she overcame her nervousness by concentrating on Miss Marsh who stood at the music stand with her eyes bulging out more than usual and her tongue flicking from between her lips. Was she sticking out her tongue on purpose, trying to make them smile, or was she nervous? Whichever it was, the choir began to giggle, their laughter rippling up and down the rows. Before they got carried away, Miss Marsh clapped her hands, and soon they were singing with a gladness they had never felt during practice. By the time they were finished the second song, Miss Marsh was smiling and Sadie knew that they had done a good job.

Second on the program were twelve girls dressed in fancy gowns dancing a minuet, and third on the program was Flora's play entitled *L'arbre de Noël*, directed by Miss Beamish, the French teacher. From the back of the theatre where the choir had moved during the minuet, Sadie watched as each girl, costumed to represent a letter in the title, lined up on the stage. When it was her turn, Flora, dressed as a donkey, stepped out of the row and holding the letter "a" said, *Je suis l'âne qui est près de Jesus*. That was it. All Sadie's efforts that had gone into making a costume so that Flora could say those few words. When the play was over, the audience refused to let the children leave the stage, clapping them into taking one bow after another. Other plays, recitations, dances and songs followed.

It was nine o'clock before the concert was over and the prize-giving began. Miss Witherspoon began reading her yearly report. Sadie didn't listen. It was hot and stuffy at the back of the theatre and all she could think of was stepping out in the fresh night air with her father and sister. By now even the satisfaction of admiring the decorated stage had worn thin. At last they were singing "God Save the King" and the fall term was officially over. Looking at the crush of people in the aisles, at her handsome father in his velvet vest and trimmed hair, Sadie was overcome by happiness. Christmas holidays had finally begun and she had twelve whole days to do as she pleased with the two people she loved most in the world.

On Christmas Eve morning Sadie, Flora and their father went down to Water Street and bought a small spruce tree, a box of ornaments and a gold star, which they carried back to the hotel. Even with the star on top, the tree was shorter than Flora, but once it was lifted onto the coffee table in their father's sitting room, it satisfied the sisters. In any case there was a huge tree downstairs in the lobby lit with electric candles. Later that afternoon, Sadie and Flora again put on their good clothes and went downstairs for supper—dinner, they called it at the hotel.

Tonight they were eating with Sour Olive. "How could you?" Sadie had said when her father told her he had invited Mrs. Hatch. "When she's so mean!"

Flora said, "Sour Olive will spoil everything."

"Surely being kind to a widow on Christmas Eve won't spoil anything," their father said mildly. "I thought kindness to others was part of the Christmas spirit."

The sisters of course had no answer to that. Sadie said, "I didn't know Mrs. Hatch was a widow."

"That was how the reverend introduced her to me when we met in the church hall in September after the service."

Sadie told their father about meeting Wanda and about Thomas who had died in the war, but she had stopped short of telling him about having gone into his room. She didn't want him to know that she had entered a place she had been told was out of bounds, and she didn't want to give Flora the chance to say that she had seen Sadie leaving the room.

Mrs. Hatch arrived for dinner wearing her church clothes: a green felt coat and matching hat with a black veil worn half-mast. Looking at her across the dining-room table, Sadie thought the veil made their landlady look mysterious, reminding her that there was a completely different woman concealed inside. Whenever Sadie's father spoke, Mrs. Hatch smiled, as if everything he said met with her wholehearted approval.

After the soup bowls had been taken away, Mrs. Hatch dabbed her lips with a napkin and looked across the dining room, where a fierce-looking, fleece-haired woman was presiding over a brood of young children. The woman stared boldly at the Morins and at Mrs. Hatch, who quickly looked away. Sadie thought the woman must be trying to figure out if they were visitors or strangers living in St. John's.

"That's Ellie Bell. She's a Crosbie," Mrs. Hatch whispered.

She looked at the woman again but Elsie Bell had turned away. Leaning toward Sadie's father, Mrs. Hatch confided, "Ellie ran the hotel until her son Charlie took it over. He's managing it now."

Teddy's parents worked for Charlie Bell.

"Mr. Bell's not here," Sadie said. "He's gone to New York for Christmas." After she'd blurted this out, she bit her lip, realizing that she might be asked how she knew Charlie Bell was in New York. She didn't want anyone to know that Teddy had told her, that they had become used to confiding in each other. But no one asked and Mrs. Hatch continued talking about about the Bells. "Charlie's father, Sam Bell, was a famous shipbuilder in his day. Ellie is a first-rate business woman."

"Is that so?" Sadie's father said, a smile sliding toward his ear. This was the half smile he used when he was teasing, but Mrs. Hatch mistook it for a sign of interest and, bobbing her head toward him, confided that the Bells were "new money." She spoke these words grudgingly as if she thought "new money" was less valuable than "old money."

The main course arrived and Mrs. Hatch picked up her fork and said, "I've heard that Ellie collects antiques. Have you noticed antiques in your room?"

"I can't say that I have."

"I'm told the hotel is full of antiques."

Flora piped up, "There's an old wooden box in your suite, Dad. It's on legs that have flowers carved on them."

"You must be referring to the smoking cabinet," he said.

Mrs. Hatch placed her fork carefully on her plate beside the knife, then pressed the napkin to her lips. "I don't believe I've ever seen a smoking cabinet!" She sounded girlish and coy, which wasn't like her at all. *She's trying to wheedle her way upstairs,* Sadie thought. Before her father could offer to show her the smoking cabinet, Sadie leapt into the conversation. "Tell us about Buchans, Dad. You've hardly told us anything about it."

"So far there's not much to tell," he said, but he seemed to know what Sadie was up to because he grinned at her and went on to describe the plan to build the town of Buchans. There was to be a school, churches, a store. "Construction will begin in the spring."

"Will you be moving there when the town is finished?" Mrs. Hatch inquired.

"No."

Sadie's father rarely used this kind of "No," but when he did she knew it meant that he was putting an end to the subject.

During dessert he encouraged his daughters to talk about school and Sadie did her best to keep the conversation away from Mrs. Hatch.

When the meal was finished, all of them, including Mrs. Hatch (would they be stuck with her all night?), went to the Church of England cathedral whose stone columns were decorated with spruce boughs and red bows. The decorations softened the starkness of the grey stone walls, and it seemed to Sadie that the congregation was gathered not beneath stone arches soaring high above but within a circle of enclosing trees. They were in a place in the woods, a clearing that provided refuge and hope. The clean spicey smell made Sadie homesick for Christmases in Copper Cliff with their mother, a memory she resolutely pushed away. The choir entered the church in a procession, holding candles which illuminated their faces in such a way that even the most worn and wrinkled looked smoothed of care. It was as if the choir had been transformed into angels for the occasion. Sadie was by now swept up with the spirit of Christmas and, when they were singing "Oh Come

All Ye Faithful" was infused with a feeling of goodwill that embraced everyone in the cathedral, including the woman in the green coat who was standing beside her.

After the carol service Mrs. Hatch invited them up to Willicott's Lane for fruitcake and tea, which the Morins ate in the front room. While they waited for Mrs. Hatch to bring in the tea tray, Sadie went upstairs and returned with a gift, which she slipped under the tree. The tree, which was about two feet high and made of pale green net on which tiny ornaments had been sewn, was prettier than she had expected.

"A fairy tree," Flora said, and it did look like the kind of tree around which fairies might dance.

Mrs. Hatch saw her looking at it.

"I bought it years ago at the church sale."

Their father asked Mrs. Hatch how she would be spending Christmas Day. For an awful moment Sadie thought he would ask her to join them for Christmas dinner, but then she remembered that he had already accepted the Dodges' invitation for Christmas dinner in their hotel suite. The invitation, she knew, was Teddy's idea.

"I'll be spending the day at the prison."

"With murderers and thieves?" Flora said, stuffing her mouth with cake.

Her father smiled.

Mrs. Hatch frowned and said, "Only one murderer. Our Home Mission Association cooks the inmates' Christmas dinner and gives them presents we have made. Which reminds me . . ." She lifted the pillow where they had been concealed and gave each of the girls a gift.

Neither sister had been expecting this.

"I think I'll wait to open mine," Sadie said.

"Me too," Flora said.

Sadie thought if they opened their gifts now that Mrs. Hatch might open hers, and she didn't want to be here when she did, because the cap had been intended more as a joke than a gift.

After the Morins had wished Mrs. Hatch Happy Christmas and were returning to the hotel, their father said, "That wasn't so difficult, was it?" and Sadie had to agree that it wasn't.

At six o'clock on Christmas morning, Flora woke up and shook Sadie.

"Let's open our presents."

"It's too early," Sadie mumbled, pulling the sheet over her head. As a little kid, Flora always wanted to open presents right away but Sadie wanted to savour the anticipation of opening them for as long as she could. If she refused to get up, Flora would grow tired of waiting and go back to sleep, which was what happened, though it took a while. At nine o'clock the family dressed and went downstairs for a breakfast of bacon and eggs. By ten o'clock they were upstairs opening gifts beside their tree.

One of Sadie's gifts from her father came in a blue velvet box. When she opened it up and saw a watch with a silver clock face and a black leather strap, she threw her arms around her father, whose crooked grin stretched from ear to ear. "Oh, Dad! It's perfect!" she said. "I never expected anything like this!"

His gift to Flora was inside an even larger blue velvet box. It was a silver music box with a winding key on the bottom and a picture of a girl who had red hair like Flora on the lid. Flora lifted the lid and the three of them heard the lively notes of "Yankee Doodle" coming from the box. "It's for your valuables," their father said.

"I haven't got any," Flora said.

"No hair ribbons or candies?" her father asked.

He had also given them new velvet dresses and patent-leather shoes. The Irish aunts' gifts were pleated skirts and wool cardigans. Flora's gift to Sadie was a green change purse. Mrs. Hatch had given them each a pair of knitted bed socks. As well there was an assortment of books, puzzles and notepaper from their father.

The sisters put on their new dresses and shoes and their father the brown velvet vest he wore on special occasions, and they went downstairs to the Dodges' apartment, five rooms at the back of the hotel behind the main desk. Teddy opened the apartment door and Sadie immediately noticed how grown up he looked in a red Christmas sweater, his dark hair neatly combed.

"Step in," he said, "and I'll introduce you to everyone."

Behind him was a large noisy crowd. These were the family relatives who were all talking at once: his mother's three sisters and their husbands from Carbonear, her brother's family from Gander Lake and four cousins from Harbour Main, making twenty-three people squeezed into the suite for dinner, five of them small children who ran shrieking between tables set up to accommodate the guests. There was so much commotion that it was impossible to hear the carols playing softly on the gramophone, but nobody seemed to care. Teddy led the Morins into the dining room, where a large Christmas tree stood in the window, and asked if they would like some raspberry punch. Sadie took some punch but Flora didn't want any. She spied a girl about her age and went off to play. Sadie's father began talking to one of the uncles, and Teddy told Sadie that he had something he wanted to show her in his bedroom.

The idea of being invited into the privacy of the room where he slept made her feel odd and special. There was something intimate about being invited into a person's bedroom, even when the person was dead like Thomas Hatch. Sadie felt that she was being trusted with a part of Teddy's life others didn't see and she stood just inside the door, nervous yet eager. What did Teddy want to show her? Maybe he had only said that as an excuse for getting her alone so that he could kiss her. She didn't know what she would do if he kissed her, but she was interested in finding out.

Teddy went to the bed, reached under the pillow and pulled out a small box wrapped in tinfoil.

"For you."

Sadie blushed a bright scarlet. She was embarrassed that she hadn't even thought of buying Teddy a Christmas present, and here he was giving her a present he had kept under his pillow. He might even have slept on it, for heaven's sake.

"Merry Christmas," he said.

"But Teddy . . ." She couldn't risk looking at his face. It was obvious now that he liked her more than she knew. She liked him too, but she didn't want their friendship to move too quickly. She didn't think she was old enough to have a boyfriend, and anyway, depending on her father's job, in a year she and Flora might have to move some place else. If she became too close to Teddy, it would make it that much harder to leave.

"Aren't you going to open it?" He was watching her closely.

"Yes, of course." Flustered, she tore the off the wrapping and lifted the cover. Inside was a silver musical note the size of her fingernail.

"It's to wear on your lapel. I saw how much you liked to sing."

"You went to the concert?"

By now Teddy's face was as red as his sweater.

"I didn't see you there."

"I know." Looking unguarded and open, he leaned toward her. Now he really was going to kiss her and she was waiting for him to do exactly that. He would have too, if at that moment Flora hadn't burst into the bedroom with the announcement that dinner was ready and that they were to come right away and get it.

The dinner was wheeled in on trolleys from the hotel kitchen. Platters of goose and chicken, stuffing and mashed potatoes, whipped parsnips and carrots, jugs of gravy, an assortment of jellies and pickles were laid out on a makeshift table where people were encouraged to help themselves. The Morins filled their plates and carried them into the living room where they sat with the Harbour Main cousins, who entertained them with a story about Eldred Murphy getting stuck in the chimney on Christmas Eve. "Was he pretending to be Santa?" Flora asked. She had stopped believing in Santa soon after she had started school. When it came time for dessert, everyone crowded around the table to watch Teddy's father pour a spectacular river of blue flame over the plum pudding. Besides the pudding, there was trifle and spotted dick. By four o'clock Flora was groaning that her stomach was about to burst.

"Time for a walk before it gets dark," their father said and they fetched their coats and walked along Duckworth Street to Queen's Road. From here they walked uphill to Lime Street and Codner's Lane, the houses becoming poorer and more derelict the farther they went. There were no sidewalks or curbs and boards had been put down where the road was muddy. Sadie remembered Mrs. Hatch telling her that in this part of town there was no electricity or plumbing. Instead, water "fountains," tall hydrants with a tap at the top, were placed at intervals. The ground beneath the taps was frozen from dripping water, but in the open gutters on one side of the road stinking sewer water trickled down the hill.

"I've been told the Irish poor live here," their father said, and though he rarely mentioned the aunts, in the wry teasing voice he sometimes used, he added, "Not many Irish are as wealthy as your mother's sisters."

The people looked poor: children, hatless and coatless, wearing shabby sweaters against the cold, played with sticks and tin cans on a road gutted by snow and rain; women with grey faces and sagging bodies, some of them with babies propped on their hips, stared from the sooty windows of unpainted houses; bony-ribbed dogs roamed the street, one with a chewed rope around its neck. The dog snarled as they passed and Sadie thought it had probably chewed itself free in order to forage for whatever garbage could be found. She thought the children playing on the street were those for whom the presents that had been collected on Santa Claus Day were intended.

They came to Lime Street and Sadie wondered which house was the one where Wanda lived. Not that one looked much different from the other: in the waning light all of them were a discouraging weathered grey. From Lime Street, the Morins went to Codner's Lane and from there down Barter's Hill to George Street, which they followed until it brought them to Duckworth Street and the comfort and coziness of the Crosbie Hotel.

That evening their father treated them to the Arlie Marks Vaudeville Show at the Casino theatre where Teddy sat at one end of four seats, beside Sadie. She was wearing the silver note pinned to her lapel but he didn't mention it or speak. Like her, he kept his eyes on the stage, waiting for the show to begin. It was as if the moment in his bedroom had never been.

The first act was a sister and brother duo called the Dancing Demons. The duo tap-danced both onto and off the stage, never missing a beat. Next were two magicians who, among other things, juggled and did tricks with boxes and hats and delighted the children in the audience by allowing a rabbit loose on the stage. Apparently the rabbit was accustomed to being on stage, for it made no attempt to bolt but hopped about the stage as if it was grazing in a meadow.

The main feature of the evening was a musical play, *Dancing Youth,* in which Arlie Marks had the starring role. Arlie played a rich girl who pretended to be poor and joined a chorus line. A row of chorus girls, dressed in strapless dresses and beaded skirts, kicked their legs high behind Arlie as she belted out one song after another. Flora was dazzled by Arlie Marks's performance and vowed to become a chorus girl when she grew up.

The week following Christmas was clear and cold though mild for winter. Sadie's father took Flora and her for a ride on the shiny red streetcar. He took them up Signal Hill and down to the Battery and beneath the fish flakes along the harbour. The flakes were empty—it wasn't the season for making fish. Sadie didn't see anyone by the harbour who looked like a murderer, a thief or a hangashore. In fact, wherever she looked in the coves behind the merchant warehouses where finger wharves pointed into the harbour, men were busy unloading bags of salt and barrels of molasses and rum. All around her was evidence of work: piles of glistening coal, row upon row of fish casks, barrels of cod liver oil piled high, thick coils of tarred rope. Sadie liked the pungent smell of tar and salt, the way the masted schooners anchored in the harbour looked like a forest of leafless trees, their ropes and guywires a screen of branches so thick they cut the sky into jigsaw pieces.

One afternoon her father hired a horse and wagon and they went skating on Burton's Pond. While Sadie and Flora, who were good skaters, circled the pond with their father, Teddy skated by pushing a chair across the ice. On Friday their father took them to the movie matinee at the Nickle theatre, where they watched *Rin Tin Tin, A Hero of the Big Snows* in which Rinty saved a little girl who had been attacked by a pack of wolves.

On Saturday when the weather turned wicked, bringing howling wind and stinging rain, their father proposed having a picnic in the suite. He ordered up egg sandwiches and cookies, which they ate lolling on a blanket spread on the floor. Their father commented on the duck swimming in the lake and on the hot sun warming his back. He picked up a smooth pebble and skipped it across the water. He took off his shoes and socks and urged Sadie and Flora to do the same, and the three of them paddled along the make-believe shore. It had been a long time since their father had been so carefree. Before their mother died, he had often been playful, making up stories about trilobites and brachiopods, which he would pretend were furry creatures with squeaky voices instead of lifeless fossils imbedded in rock. Sadie had almost forgotten how funny her father could be. He had a lightheartedness about him, what her mother had called a careless charm, that made him good company. But he also had a heavier, melancholy side. More than once during the holiday, she saw how his mouth drooped, how he stared at nothing in particular as if his thoughts were locked away in the place where he kept his grief.

"Are you all right, Dad?" she said.

He jumped. "Me? All right?"

"You look sad."

He grinned and the sadness vanished. "I'm not sad when I'm with my girls."

The Sunday before New Year's, after Mrs. Hatch had gone to the church hall to serve coffee and tea, Sadie's father told her to take Flora back to the hotel while he talked to the Reverend Mr. Eagles about the availability of other boarding-houses close to Bishop Spencer. The sisters took their time walking back and had no sooner taken off their coats and seated themselves on the davenport when he returned. He looked glum, and right away Sadie knew that the reverend had been no help.

"According to the reverend, most respectable boarding-houses won't take families. They don't want the responsibility of looking after several children. They prefer single boarders," her father said. "He said that if you girls were willing to live apart, other accommodation might be found."

"We won't live apart."

"Of course not. I told him that was out of the question." Her father sighed. "I'm afraid you and Flora will have to put up with Mrs. Hatch for six more months."

They moved back to Willicott's Lane on New Year's Day to make themselves ready for school the next day. Although her father stayed in St. John's for the rest of the week, as far as Sadie was concerned, once she and Flora moved out of the hotel, the good times were over. At night when she lay on the iron bed, she folded her hands over her chest and prayed for a heavy snowfall, preferably a blizzard, a momentous storm that would dump enough snow on the railroad tracks to keep the train from running and their father from leaving. It rained instead, a harmless mizzling rain that in no way altered the train's departure.

The night before he left, when they were eating supper at the hotel, in desperation Sadie burst out, "Do you have to go? Couldn't you get a job here in town?"

Her father said, "I would never find a job here that pays me as well as the one I have now. Besides it won't be for long."

"Then what will you do?"

"It's too soon to say," he said mysteriously. "But I'm hoping to find something that will earn me enough money so that we can pick and choose where we want to live."

"I thought you already had enough money," Flora said, stirring chocolate sauce into her ice cream—she had eaten the same dessert every night for the past two weeks.

"I did have," their father said, his mouth crooking up, "but my youngest daughter ate it up."

"You're so funny, Dad," Flora said and laughed.

But Sadie didn't laugh.

"Cheer up and look ahead," her father said. "In three months it will be Easter and we'll be sitting here again."

"Three and *a half* months," she said.

The night after her father boarded the train, Sadie dreamed that he was a magician performing on the stage of the Casino theatre. There he stood in front of the footlights, looking like a debonair showman in a top hat and carrying a wand, a shining glass globe on his outstretched hand. The globe shimmered with promise and hope, with the fleeting certainty that whatever would make her happy was inside the globe. But then her father, the magician, passed a gloved hand over the globe and poof! both he and the globe disappeared. Sadie awoke in a panic—her chest was tight and she was unable to breathe. She sat up in the chilly darkness and thought, *Where is Dad?* Had he really been here or had she dreamed it? She touched her silver wristwatch and was reassured that yes, her father had been here. Hadn't he given her this watch for Christmas? He was gone now but he had definitely been here. With this thought came a welcome gasp of relief that loosened the tightness in her chest. The gasp was followed by another and another until she was breathing normally. Then she lay down and, turning toward her sister, went back to sleep.

9

The Fouled Mug

THE DAY AFTER THE TRAIN CARRIED HER FATHER AWAY, Sadie awoke inside the house on Willicott's Lane to a frigid room. There was a draught on her neck and her nose was cold, but at least with bedsocks on, her feet were warm. She and Flora dressed quickly and went downstairs for breakfast, which Sadie ate while staring glumly outside. She hated the winter dark and this morning the greying light outside the window mirrored the sadness she felt now that her father had gone. Later when she went upstairs to get her toothbrush, she noticed the first tentative streaks of dawn brightening the sky over the Southside Hills and gradually her melancholy began to lift. There had been a freezing rain overnight, what Mrs. Hatch called a silver thaw, and now the electrical wires were necklaced with ice which glittered and winked with light. The same light transformed the icy tree branches into crystal chandeliers. The freezing rain meant that before leaving for school, Sadie and Flora had to spread ashes from the stove in front of the back door and along the sloping lane. Otherwise, Mrs. Hatch said, they would fall and break their necks.

With their father gone and the sisters back at school, Mrs. Hatch seemed to think it necessary to increase their chore load. She said that during the holiday they had fallen behind in their housework and must work hard to catch up, and with the cold weather added coal hauling to the list. Every morning after breakfast Sadie and Flora filled the kitchen coal box as well as the scuttles in the front room and in Mrs. Hatch's bedroom. It rankled Sadie that they had to fetch coal for fireplaces she and Flora never used. Last fall when their father had inquired about how his daughters' bedroom would be heated, Mrs. Hatch had pointed to the register in the ceiling above the kitchen stove and said the heat from the stove would keep their bedroom warm in the winter. This wasn't true—there wasn't even enough heat coming through the register to melt the ice crystals on their bedroom window. Sadie thought their bedroom had probably been Wanda's—it was Thomas who had been given the room with a fireplace.

In addition to hauling coal, the lamps had to be filled with oil and their blackened lanterns cleaned. Although electric light bulbs dangled from the ceiling of every room, they were seldom turned on, because Mrs. Hatch claimed that it was more economical to use oil lamps. On top of these chores, there were floors to mop and wash, furniture to be polished, the bathroom to scour. There were clothes to iron, uniforms to sponge and press, shoes to shine. When Flora grumbled about the amount of work, Sadie reminded her that Mrs. Hatch had told their father before he left that once their chores were caught up, they could join Brownies and Guides. Sadie was certain that if he could see for himself the amount of work they were required to do he would remind their landlady that she and Flora were boarders, not servants. Sadie felt she was being treated like a servant most of the time. Do this, do that, Sour Olive said as soon as they took off their boots at the door. And she never thanked them for the work they did or told them that they'd done a good job.

Classes at Bishop Spencer had been underway a week before Millie, Gert and the Aspell twins returned. The morning they showed up at school, the four girls spent half an hour behind Spoony's closed office door and Sadie noticed that when Millie came into Miss Bugle's class afterwards, she was sullen and red-eyed. Miss Bugle didn't comment on her late arrival or on the geography test that Millie had failed. The exams students had written before Christmas were gradually returned and reviewed question by question, after which the correct answers were provided.

After Miss Bugle's class, Spoony returned the literature test, two lengthy essays about "The Rime of the Ancient Mariner" and another poem they had studied last term, "The Lady of Shalott." Sadie had been given 95 per cent on the test which, Spoony said, was the highest mark in the class, adding that the lowest mark , 48 per cent, was Millie's. The headmistress didn't ask Millie to read from her test. Instead, she asked Eunice, who had made 90 per cent, and Nelly, who had made 55 per cent, to read their essays aloud as an example to the other girls as to how they ought and ought not to be done. When Eunice had finished reading, Miss Witherspoon looked at her and then at Nelly and said, "Do you see how it's done, Nelly? You must try harder next time. You don't want to be at the bottom of the class with Jane Miller, do you?"

There was an intake of breath, a collective gasp in the room and except for the cooing pigeons huddled above the windows outside, silence. This was followed by a scattering of titters, but not many—most of the girls were shocked by Spoony's unkind remark, because though firm she was usually fair. Behind her, Sadie heard Millie sniffing. As soon as class was over, she turned, wanting to offer comfort, but her friend was already at the end of the aisle, churning toward domestic science class.

Sadie's next class was Latin with Miss Marsh. Sadie had made 92 per cent on her Latin test, which meant that during class she was called upon to supply correct answers. She did this mechanically, thinking all the while about how terrible Millie must feel to have been reminded that she was where no one in school wanted to be—at the bottom of the class. Why had the headmistress been so mean? Was the meanness an awkward attempt to encourage Nelly, or didn't she care about Millie's feelings? Whatever the reason, Sadie was angry that Miss Witherspoon had been so thoughtless. If her father were here, he would say that Sadie's Irish was up. It was what he used to say about her mother when she was provoked. At times like this Sadie most missed her mother. She missed not being able to sit across from her at the kitchen table and tell her what Miss Witherspoon had said to Millie. Her mother would have understood how helpless she felt having to sit there silently while Millie cried. Before she became ill with pneumonia, her mother had been spirited and feisty. She had a particular distaste for snobs and when a neighbour, Lydia Cross, remarked that immigrants were taking over Copper Cliff and was against the Halvshchaks moving from Shantytown to the company house next door, Sadie's mother reminded her that she and Lydia were immigrants from Britain and that personally she liked living next door to the Samulskis, who had recently immigrated from Poland.

After the noon bell, Sadie searched for Millie so that they could walk to Rawlin's Cross together, but she was nowhere to be found. After school, Sadie and Flora looked for her in Spencer Lodge, but she wasn't there either. Gert Green didn't know where she was but she agreed to put Millie's Christmas present beneath her pillow.

Walking to school the next morning, Sadie told Teddy what had happened. As usual, Teddy listened intently until she finished explaining, making no attempt to interrupt or to change the subject. Because of his quiet way of listening, Sadie was surprised when he burst out, "Some of the boys at Bishop Feild are meanly treated by the masters. That won't change until more Newfoundlanders are teaching in our schools."

Sadie was surprised by the passion in his voice. "Is that what you intend to do, become a teacher?"

"Yes." Teddy flushed. "No. I haven't decided. All I know for sure is that I'm fed up with the British treating us as if we're slow-witted and backward."

During Friday recess, Millie came up to Sadie as she was leaving the cloakroom with her cocoa mug.

"Thanks for the playing cards," Millie said. "I would've thanked you sooner but I've been feeling out of sorts."

"That's all right."

"I wants you to know that I'm pleased you got all them high marks."

Sadie had led the class.

"The reason they're high is because I'm repeating the grade. I've studied most everything before."

"I'm repeating the grade too but my marks is worse than last year," Millie said and giggled, to make it a joke.

"I'm not sure that I want to lead the class," Sadie said. "It's only made Eunice hate me more. You've seen Tina and her passing notes about me in class."

"How do you know the notes are about you?"

"I opened two of them. SUCKER was printed on one in big letters and TEACHER'S PET on another."

"You should hate her back."

"Eunice or Tina?"

"Eunice. Tina's only doing what Eunice wants."

Millie picked up her mug and together they took them to be filled. Afterwards they stood in the corner in a space behind the stairs and talked.

"Eunice is scared you'll get a blue sash instead of her," Millie said.

As Spoony had explained during an assembly, at Spencer a coveted blue sash was awarded to those girls who demonstrated outstanding qualities of character such as self-control, courtesy, enthusiasm and cheerfulness. The chosen girl also had to be an all-round person, which meant being able to do other things besides study, such as sports.

"There's no chance of me winning a sash," Sadie said. "I'm a Canadian and I'm hopeless at sports."

At Spencer girls earned points for their houses through sports and so far Sadie hadn't earned a single point for her house. There were five houses, each one having a different coloured ribbon as a flag. Sadie had been assigned to St. George's house, whose ribbon was red, and Flora to St. Michael's, whose ribbon was purple. Neither of them had what she wanted, because they both wanted to be in St. Patrick's house, with its green ribbon. The houses were intended to build cooperation and team solidarity in sports, and whenever points were gained during games, they were assigned to a house. So far the only game Sadie had played was basketball, which she disliked. Unlike Eunice, she was awkward, and whenever she got the ball, either dropped it or tripped over her feet. She much preferred gymnastics, which required the girls to arrange their bodies into rectangles, circles and triangles Miss Fraser, their gym teacher, called pyramids. This required good balance and the ability to stay still, both of which Sadie possessed.

It was during a gym class in late January that Millie first took sick. The class began with Miss Fraser instructing the girls to leap over a wooden horse, then tumble head first onto the padded mat where they were expected to do a somersault. Sadie wasn't too bad at this, having practised somersaults on the living-room carpet in Copper Cliff when she was younger. More recently she and Flora had somersaulted on the carpet of their father's sitting room at the Crosbie Hotel. Millie was the best somersaulter in the class and had a knack of tucking herself in until she looked like a ball rolling across the mat.

They had finished tumbling and were dragging the mat to the back of the gym when Millie fainted. Her eyes closed, her legs buckled and she fell to the floor with a thud. Sadie thought the smell of Dustbane might have made her faint. Mr. Buckle used the oily green cleaner when he swept the floor, leaving a sickly sweet odour behind.

"Back away, girls," said Miss Fraser, whose freckles and smallness made her look like a girl herself. She knelt beside Millie. "Back away. She needs air. Sadie, go to the washroom and bring me wet towels."

"Use cold water," she called as Sadie ran from the gym.

By the time she returned with the wet towels, the rest of the class had retreated to the far end of the gym and Millie's eyes were open. Miss Fraser held the cold towels to Millie's forehead.

"Can you sit up?"

"I think so."

"My head hurts."

"Where?"

"Back here."

"You must have hit it when you fell." Millie sat up and Miss Fraser leaned over and examined her head. "There's a bump there where you've been bruised. Can you stand?" She held out her hand.

Millie took the hand and pulled herself up.

"Now look at me." Miss Fraser stared at Millie's eyes. "Your pupils are normal, which means you don't have a concussion. Even so, I think it's best if you stay on your feet. If you feel sleepy, don't lie down." The gym teacher looked at Sadie. "Can you walk Millie to Spencer Lodge? I will tell the headmistress what has happened. She will look in on you later."

Outside, on Bond Street, away from the school, Sadie and Millie walked arm in arm, laughing and chatting. Millie had completely recovered and by the time they reached Rawlin's Cross, the fainting spell was almost forgotten.

"I don't feel like going to the lodge," Millie said. "Why don't we go to your boardinghouse and you show me your bedroom?"

"All right." Sadie knew Mrs. Hatch wouldn't be home because her church group met on Wednesday afternoon.

Leaving their gaiters by the back door, the girls walked through the kitchen, which was cold now that the stove fire was banked, and Sadie showed Millie the house room by room. She even took her into Thomas Hatch's room, where she made Millie swear on the open Bible not to tell. Sadie noticed that the pages had been turned to "Matthew, Chapter 23" where "And call no man your father upon the earth; for no one is your father, which is in heaven" was underlined. Millie looked around the room and said there was a woman in Heart's Content who kept a room like this for her son who had died in the war.

"It has an open Bible in it too, but it's a sadder room because it has a helmet and gas mask on the pillow and the soldier's uniform is laid out on the bed."

Sadie was disappointed that Millie wasn't more impressed. But she was impressed with the pictures of Sadie's parents. There were two pictures in hinged silver frames that faced each other like the pages of a book. One picture showed Sadie's parents together, her father standing slightly behind her mother. Mary Morin was wearing a high-necked blouse and her hair was piled thickly on top of her head; Russ Morin was wearing a suit and vest, a felt hat tipped at its usual angle at the back of his head. The other picture was of Mary by herself. A half-smile hovered about her lips and her eyes were averted. Their expression was dreamy, reminding Sadie of the day long ago when she and her mother, who was holding Flora, drove with the aunts through the Irish countryside.

"She's beautiful," Millie said.

"She looks like Flora."

"Don't be daft. She looks like you. I may not be smart in school but I knows that much."

It was next day during recess when Millie was in the washroom and Sadie was drinking cocoa near the staircase that Nelly asked her about Teddy. She said she knew Sadie and he knew each other because she had seen them walking along Gower Street together. "Is he your boyfriend?"

The question gave Sadie such a start that she slopped cocoa onto her white cuff.

"He's a friend," Sadie said guardedly. "Not a boyfriend."

"But you like him."

"Sure, I like him."

"Are you going out with him or anything like that?"

"We walk to school together. Why are you asking me this?"

"Because I have a huge crush on him," Nelly said. "I first noticed him back in the fall and have been dying to meet him since. Could you introduce us? I mean, I wouldn't want him to think I was chasing him or anything like that."

"Sure I'll introduce you," Sadie said, trying not to show that she was upset by Nelly's request. It was true that Teddy wasn't exactly a boyfriend, but he was more than a friend. Nelly had lots of her own friends. Why did she want Sadie's too? But she had to do as Nelly asked, if only because she didn't know how to refuse.

They arranged to meet next morning, seemingly by chance, at the corner of Gower and Prescott streets. As far as Sadie could tell, Teddy took this "accidental" meeting in his stride and was the usual polite Teddy, asking Nelly questions about herself. When she said she was a Goodyear from Grand Falls, he told her that his uncle on his mother's side lived there. It turned out that Nelly had minded his uncle's children and had been in first grade with one of his cousins. The rest of the way to school, they chatted about family and relations. Listening to them talk, Sadie was filled with envy and longing. She couldn't help it. Their talk made her painfully aware that, except for the Irish aunts and her father's brother who lived in California, she didn't have any relations. She didn't even have a place she could call home.

When Teddy left them at the front of the school, Nelly whispered, "I think he likes me, Sadie. Maybe he'll ask me to a movie or something."

But on Friday morning when Sadie was walking to school with Teddy, he invited Sadie to the movie matinee the next afternoon. "There's a western playing at the Queen. Can you come with me?"

Sadie was caught unawares, but she was pleased that he had asked her to the movie, and relieved that he had asked her and not Nelly. But then she thought, *If I say Yes, am I being disloyal to Nelly?* "I don't think I can go," she said. Pleasing friends was so confusing. She wanted to be loyal to Nelly but not at the risk of losing her friendship with Teddy.

Teddy looked at her over his glasses, which had slid partway down his nose. "Why not? Won't your chores be finished by then?"

"I have to look after Flora. I can't leave her with Mrs. Hatch." Now was the chance for Teddy to say that Flora could come along. It was a lame excuse but it was also a solution. Surely Nelly wouldn't think Sadie was disloyal if she went to a movie with Teddy *and* her little sister.

"Couldn't Flora stay with Peggy's mother?"

"I suppose she could," Sadie said doubtfully.

"Sadie, you can't do everything with your little sister," Teddy said. "You have to have a life of your own."

Sadie bit her lip. She felt angry heat rising in her cheeks. She glanced sideways and noticed the tips of Teddy's ears were red. For some reason this softened her anger and rashly, impetuously, she agreed to go. Nelly was a friend of hers, but so was Teddy.

"You're sure?"

"Yes, but I'll have to meet you at the corner because I don't think Mrs. Hatch would approve of me going. And I'll have to ask Mrs. Collins if Flora can play over there."

Saturday afternoon after their chores were done and Flora went off with the Collinses, Sadie put on the skirt and sweater the Irish aunts had given her for Christmas and pinned the silver note on the sweater. She put on her coat and buttoned it up so that Sour Olive wouldn't ask why she was dressed up. She needn't have bothered because her landlady called upstairs to say that she was going out to do some errands. Sadie waited in the window until she saw Mrs. Hatch reach the end of the lane before putting on her boots and going out to meet Teddy.

The theatre was nearly full when they arrived, but they managed to find two seats at the back. The movie, *The Cowboy Musketeer*, featured Tom Tyler, a hard-riding, hard-shooting cowboy hero. He and his pals risked racking water and jagged cliffs to rescue a six-year-old boy and his dog. There was a scene when Tom and the heroine, Laura, came face to face with doom, but there was nothing sappy about their romance, nothing that would embarrass Sadie in front of Teddy. What a treat to be able to watch a movie without having to push past irritated people on her way to the washroom because her little sister insisted she had to go. Or having to put up with sleeve tugging and whispering when they reached a part of the movie Flora didn't understand. This afternoon Sadie could sit in the theatre without being expected to do anything but enjoy the show. She sat straight-backed, hands in her lap in case Teddy should try to hold hands. If they were alone, she would have wanted them to hold hands, but not when they were surrounded by people. Teddy must be feeling the same way, because he made no attempt to do this or to put an arm around her seat, but like her, sat and watched the movie as if he was nothing more than a casual friend.

When the movie was over and the lights came up, Sadie sat watching the people in front of them who were leaving their seats and edging up the aisle. It was then she saw Nelly and Eunice sitting five rows ahead. This was a surprise. Sadie didn't know that Nelly and Eunice were close enough to attend a movie together; if she had known, she would never have asked Nelly about how to get along with Eunice, because Nelly was the kind of person who would pass it on. Nelly stood up and turned, looking for a scarf, perhaps, or a glove, and saw Sadie with Teddy. Sadie saw her mouth open in a mixture of surprise and dismay before she turned away and whispered something to Eunice. While Teddy made his way to the end of the aisle, Sadie stood unmoving, caught in a snare of tangled feelings: guilt, disappointment, fear, she didn't know which one rankled her the most. She stared fixedly at Nelly, wanting her to turn, to smile or wave, to show that they were still friends, but Nelly ignored her and Sadie knew that her feelings must be hurt. She probably thought she had been lied to when Sadie said that Teddy wasn't her boyfriend. She might even think that Sadie has asked him to the matinee herself.

On Monday morning when Nelly wasn't waiting at the usual spot for Sadie and Teddy to come along Gower Street, Sadie knew that she had to talk to Nelly and explain. She'd do it first thing after school. She had to wait until then because it was her day to clean the blackboards, which would take most of her recess time. Halfway through their first class, there was a surprise fire drill, and when Sadie filed outside with her classmates to stand in the shivery cold, she thought she might get a chance to talk to Nelly, but she was too far back in the line. Later, during recess, Sadie was outside whacking the blackboard brushes against the stone wall to get rid of the chalk dust when Nelly opened the door and called, "Do you want me to pour you some cocoa while there's still some left?" So she wasn't put out; they were still friends.

Sadie smiled. "No thanks. I'll get it myself," she said and when she finished cleaning the brushes and returned them to the classroom, she went downstairs to the cloakroom to fetch her cocoa mug, which she had hung on the hook beneath her coat. Reaching beneath the coat, she groped for the mug but it wasn't there. Although Sadie had said she would get the cocoa herself, Nelly must have taken the mug away to fill it. She was about to look around for the mug when she caught a whiff of something foul coming from the box where she kept her boots. She reached down and pulled out her boots and saw a mug of excrement shoved into one of her gaiters. Her mug. It was full of poop.

An "Oh!" escaped before she clapped a hand over her mouth. She stood there shocked, her heart pounding. Then she looked carefully around the cloakroom which, because recess was nearly over, was empty. In a way the emptiness was a relief because it saved her the embarrassment of having someone else see what was inside her mug. She picked up the boot and carried it into the dingy green washroom. One of the four cubicles was occupied but the others were free. Sadie carried the boot inside an empty cubicle and hooked the door. Grabbing a handful of toilet paper to cover the poop, she lowered her hand into the boot and lifted out the mug. Then she dumped the poop into the toilet and flushed. She wrapped more paper around the mug and put it into the waste can, knowing that even if it was cleaned with boiling water that she would never drink from it again. She waited until whoever was in the next cubicle had left before coming out of her own and washing her hands. She didn't look in the mirror, afraid she would cry if she did.

She went back into the cubicle, locked the door, sat on the toilet and tried to think. Who would do such an awful thing? She didn't know which was more upsetting: to have someone so thoroughly dislike her that she took the risk, not to mention the trouble, of collecting someone's excrement and putting it into her mug; or to be completely humiliated and shamed by the ugliness of the prank. But this wasn't a prank. A prank was meant as a joke and this wasn't a joke. This was a mean-hearted and cruel attempt to make her feel miserable.

Who would do such a thing? One thing was certain: whoever had done it was from Sadie's class and knew that today was her turn to clean the blackboard brushes, which meant Nelly, who she had mistaken for a friend, had been in on it, leading her to the mug by offering to pour her cocoa. The offer had been a reminder not to forget to get cocoa so that when Sadie went to get her mug, she would find the poop before Mr. Buckle or the housekeeper, Mrs. Collins, found it. If either of them found the mug, it would be immediately reported to Miss Witherspoon, who could begin an inquiry that wouldn't stop until she got to the bottom of it. It had all been cleverly planned. Was Nelly clever enough to have planned it? Or did Eunice plan it after she and Nelly left the movie?

The end-of-recess bell rang and still Sadie sat, trying to decide what to do next. She could feign sickness. She could tell the headmistress that she wasn't feeling well, which was true, and ask to be excused from school. But if she didn't return to the classroom, whoever had done this awful thing would know that Sadie had been unable to face the class and would assume that she had been defeated by hate, and meanness would have been rewarded.

Sadie couldn't let that happen, she just couldn't. Stubbornness and a fierce pride were taking hold. She knew that no matter how humiliated and ashamed she felt inside, she couldn't creep away. She would have to stand up for herself. No one else would. After what seemed like hours but was only a few minutes, she got up and washed her hands, this time to get rid of the feeling that they had been contaminated. She picked up the boot and returned it to her box. Then she went upstairs, passing Miss Witherspoon's closed door. It crossed her mind that she could tap on the door and if the headmistress was inside, she could tell her what had happened. But if she did, weeks of humiliation and shame would follow, because once Miss Witherspoon began an inquiry, the entire school, including the elementary girls, would know what had happened. Girls would tell their mothers who would tell their fathers and soon all of St. John's would know about the fouled mug. No, she couldn't tell the headmistress about the mug. Sadie continued resolutely along the hallway and took her seat in Miss Beamish's history class. Miss Beamish was absent from the room and HONOUR SILENCE was printed in large letters on the blackboard. No one appeared to notice Sadie's entrance but of course they did. She looked around at the green wainscotting on the walls and above it the regal pictures of King George and Queen Mary, meant to establish the orderly presence of Britain. She looked down the rows of wooden desks where, except for Millie who glanced up when she entered the room, her classmates kept their heads bent over their books as if the only thought in their heads was to be studious and obedient. If Miss Beamish, Miss Witherspoon or any of the teachers were to come into the room now, they would say to themselves, "This is the honour system at work; this is the trustworthy behaviour we expect of our girls." They might even think it was a happy class.

10

Millie

A DAY PASSED, ANOTHER, THEN ANOTHER, AND STILL
Sadie told no one about what she had found inside her
boot. It wasn't that she didn't want to tell someone. She did.
She was desperate to tell someone. She was tired, worn out
from the effort of keeping her feelings inside and wanted to let
the shame and anger spill out. But who would she tell? She
certainly couldn't tell Flora, who would be deeply frightened if
she knew what had happened.

One morning, a week after Sadie's mug had been fouled and
she was brushing her hair in front of the mirror, Flora asked
why she was whacking her head with the brush.

"Don't be silly. I'm only trying to flatten my hair."

"You're whacking yourself," Flora insisted.

"Isn't it better that I whack myself instead of you?" Sadie
said. She had never whacked Flora in her life but she felt like
doing it now. She wanted Flora to leave her alone. She wanted
her to get out of bed for once without having to be told. In less

than an hour they had to be in school, and there was Flora sitting up in bed in one of Sadie's old nightgowns, as if she had all the time in the world.

"Don't you like yourself, Sadie?"

"Of course I like myself. NOW WILL YOU GET UP?" she yelled, completely forgetting that Mrs. Hatch could hear her through the floor register.

As if that wasn't enough, half an hour later, on the way to school, Teddy asked if she was she feeling all right. "Lately it seems like something's been bothering you."

"I'm fine, thank you."

"Did you hear some bad news?"

"No."

"Are the girls at school ostracizing you?"

"What do you mean?"

"I mean ignoring you, leaving you out."

"Well, yes, in a way they are."

That was all she would admit.

"It's probably because you're a new girl. I was ignored when I first moved here from Carbonear."

"Nelly's from Grand Falls and she's not ignored."

"Yes, well, you're from Canada and she isn't."

"So that explains it."

"Sarcasm doesn't suit you, Sadie," Teddy said earnestly.

"It suits me when I'm fed up and I'm fed up now."

They walked the rest of the way in silence. Before Teddy crossed the street to his school, he said, "If you want to talk about what's bothering you, you know I'll listen."

She couldn't tell Teddy about finding a mug full of poop. It was too ugly and humiliating. If she told him, he might think less of her; he might think there was something shameful about her that he didn't know. And she couldn't tell her father.

She had written him a letter telling him about their first-term results, but she hadn't written a word about what she had found in her cocoa mug. She couldn't tell her father for the same reason she couldn't tell the headmistress. If her father was told about the mug, he would be so distressed that he would write to the headmistress requesting an explanation as to how such base behaviour could happen in a school whose aim was to encourage high standards of deportment and character. Upon receiving the letter Miss Witherspoon would summon Sadie to her office and demand an explanation she couldn't provide. There would be an announcement in assembly followed by an investigation that would probably fail because no Spencer girl would own up to having done such a disgusting thing. Whether or not it failed, before the investigation was over, everyone in the school and the city would know about Sadie's mug.

There was one person in school she could tell and that was Millie. But Millie hadn't been herself lately and since the day she fainted in gym class had been feeling poorly. Sometimes she didn't come to school until mid-morning, when she showed up in class looking red-eyed and out of sorts. If Sadie had gone downstairs during recess, she might have met Millie, but she had stopped going downstairs, preferring to spend recess in the classroom alone. No one, not even Millie, seemed to notice that she wasn't downstairs during recess. She had become invisible. Eunice and Tina no longer bothered to pass notes about her in class. It was as if by humiliating her, she had been taught a lesson and could now be left alone. Sadie had no experience in dealing with girls who were mean. In Copper Cliff, her best friend had been Marie Bernier. Until the Berniers moved to Quebec six months before the Morins moved to Newfoundland, the girls had been inseparable, and not once had they been mean to each other. Sometimes Marie threatened to go home if she didn't get her way, but that was the worst of it.

The grey slushy days dragged on and every day after school Sadie and Flora did Sour Olive's chores. Finally, near the end of January their landlady told them that now that their housework was caught up, they could join Brownies and Guides. She made this pronouncement self-importantly, as if joining these groups was her idea, and not their father's. Flora joined Brownies but Sadie had no intention of joining Guides. What was the point? Eunice and Tina were in Guides and would only make her life miserable if she joined.

On Flora's first Brownie day, while Sadie waited for Flora and was downstairs in the washroom after school, Millie came out of a cubicle, a speck of toilet paper stuck to her lower lip. Millie washed her hands and looked in the mirror, oblivious to Sadie, who stood near the wall. Except for them, the washroom was empty, school having been dismissed half an hour earlier.

Sadie blurted out, "Millie, I have to talk to you. It's important. Can we go for a walk?"

Millie looked at Sadie, startled that she was there. She was like a sleepwalker who had been nudged awake.

"Now?" she asked.

"Yes. Now. I know it's cold outside, but what I have to tell you won't take long. I have to fetch Flora in half an hour."

"Sure, Sadie."

They put on their coats and hats and mitts and walked arm in arm along Gower Street.

"It's freezing. Let's go to the church," Millie said. "Sometimes I goes in there and sits."

When they reached the old garrison church they found that the door was locked, so they walked around the outside of the church instead, ignoring two boys who were playing hockey on a scrappy sheet of ice. The girls buried their chins in their scarves—a brutal wind was blowing through the Narrows—and kept their eyes on their feet to avoid slippery patches. While they walked, Sadie told Millie about finding the mug in the cloakroom, letting it all pour out, the anger, the humiliation, the shame. As she spoke, the wind snatched up her words so that she had to shout. Shouting made her feel better because it was as if she was emptying herself of all the outrage and the wind was carrying it away.

Millie waited until Sadie had finished and then she let loose. "Those hags," she shouted, "those witches. A mean-hearted crowd, some of these townie girls are. Eunice Baird may have piles of money but she wouldn't last ten seconds in Heart's Content. If she put a turd into someone's mug, she'd get her arse kicked from here to kingdom come."

What a relief it was to hear those words. Sadie reached out and hugged Millie. "Thanks," she said.

"They burns me up, they do."

"Do you think Eunice did it?"

"It was her all right," Millie said. "See, she's used to lording it over everyone. When she's in one of her crooked moods, she thinks she can treat the rest of us any way she wants. Then you come along and you don't kowtow. To make it worse, you lead the class instead of her. That's why she's trying to get back at you. Like you said, Nelly was in on it and maybe others too, but Eunice was the main one behind it."

"It's terrible to be hated so much."

"I knows," Millie said and went quiet. Then she reached over and squeezed Sadie's hand. "Sadie, you got it all over Eunice Baird."

Sadie laughed. It felt so good to have finally told someone who was as offended as she was by what had happened.

"You won't tell," she said though she knew Millie wouldn't.

"I won't. Now I got to tell you something, a secret not even Gert knows."

"What?"

"I'm going to have a baby. See Ray and me did it at Christmas, the day after I got home. He wanted to get married afterwards but I said no, I got to go back to school and finish up."

"A baby!" Sadie shrieked into the wind and immediately felt foolish. A baby was the last thing she had expected Millie to say. She remembered a girl a grade ahead of her in Copper Cliff getting pregnant and some of the other girls in school saying she was bad. A wicked, shameful girl was what they said. It was the absolute worst thing that could happen to you. And now it had happened to Millie. Sadie didn't know what to say. She wanted to be as good a friend to Millie as Millie was to her, but the only helpful thing she could think of to say was to ask how Millie was feeling.

"I feels rotten most of the time. I throws up every morning and am off my food."

"I mean, how do you feel about having a baby? Do you want to have it?" Sadie wouldn't want a baby. When she was grown up, maybe she would, but not now.

"I wants it. Two of my friends at home are expecting babies. And I loves Ray. He's as good as gold. I knows I'll be happy being his wife. It's me auntie that has me worried." Millie began to cry. "She wanted me to get an education and I let her down."

Sadie reached out and dried Millie's tears with her scarf. "But you are getting an education. You'll have your grade ten."

"I can't finish grade ten. I can't make it through to June. Besides, when Spoony finds out, she'll send me home. I got to tell her soon," Millie said grimly, "before I shows."

"I'll go with you if you want," Sadie said. "To Spoony's office, I mean." It was the least she could do, considering how much Millie had helped her.

"Thanks. I dreads telling her. But I dreads telling Auntie Jane more." The tears began afresh.

Sadie gave her friend's arm a squeeze. Though it was bitterly cold, she wanted to keep walking, to walk until Millie felt better, but Flora came to mind. Always she had to think of Flora. "I've got to get back to the school," she said, "to collect my sister. She gets frightened if she has to wait." What a nuisance Flora was. Sadie couldn't do anything without having to see to her little sister. And Flora didn't appreciate it. She took it for granted that Sadie would be there to walk her back to Willicott's Lane.

"We'll collect her together," Millie said and she and Sadie returned to the school.

Flora was bubbling over with what had happened during Brownies. The leaders had dressed up in costumes and acted out a play called *Amelia's Dream* and after the play Guides dressed as Yankees sang "Lucky Lindy" and "Polly Wolly Doodle."

"You should have joined Guides, Sadie," Flora said. "They have loads of fun."

"I don't think I'd like their idea of fun," Sadie said. "Would you, Millie?"

"I sure wouldn't." Millie winked at Sadie. "Because Guides don't have as much fun as Brownies."

"Yes, they do," Flora said.

"How would you know?" Sadie almost said but didn't because having just finished a grown-up conversation with Millie, she couldn't be bothered squabbling with an eight-year-old.

During the next few days Millie couldn't stop talking about her life with Ray. She told Sadie that after she and Ray were married, they would live with his father and she would keep house for both of them. Ray's mother had passed away the year before and his father was lonely. It would be cruel leaving him by himself and his father would be no bother. Most of the time he was on the water or out with his buddies and she and Ray would have the house to themselves. They had spent most of the Christmas holidays in the house. She had got pregnant on Ray's bed, which squeaked something fierce. Sadie blushed when Millie told her that she had never felt so good as when she was on that bed.

This was a revelation to Sadie who knew next to nothing about what went on between a man and a woman in bed and was embarrassed by the merest mention of it. While Millie was talking about what had happened on Ray's bed, Sadie imagined herself and Teddy on the bed where they had put their coats on Christmas Day. Just the thought of lying beside Teddy turned her cheeks crimson and made her breasts prickle in an alarming way. If her thoughts could so easily overwhelm her body, what would happen if she and Teddy really were on a bed?

A week before Valentine's Day, Teddy sent Sadie a valentine which she opened in the bathroom to avoid Flora's curiosity. The valentine was a large red heart with "Thinking of You" written across the top and "Yours, Teddy" across the bottom. The same night, Sadie made him a valentine after she and Flora had finished making valentines for their father and Flora was asleep in bed. The valentine was a red foil heart pasted on a sheet of white paper on which Sadie had written "Happy Valentine's Day." Next day, she mailed the valentine at the post office when she mailed their father's. The valentines she and Flora had made for their father were more elaborate, with declarations of love written all over them. Flora had drawn a picture of a cottage in which the three of them sat drinking tea.

She called the cottage the house of hearts, because everything inside—the cups, the teapot, the clock and the chairs—was shaped like a heart.

On Tuesday when they were walking to school, Teddy mentioned receiving Sadie's valentine and asked if she had received his. When she said yes she had, he asked if she would like to go to a valentine dance on Rennie's Mill Road on Saturday. "One of my classmates, Jeff Greenslade, invited me and asked me to bring a friend."

"I can't dance," Sadie said, though she never had any difficulty keeping up with her father when for a lark he used to waltz her around their house in Copper Cliff.

"Neither can I," Teddy said. "But I'm sure we can manage to shuffle around."

"I'd like to go," Sadie said quickly before she could change her mind. "But it will depend on Mrs. Hatch. Since it's at night I can't slip away like I did to the matinee. I'll have to ask her permission."

"You can tell her the party will be chaperoned by Mrs. Greenslade and the judge."

"What time does it begin?" Sadie was thinking about Flora, and whether she would agree to stay in the house with Sour Olive. Flora's bedtime was seven-thirty. If she was in bed by then, would she let Sadie go out without a fuss? Sadie didn't ask if her little sister could come along. Asking if she could come along to a movie was one thing, but having her tag along to a grown-up party was another.

On Wednesday night Sadie waited until Mrs. Hatch returned from prayer service and Flora was asleep before going downstairs. Sour Olive was in the kitchen making the breakfast porridge. She always made it the night before, which is why it was lumpy.

"I've been invited to a dance on Rennie's Mill Road on Saturday night," she said to Mrs. Hatch's back. "I'd like to go."

"Whose house would that be on Rennie's Mill Road?"

"Greenslade. Mrs. Greenslade and the judge will be chaperoning."

"The judge! Why, he's a member of the Church Synod. Fancy you being invited to the judge's house!" she said in her resentful way. "I've lived in this city all my life but I've never set foot inside his house, though he is kind enough to speak to me in church." Then ducking her head, she added humbly, "That is something, I suppose."

"But may I go to the party?" Sadie hated having to ask but there was no way around it. She needed her landlady's permission.

A sigh. "I suppose you can go, but you must be escorted."

"Teddy Dodge can escort me."

"Who is Teddy Dodge?"

"His parents work at the hotel."

"Ellie Bell's employees," Mrs. Hatch said, as if she was putting the Dodges in their place. "What time did you say it was?"

"Eight o'clock."

"Your sister will have to be in bed before you leave."

"She will be," Sadie said with more confidence than she felt. But Flora didn't make a fuss. Saturday afternoon after their chores were finished, Sadie took her to the Royal Stores and let her pick out a chocolate bar and a *Little Lulu* comic book. Later while she was washing their hair, Sadie promised to bring Flora treats from the party, and after supper when Flora was ready for bed, Sadie read two chapters of *Five Children and It* instead of the usual one. Afterwards, Flora lay in bed watching Sadie in her new velvet dress, brushing her hair. Sadie counted the strokes aloud, forty-five, forty-six, forty-seven. She had discovered by accident after her mother died the hypnotic effect counting had on Flora, and had used it many times since to put her to sleep. By ninety-five Flora was asleep. Sadie tucked the blanket around her little sister and looked at her fondly. Flora was a sweet child, really. She could be a nuisance but at times she could be helpful and cooperative.

Sadie went downstairs and stood by the back door to wait for Teddy. She didn't want Sour Olive answering the door and asking him nosey questions. Her landlady was in the front room, probably knitting, though Sadie didn't hear the click of knitting needles. When Sadie heard Teddy walking up the lane, she opened the door and Mrs. Hatch called out, "Mind you're back by ten-thirty!" Sadie called back, "Yes, Mrs. Hatch!" and went out the door.

The Greenslade house was grand, nearly as grand as the Irish aunts' mansion in Cork. There were mullioned windows, a long sweeping staircase, crystal chandeliers, heavy folding doors between the sitting and dining rooms. These doors had been opened, revealing a table laid with plates of sandwiches and cakes, heart-shaped cookies and a bowl of red punch. There were white candles and dishes of red candy. Red and white crepe-paper streamers were strung from the chandelier to the corners of the room. Highly polished furniture gleamed in the firelight. There were two fires burning, one in each room.

All the girls in the room were wearing good dresses, and the boys, including Teddy, jackets and ties. Because Sadie was used to seeing him in his school uniform and with his shirt-tail loose, Teddy's formal appearance made him seem like a stranger. All the boys attended Bishop Feild, the girls Bishop Spencer. Except for Sadie, they were grade-eleven girls she didn't know but recognized from having seen them in assembly. This was an older crowd whose talk was mainly about their studies and where they expected to be during the Easter holidays. Esther, the grade-eleven prefect who had been awarded a blue belt at the Christmas Concert and Prize Giving, was going to Montreal with her mother and sister Vera to shop. Two boys who looked like twins were spending Easter in Halifax with cousins, and a third said he would be spending Easter in Boston. This last bit of information was imparted in a bored, disdainful way. Teddy said he was going to Carbonear for Easter, which brought loud guffaws from his Feildan fellows. No one asked Sadie where she would be at Easter, which was here in St. John's with Flora and her father.

"Everyone on their feet for a dance." Mrs. Greenslade, a large fleshy woman, was standing in the doorway clapping her hands to the sound of a polka. Teddy took Sadie's hand and together they hopped around the room like two fleas. The polka was followed by a jig, the jig by a lancer, the lancer by the goat. The goat had them dancing in a line that wound through the rooms, across the hall to the library where the judge sat reading. From there the line, led by Mrs. Greenslade, proceeded to the kitchen, then up the back stairway, along the corridor, past bedrooms on either side, then down the grand staircase and into the sitting room, where everyone except Mrs. Greenslade flopped laughing and breathless onto chairs. Despite her girth, she had outdanced them all. She was an Ayres from Fortune and had been brought up dancing the goat. The dancing had been her idea, not only to provide enjoyment but to break the ice.

After the dance everyone began mixing freely, helping themselves to food and sitting wherever they pleased. Balancing a plate on her knees, Sadie sat on the chesterfield between two

Feildans who were arguing about that afternoon's hockey game. She was so relaxed and at ease that she forgot her shyness and joined in the conversation, asking questions whenever she got a chance. When it came time to leave the party, she had no difficulty asking Mrs. Greenslade if she could take some valentine cookies home for her little sister. As well as cookies, Mrs. Greenslade insisted on giving Flora a large piece of cake and a handful of candy.

"Thanks for inviting me, Teddy." Sadie was standing in front of the house in Willicott's Lane. The house was in darkness except for a weak rectangle of light coming from the kitchen window. "I enjoyed meeting your friends."

"They can be stuffy and standoffish, but mostly they're all right," Teddy said. He loomed over her, seeming so much larger in the night. He could have kissed her in the dark and she wished he would, but he didn't, and after telling her that he would see her on Monday, he put his hands in his pockets and went down the lane.

Buchans, January 27, 1927

My darling daughters,

Here I am in the bunkhouse, writing to you with my feet inside my sleeping bag and a blanket wrapped around my shoulders. It is very cold here now and some nights I sleep in my clothing which makes me feel somewhat like a smelly sausage squeezed into a bun.

I received your letter with last term's marks and trust you received my note confirming my safe arrival here. I must say I am a proud father of two clever girls. Keep up the good work.

My work here continues as before, with Gutsy Pike and I

sharing the drilling shifts. To break the monotony, next
weekend he and I plan to cross the ice by dog team and
camp overnight on the other side of Red Indian Lake. I am
told that the next mail won't leave camp until next week,
so I will write you about our adventures on our return.

February 3

It is with some embarrassment that I report that Gutsy
and I never reached the other side of the lake. The dog
team must have recognized us as novice drivers because
they refused to cooperate and fought constantly with each
other, so that after several frustrating hours, we had to
abandon our plans. Obviously, we needed a leader like Rin
Tin Tin.

Keep up the good work.

Your loving father

P.S. I hope you recognize that my crude attempts to draw
two hearts are valentines for my beloved daughters.

On Monday Millie didn't turn up for class. Sadie assumed
that she was late again and would probably turn up at recess,
but recess came and went, then noontime came and went and
still there was no sign of her friend. All afternoon Sadie waited
for school to be over so that while Flora was in Brownies, she
could walk over to Spencer Lodge and visit Millie, who might
be feeling ill and in need of help.

Sadie's final class was literature with Spoony. Today Spoony
began introducing them to a Shakespearean play, *The Tempest,*
which she said she had chosen for study because it involved
shipwrecked castaways on an island, a situation with which

Newfoundlanders were familiar. During the next few weeks when they were studying the play, she wanted the girls to imagine it taking place in Newfoundland. After introducing the characters, she said she would assign speaking parts during the next class because they would be presenting a shortened version of the play to the assembly before Easter.

Spoony had finished her lecture and was sailing majestically toward the door when she stopped and announced that Sadie was to report to the office before she went home. Sadie collected her books with trepidation, trying to think why she had been summoned. She went to the office but it was empty, and she had to wait by the door for the headmistress while girls streamed past on their way home. It was difficult not to envy these girls going home to their mothers. Remembering how her mother often had poppyseed cake cooling on the table when she returned from school, Sadie imagined townie girls entering warm kitchens where they ate gingerbread and sticky buns fresh from the oven.

"A million miles away."

Sadie blinked. The headmistress stood in front of her, her head cocked to one side, a quizzical smile on her lips.

"Come in, Sadie, come in." Spoony gestured to the open door.

"Thank you, Miss Witherspoon."

The headmistress left the door open.

"This won't take long." She didn't invite Sadie to sit but picked up a parcel from the desk and gave it to her.

"Before she left, Jane Miller asked me to give you this package. She was most insistent that you have it."

"Did she go to Heart's Content?"

"Yes. Family matters required Jane to go home. She will not be returning to Bishop Spencer."

Though Sadie had known this day would come, she had imagined it differently. She had never imagined that Millie would leave St. John's without telling her.

"When did she go?"

"On Saturday morning."

Sadie felt tears rising. She bit her lip, willing them to recede.

"I wanted to see her."

"I am sure you did," the headmistress said briskly. She went behind the desk and sat in her chair. "But her leaving really is for the best. Jane Miller was not cut out for scholarship. A domestic life will suit her better. She never belonged to Bishop Spencer, whereas you, Sadie, do belong."

Sadie wanted to tell the headmistress that she was mistaken. She didn't belong in Bishop Spencer. Her classmates were making sure of that.

Miss Witherspoon said, "You will be far better off without Jane."

"I don't think so," Sadie said. "She was my best friend."

"She was not a good influence on a girl like you."

"Yes, she was. She was kind and helpful and never mean." Sadie was aware of the Bishop Spencer rule that the headmistress must never be contradicted, but she was determined to speak the truth and she wasn't finished yet. She said, "Millie is a far better person than some of the other girls in my class."

Miss Witherspoon was so taken aback that she had nothing to say to this, and Sadie left the room without waiting to be dismissed. This was also against school rules but she couldn't hear another unkind word said about Millie. She went downstairs to the washroom, which fortunately was empty, and sat in a cubicle to open the brown paper package tied with butcher cord. Inside was Millie's cocoa mug with a picture of a Newfoundland dog on one side. Tucked into the mug was a note.

Dear Sadie,

I'm sorry I never got the chance to say goodbye. Spoony cornered me Friday after school and ordered me to leave. The mug is for your cocoa. Write to me please.

Love, Millie

Millie's handwriting was large and childlike but there wasn't a single spelling mistake. This, as much as Millie's message, brought the tears. Sadie let them roll, dabbing her eyes and blowing her nose until it was time to pull herself together and take her sister back to Willicott's Lane.

11

Flipper Pie

IT WAS TWO WEEKS BEFORE SADIE SCRAPED UP THE courage to carry Millie's cocoa mug downstairs to the basement. Outside the school windows the sun was hidden behind cloud, only a ring of pale gold showing. It was the kind of bleak, cold morning on which she needed the comfort of a warm drink. Today Esther Murray was pouring. Recognizing Sadie from the Greenslade party, she said, "I haven't seen you down here for a while."

"I usually stay in the classroom at recess and do my homework."

Esther looked at her closely. "Well, I'm glad you came downstairs today."

Sadie held out her mug, but before Esther could fill it, Eunice came from behind and shoved her mug in front of Sadie's.

"You've already had cocoa," Esther said.

"But there's lots left," Eunice replied, using a little-girl whine, "and recess is nearly over."

"Why don't you grow up, Eunice?" Sadie heard the exasperation in Esther's voice.

Muttering something about Esther not being able to take a joke, Eunice stalked off and joined Tina and Nelly at the bottom of the stairs. Esther frowned at the three girls and asked Sadie if she felt like a fish out of water in the grade-ten class. "You seem much more mature than those girls."

"I'm supposed to be in grade eleven but Spoony insisted that my sister and I repeat a grade when we moved here from Canada."

Esther laughed. "That's typical of Spoony. She likes to think Spencer girls are in a class by themselves. My cousin in Montreal who's in grade eleven is far ahead of me in every subject, but of course I would never tell Spoony that. She has dedicated her entire life to establishing Spencer's scholarly reputation."

The first bell rang and Sadie finished her cocoa and headed for the washroom to rinse her cup. "If you ever want company at recess, Sadie," Esther called after her, "you can always talk to me. I'm a little shy myself."

Was she really shy or was she trying to be kind? Whatever the reason, Sadie was grateful for Esther's invitation, which took away some of the sting she felt about missing Millie. The day before, Sadie had received a letter from Millie describing the wedding which had taken place in the Methodist church in Heart's Content. Millie wrote that it was a good thing that she had been able to wear her mother's wedding dress because there wasn't time to get one made. After the wedding, there was a dance in the church hall that had lasted until midnight. Millie wrote that she was now cleaning Ray's father's house from top to bottom and that she wished Sadie and Flora could come for a visit sometime. The letter was signed "Mrs. Ray Chaulk."

How Sadie longed to visit Heart's Content. Its name alone drew her in. From everything Millie had said about it, Heart's Content sounded like an enchanted place that no one who lived there wanted to leave. If Sadie went there, would she feel the same way, that she wanted to stay forever? But she couldn't go to Heart's Content, at least not while school was in. Hadn't Miss Marsh said that it was a difficult place to reach from St. John's? Maybe she could persuade her father to take Flora and her to visit Millie during the Easter holidays.

The third Sunday in March, when Sadie was at the kitchen sink washing the breakfast dishes and Flora was at the table trying to persuade herself to swallow the last mouthfuls of fried bread, Sadie heard the back door open. She felt a draught of cold air against her ankles but she didn't turn around, assuming that Mrs. Hatch, who had left for church a few minutes earlier, had found a reason to come back. It was a shock when she felt a pair of cold hands cover her eyes and a smoky voice whisper in her ear. "Guess who!"

"Wanda!" Flora leapt to her feet. "It's Wanda Hatch!"

Wanda dropped her hands just as Sadie said, "Wanda, is it really you?"

"It's me all right. I been having a smoke in the shed, waiting until Ma left for church. I come to see how you girls are getting on."

Sadie's warm soapy hands reached for Wanda's, which were cold and yellowed with nicotine. "It's so good to see you."

Wanda grinned. "Does that mean you'll stay home from church and visit with me?"

"It's not home," Sadie said.

"It's not home to me either, girl, and I grew up in this house."

"We won't go to church," Flora said. "Will we, Sadie?"

"Of course not." Sadie knew that their absence from church would be noticed but quickly decided that a visit with Wanda was worth having to put up with one of Sour Olive's harangues.

"Let's have a spot of tea," Wanda said. "I brought along some shortbreads in case I could persuade you to miss church." She dug into the pockets of her mangy fur coat for the cookies and put them on Flora's plate before dropping her coat to the floor. For the first time Sadie noticed how thin Wanda was and how deep the pocked scars were on her face. Wanda sat down and, hooking her shoulders over the chair back, spread her knees wide, which further delighted the sisters since they were often reminded at school that this was not the proper posture for a young lady. "So, how's life been treating you two?"

While Sadie made the tea and poured them each a cup, Flora launched into the tale of the scalding, rolling down her stocking to show where her leg was a shiny pink. Sadie let her talk. How she wanted to tell Wanda about the mug of poop and Millie's pregnancy, but of course, she couldn't speak of these things in front of her little sister. All she said was that she was lonesome for her best friend who had left Spencer and returned to Heart's Content.

Wanda bit off a bit of fingernail and said, "If you've been lonesome, why didn't you come and see me?"

"I didn't know where you lived," Sadie explained. "When we were out walking with our father at Christmastime, I wondered which house on Lime Street was yours."

Wanda didn't say which house on Lime Street was hers. Instead she told Sadie she could visit her at the Anchor and Chain in Steer's Cove. "I told you where it was. Why didn't you come?"

Why hadn't Sadie gone to see her at the Anchor and Chain? Remembering Wanda's puffy face and swollen lip, was she afraid of what she would find? Was it because Wanda worked in a bar, what Mrs. Hatch called a place of ill repute?

As if she was reading Sadie's mind, Wanda said, "It's safe coming to see me in the afternoon. The drinkers don't come into the bar until supper time. After that they pile in and I work till I drops." She yawned and stretched her arms above her head. "Since the sealers come back, I've been working half the night."

Sadie remembered the day two weeks ago when two sealing ships left St. John's harbour for the ice. For some time now when she looked out her bedroom window she'd been seeing a band of pack ice on the sea beyond the Narrows laid on the blue like a vast white sheet. According to Teddy, the ice where the harp seals birthed their young was Newfoundland's sign of spring.

"I saw the sealers leave," Sadie said.

"So did I," Flora said. "We were allowed to watch from the school windows."

That day when church bells rang over the city and the blast of car horns and ship whistles filled the air, Miss Bugle encouraged the grade-ten class to leave their seats and watch the sealing ships steam through the Narrows, the men aboard waving and shouting at the crowd gathered on shore.

Wanda said, "My boss ran a raffle based on the number of pelts the ships would bring back. Benny Mercer won. He guessed five thousand and nine seals."

"The seals are dead, aren't they?" Flora said.

"Yes, they are."

"That makes me sad." Flora's eyes filled with tears.

"I know, girl, but we got to eat." Wanda reached out and put an arm around Flora who sat with her lower lip jutting out, a sure sign she was upset. "But you hates eating, don't you?" Wanda sighed. "And those poor cookies disappeared all by themselves."

Flora giggled.

"Next time I sees you," Wanda teased her, "I won't give you any shortbreads. How's that?"

"But I love shortbreads!"

Wanda grinned and took a last cookie out of her pocket. "I knows. That's why this one is for you."

Flora pounced on the cookie and Sadie began pouring more tea. Wanda put a hand over her cup. "No more for me. Now that we've had a little visit, I'm going back to bed." She yawned. "Sunday's the day I sleeps in."

Flora said helpfully, "You can sleep upstairs."

"I know, but I gotta get back before my boyfriend wonders where I got to."

Did she sleep in the same bed with him?

"And I'm dying for another smoke." She stood up and stretched. "Can't smoke in here, now can I? Ma would know I was here for sure."

After Wanda left, Sadie swept up the cookie crumbs and washed the teacups. By the time Mrs. Hatch returned from church, she and Flora were upstairs in their bedroom, pretending to be doing their homework. Sadie heard the back door open and visualized their landlady hanging her coat and hat on the peg by the door, bending over to take off her gaiters, then putting on her slippers and padding across the kitchen floor, her thin body bent forward. She could imagine the small head swaying back and forth as Sour Olive looked into the front room and the hall before coming to a standstill beneath the heat register.

"Girls?" she called querulously. "Are you up there?"

The sisters sat, Sadie on the bed, Flora in the chair, hands over their mouths to muffle their giggles.

"Sadie! Flora!" The voice was strident now. "Are you up there?"

"We're up here!" Sadie said.

"Come down at once!"

"I'll go," Sadie whispered and went down to the kitchen.

"I didn't see you at church," Sour Olive said.

"We intended to go but at the last minute decided not to."

Mrs. Hatch peered at her. "And why was that?"

"We weren't feeling well and went upstairs to lie down."

"You look well enough to me."

"We won't want any dinner. It might upset our stomachs," Sadie said, her stomach full of Wanda's shortbreads.

Sour Olive said, "It's all the same to me. Dinner's already made and you can eat it for supper. Afterwards you can go to evening service."

Sadie went upstairs and when she and Flora heard Sour Olive's rocker in the front room, they burst into another round of giggling. Wanda's visit had made them feel carefree and high-spirited and they wanted to continue the pleasure of having put one over on their landlady for as long as they could. Sadie knew that by deceiving Mrs. Hatch, she had told another lie, not a huge lie because she really had intended to go to church, but it was a lie nonetheless. She could blame the deception on Sour Olive's strictness, which in a way *forced* her to lie, but she also knew that, as her mother often said, if you lied once, you were more apt to lie again, and she didn't want to become a dishonest person.

The supper was seal flipper, which Mrs. Hatch had boiled with onions and put in a bowl, then covered with mashed potatoes. She called the scummy mixture seal flipper pie and said

Sadie and Flora were lucky that the seal meat was so tender. Flora refused to touch it but Sadie made an attempt. The flipper tasted oily and fishy, but she forced down a mouthful as if it was a penance she had to undergo to make up for being untruthful.

12

The Silver Brush

Buchans, March 9, 1927

Dear Sadie,

This is not a proper letter, only a note that one of the Lucky Strike officials who is leaving camp shortly has promised to mail for me. Could you use the enclosed dollar to buy something special for Flora's birthday? Thanks.

Your loving father

P.S. I will be writing to you both soon about future plans.

Sadie tucked the note into the underwear drawer where Flora wouldn't see it. She had no sooner put the note away when she took it out and reread it. She was puzzled by the postscript. What did her father mean by "future plans"? Did he mean his future plans for work after he had finished his job at Buchans or did he mean Easter plans? Telling herself that he must mean Easter plans, like when he would be coming to St. John's and so on, she buried the note with its dollar inside beneath her underwear. If she had put the birthday money inside Madeleine's pantaloons, there was a good chance of Flora finding it. Every once in a while her little sister liked to count what was left of the ten dollars spending money their father had given them at Christmastime to cover day-to-day expenses.

Besides the spending money inside Madeleine's pantaloons, Sadie had more money hidden away. This was a twenty-dollar bill her father called emergency money, which he had advised her to put it away somewhere safe where it wouldn't get mixed up with the daily expense money. He didn't think she would need it but he felt better knowing that she had the money. He called it the mother lode which, Sadie knew, was a mining term that meant where the main body of ore is located. Sadie had rolled up the twenty-dollar bill and put it inside the hollow handle of the silver brush. Her mother had shown her this hiding place when she was six years old.

It had been during a heat wave in Copper Cliff when the air was so hot it shimmered and seemed to bend and wave in the light. She remembered standing outside in the cinder yard, the sun beating down on her bare head while rods of speckled light quivered and danced in front of her eyes. It seemed to her now that she must have stayed in the yard a long time, because she became so flushed and heavy-headed that suddenly she was desperate for the cool shelter of the house. Inside, she had stood for a while on the mat, blinded by the darkness after the dazzling outdoor light. When her eyes adjusted, she walked down the hallway toward her mother, who was sitting on the curtained stool in the bedroom, brushing her hair at the dressing table. Flora, four months old, was asleep in the corner of the room. Sadie went to the cot and looked at her baby sister's heat-prickled skin.

"Come here, sweetie," her mother whispered.

Sadie went to her mother and leaned against her thigh where her cream silk dressing gown had fallen away.

"Watch this." Her mother unscrewed the handle of the hairbrush. "Look." She held the handle close so that Sadie could peer inside. "It's our hiding place."

"Yours and mine?"

"Yes. You try it."

Sadie screwed and unscrewed the handle several times.

"It's our secret, Sadie," her mother whispered. "Yours and mine. Nobody else's. Can you keep it secret?"

"Yes."

And she had. No one, not even her father, knew about the hollow handle, and certainly not Flora. Sadie had never told her and though her little sister was a snoop, Sadie didn't think she knew. Neither had Sadie told her about the twenty-dollar bill. Twenty dollars was a lot of money and if Flora knew about it she might spend it. She was impetuous and entirely capable of doing something rash.

On Tuesday, Sadie took her father's birthday dollar and went down to the Royal Stores and bought her sister a fifteen-cent bag of marbles. There was a patch of dry gravel behind the Collinses' house where, if it wasn't too cold, the girls played marbles, bouncing them against the side of the house, then measuring their position by using a thumb and a little finger. Flora would be glad to have her own marbles again instead of borrowing Peggy's—soon after they'd moved to St. John's, she'd lost her own bag of marbles. With the leftover money

Sadie bought balloons, candies, cupcakes and candles and took them over to Mrs. Collins, who agreed to have a birthday supper—Sadie hadn't even bothered asking Mrs. Hatch. On Wednesday before they went down to breakfast, Sadie gave Flora the marbles and a bag of saltwater candies she could share during recess. After school while Flora and Peggy played marbles outside, Sadie went to the Collinses' house and decorated the cupcakes with nine candles and blew up the balloons. At five o'clock the girls were called inside for a meal of bangers and beans. After the cake and ice cream had been eaten, Flora opened her presents: a jigsaw puzzle picture of kittens in a basket from Peggy, and a flowered cotton nightgown from Sadie. Flora put the nightgown on over her clothes.

"Thank you, Sadie, for giving me something new to wear."

Flora put on the nightgown again as soon as they were upstairs in their bedroom. "I'll do your chores," Sadie said. Sour Olive had agreed to them having supper at the Collinses' as long as the chores were done afterwards. Sadie swept and mopped the downstairs floors and filled the coal box. By the time she went upstairs Flora was asleep, wearing the new nightgown and clutching the balloon string in her hand. Sadie was overcome by tenderness for the little girl lying in bed flushed and happy, her hair stuck to the smudge of icing on her cheek. It was a nuisance having to drag Flora everywhere, and it was irritating the way she kept losing things, but she really was a good little girl. What made Sadie feel especially protective and loving toward her was how easily pleased Flora had been today. It hadn't been much of a birthday but Flora was satisfied, and Sadie was grateful to her for that.

∾

The next morning in school, the headmistress began casting *The Tempest.*

"Sadie, you are to play Ariel," she said, speaking in the queenly way few would dare challenge. "Nelly, you are to play Miranda. Eunice, you will be Caliban. Sandra, you will play Prospero. Patricia, you will play Antonio." She continued assigning parts until fourteen parts were taken. "The rest of you will be boatmen and airy spirits as required. We will, of course, begin with Act I, Scene I, but will not act out the entire play."

Miss Witherspoon proceeded to guide the class through *The Tempest* a second time, telling them which passages would be omitted in order to work from a script that had an hour's playing time. "For this occasion and this occasion only, you may indicate the omissions lightly on the margin in pencil."

"Costumes will be minimal—trousers for the men, a skirt for Miranda, wings and scarves for Ariel. The performance is intended to familiarize you with how Shakespeare transformed an island setting into a magical place. Though we will perform the play during the last assembly before the Easter break, it is not my intention to perform in public. Are there any questions?"

Eunice got to her feet and said in a timid voice, with no hint of the usual boldness, "Miss Witherspoon, do we keep our assigned parts or will we be changing them later on?"

"Unless I am persuaded otherwise, Eunice, you will stay with the part I have assigned. Why do you ask?"

"I don't want the part of Caliban. I don't think I can play the part of a misshappen monster, but I could play the part of Ariel."

"On the contrary, Eunice," the headmistress said. "I think you will manage Caliban's part quite well, and once we find you a hair suit or some such costume, you will look every inch like a cave-dwelling outcast."

"But I want to play Ariel," Eunice insisted. Again Sadie heard the whine in her voice but this time she wasn't pretending.

"Ariel's part will be acted by Sadie," Miss Witherspoon said firmly. "Ariel is a lithe, airy spirit and Sadie has a better physical presence for playing the part than you. You may sit down, Eunice."

Sadie was surprised that Miss Witherspoon had taken her side and put Eunice in her place. This meant the headmistress must have excused Sadie for contradicting her the day she had stood up for Millie. Why had she assigned her a role that most grade-ten girls wanted? How odd that she had given Sadie a role that she wasn't sure she wanted. Well, part of her wanted it and part of her didn't. The shy part preferred to stand in the back row where she wouldn't be noticed. She imagined herself telling the headmistress that she didn't want to play Ariel, that the role should be given to Eunice, who wanted it more. She imagined the headmistress replying that she was the best judge of how the roles should be assigned, and that she was sure Sadie would come to enjoy playing Ariel. The part of Sadie that wanted the role was the part that liked to imagine herself flying over the sea where she would use her magical powers to call up mountainous waves high enough to sink a ship, then afterwards whisk passengers safely ashore. She liked the idea of being able to arrange the weather to suit a purpose.

St. John's, March 15, 1927

Dear Dad,
      You'll never guess what happened to me today. Miss Witherspoon assigned me the role of Ariel in The Tempest. We won't be performing the play in public, but if you can

make it here for the last assembly before Easter, you'll be able to see it. I know I'll have stage fright acting the part in front of the whole school, but it will help knowing you're there in the audience.

Flora enjoyed her birthday party. I bought her a bag of marbles with your money and Mrs. Collins had us over for a birthday supper. She's outside now playing with Peggy, but when she comes inside will probably draw you a picture of her party.

I can hardly wait until Easter to see you again.

Love,
Sadie

When Sadie told Teddy about being in *The Tempest*, he immediately began reciting a verse in the play.

Now my charms are all o'erthrown,
And what strength I have's mine own,
Which is most faint, now, tis true,
I must be here confined by you.

"Is there anything you don't know?"

He grinned. "I played the role of Prospero in grade ten. Does this mean that Spoony will be mounting another magnum opus?"

"Magnum opus?"

"A grand performance. Will I see you at the Casino flying across the stage on gossamer wings?"

"Oh no!" Sadie was horrified at the thought of acting in a theatre. Singing in a choir was one thing, but acting a part was quite another. "But we may put it on for assembly."

Two weeks after she had been assigned the part of Ariel, Sadie walked into the kitchen on Willicott's Lane one afternoon after school and saw, leaning against the spoon jar, a thick envelope addressed in her father's handwriting to Flora and herself. Snatching up the bulky letter, she raced upstairs to read it before Mrs. Hatch came home. She didn't bother taking off her coat but flopped onto the bed and slit open the envelope with her fingernail.

Buchans, March 28, 1927

My darling daughters,

It is with a heavy heart that I must tell you that I will not be joining you in St. John's for Easter. This will come as a disappointment to you, I know, but as the breadwinner of our family, I must make long-range plans.

The mining engineer, Mr. Gilchrist, has told me that now that the Lucky Strike find is moving into production, there will be no employment for a prospecting geologist like myself unless I continue to spend long hours working underground, which I am not prepared to do. Underground work is routine and monotonous and does not challenge my abilities. For this reason, Gutsy Pike and I have decided to head west to look for gold. Gutsy, who has already prospected for gold near a mine in Sop's Arm, thinks we have a good chance of making our fortunes there. Though there's been a considerable amount of gold prospecting on the island, he thinks the richest veins are still undiscovered. If we strike the mother lode, we will be set for life. As a rich man I will be able to keep my daughters in style.

If you look on the map of Newfoundland, you will see that Sop's Arm is at the bottom of White Bay. When Gutsy and I leave here tomorrow, we go to Howley by train. From Howley we travel to Hampden where we take a boat to Sop's Arm. Gutsy estimates the journey will be about two weeks. Since Sop's Arm is a small outport without a postal service, you should send letters to me in care of Mr. & Mrs. Leeson in Corner Brook, which will be closer to me than St. John's. I will contact the Leesons and ask if we can stay in touch during the next few weeks through them.

I am mailing Mrs. Hatch three months' rent, which means your room and board will be paid for until the end of June by which time I expect to be back in St. John's. I will post her letter along with this one.

I enclose five dollars for you and Flora to treat yourselves at Easter. I am sure you can find some interesting things to do in the city during the Easter holiday. I am sorry that I won't be there to do them with you, or that I won't see my daughter speak Ariel's lines at assembly. I am confident that you will speak them with grace.

It is my hope that when I see you in June, you will be looking at someone on his way to becoming a rich man and we can spend the rest of our lives without a care in the world.

Your loving father

By the time Sadie had finished reading the letter, she was rigid with anger. She was furious at her father for deciding not to come to St. John's for Easter, instead going into the wilderness of Newfoundland to look for gold. When they lived in Ontario, he had often spent weekends near Timmins prospecting for gold. They couldn't even go on a family picnic without their father dragging Flora and herself into the wilderness to look for gold in a chunk of quartz diorite or pegmatite in the Sudbury Basin. (Their mother always declined to join them, preferring to lie on the blanket and read instead.) Later, while their family was enjoying the lunch their mother had prepared, their father would get Sadie to recite the geological time periods as if they were books of the Bible. By the time she was seven, she could rattle off all twelve periods from Precambrian 4,600 million years ago up to Quaternary, which was a mere two million years ago. It wasn't her father's obsession with geology that angered Sadie but his obsession with finding gold, with finding the pot at the end of the rainbow. Why couldn't he settle down like other fathers and find an ordinary job? Even if the job was routine and monotonous, why couldn't he continue to work underground, at least until the summer holidays when they could be together as a family again? School work was often routine and monotonous, but he expected her to do it, didn't he? And why did he think that they needed a lot of money, that she and Flora needed to be kept in style? Didn't he know that more than anything they wanted him back? What was he thinking, going off on what her mother would have called a wild-goose chase with someone called Gutsy Pike.

Still wearing her coat, Sadie lay on her back and stared at the ceiling, for the first time noticing a spider web attached to the electrical cord. She would have to remember to sweep it down on Saturday. Through the heat register, she heard the back door open below.

"Sadie! Flora!" Mrs. Hatch was home. No doubt Flora, who was playing outside with Peggy, had spied her coming along the lane and was hiding somewhere.

"I'm up here!" Sadie called. She got up from the bed, put the letter on the dresser and took off her coat. She went downstairs and carried a basket of laundry into the kitchen. Today was ironing day. She lowered the ironing board from the wall and lifted the iron from the back of the stove. For the next hour she pushed the heavy iron back and forth across blouses, sheets and table runners, sighing, her heart heavy with the weight of disappointment, with the growing conviction that she was the only responsible member left in their family.

13

Missing Dad

SADIE WAITED UNTIL MRS. HATCH HAD GONE TO A Lenten prayer service and Flora was ready for bed before telling her that their father wouldn't be coming to St. John's for Easter, that he was on his way to Sop's Arm to prospect for gold. "It will come to nothing," she said, "as always."

"You shouldn't say that," Flora chided her. "Maybe this time he will find gold. Then you'll be sorry."

"I doubt it," Sadie said. "He hardly knows Newfoundland. And he's never been lucky finding gold."

"He might be lucky this time," Flora insisted.

"I don't believe in luck."

The next morning during recess, Sadie studied the large map of Newfoundland on the classroom wall for ten minutes before she located the body of water called Sop's Arm near the bottom of White Bay on the other side of Newfoundland, a long way from where she stood. As her father had written, the arm was close to Corner Brook, where the Leesons lived.

Although Mrs. Leeson had been a close friend of her mother's, neither Sadie nor her father had met her, and using her as a go-between made Sadie ill at ease. She would have preferred that it be someone she knew. What if Mrs. Leeson didn't want to be a go-between?

That night, after the supper dishes were washed and dried and Flora was upstairs in bed, Mrs. Hatch called Sadie into the front room, where she was knitting what appeared to be a man's sock, probably for one of the prison inmates. "Sit down," Mrs. Hatch said and continued knitting even after Sadie had found a place on the sofa.

"I know you received a letter from your father yesterday. Did he say exactly when he would be arriving for Easter?"

"Didn't you get a letter from him explaining the situation?"

The knitting needles stopped. "What situation?"

"He said he sent you a letter."

"I received no letter."

"Are you sure?"

"Of course I'm sure," Mrs. Hatch snapped. "I go to the post office every weekday."

"He said he had sent you enough room and board money to carry through until he arrives at the end of June. He won't be coming to St. John's for Easter because he'll be prospecting in Sop's Arm."

"Prospecting in Sop's Arm! Why would he do such a thing?"

"He's looking for gold."

"Well, I never." Mrs. Hatch's shook her head as if she couldn't quite believe the news. She shoved the knitting between her thigh and the armrest on the chair. "And what of his responsibilities here? I'd like to know that!" She narrowed her eyes, which made her look more ferrety. "Thanks to him, I'm landed me a fine kettle of fish. I intended to visit my brother in New Harbour over Easter. Now, without your father here, I won't be able to go."

"Couldn't someone else stay with us?" Sadie said. She was thinking of Wanda.

"There is no one else."

"We could stay alone," Sadie said hopefully. "I'll be fifteen next month, which is old enough to be left in charge."

Without Mrs. Hatch in the house, Easter might be fun. Sadie and Flora could make fudge, they could come and go when they wanted, they could stay in bed in the mornings, and they could do as they pleased.

"It's out of the question."

The knitting needles clicked again. "I have no intention of leaving you girls alone in my house."

"Maybe we could go to Heart's Content," Sadie said. "I have a friend from school who lives there and she's invited me to visit." Sadie had a wistful picture of her and Flora sitting around a table eating Easter dinner in Heart's Content.

"As long as I am looking after you girls, you can hardly expect me to agree to such a thing."

"Why not?"

"Because you are my responsibility. Not that it's anything you've ever thanked me for." Mrs. Hatch's head was bobbing up and down as if she was powerless to stop it. "I have no choice but to notify my brother that I'm unable to come to New Harbour, that it is my Christian duty to remain in St. John's."

The next morning Sadie told Teddy about the conversation with Mrs. Hatch. Whenever she confided in him, he listened closely and afterwards had something reassuring to say. Not today. Today Teddy's response was awkward and apologetic.

"I'm sorry I won't be here for Easter," he blurted out, "because if I was you might be able to move in with us for a few days while Mrs. Hatch is away. Mr. Bell will be managing the hotel while we're in Carbonear. I don't think he'd be keen on having two girls stay in our apartment unless they were paying guests."

Sadie was embarrassed that Teddy should think that she and Flora needed looking after, that they were charity cases, and immediately regretted telling him about Mrs. Hatch.

"You needn't worry about us," she said huffily. "Flora and I will get along just fine."

"I didn't mean to suggest that you wouldn't," Teddy said. "It's only that I feel I'm letting you down."

All this was said as they walked along Gower Street, neither of them looking at each other. When they reached Bond Street, Sadie looked directly at Teddy. "You aren't letting me down. You can't solve everyone's problems, Teddy. You're not God." This was unfair and Sadie knew it, but she was unwilling to take it back.

"I never thought I could," he said. Which was true; he had never presumed to be able to solve her problems. The most he had been guilty of was trying to help.

He wasn't waiting for her at the corner next morning or for the rest of the week, which made Sadie realize how much her words must have stung. Now that she'd had time to think, she knew that she had taken the anger she felt toward her father out on Teddy and she was sorry about that. Teddy was a good friend, maybe her best friend, and she'd hurt his feelings. The next time she saw him she would apologize for having been unfair.

But the next time she saw him wasn't until the end of term when he came to see *The Tempest*. The performance was over and she and the other girls were taking a bow when she saw him leaning against the back wall of the gym clapping along with the others—he must have skipped a class at Bishop Feild to come here, slipping into Bishop Spencer after the assembly bell rang. She smiled directly at him so that he would know that she was glad to see him, that she wanted them to be friends again.

Later, when she was back in the classroom after changing out of her costume, several girls remarked on her performance.

"Spoony was right to cast you as Ariel," Patricia said as they were cleaning out their desks.

"I thought you were going to fly!" Sandra said.

The fact was that for a brief fleeting moment on stage Sadie had felt she was flying. Bare-legged and armed, costumed in wings and a tunic made of scarves, she had felt airborne. She felt so graceful and light in her costume that on her way downstairs to the washroom to change into her uniform, she had hoped to run into Teddy, even though she knew he wouldn't have hung around for the rest of assembly, which had gone on for a half hour after the play. But three teachers called out to her through open classroom doors, congratulating her on a job well done.

While she was changing into her uniform, Sadie heard Eunice in the next cubicle, grumbling and cursing as she struggled to get out of her Caliban costume, made of floor mats sewn together. Sadie changed quickly, eager to get away from Eunice and to finish cleaning out her desk. Spoony had given strict instructions that before the girls went on holiday, their desks had to be emptied so that Mr. Buckle and Mrs. Collins could give them a thorough cleaning. By the time she returned to the classroom, some of the girls had gone. Sadie heard Patricia and Sandra talking about going to Halifax for Easter. A few of the girls were leaving the island, but most of them were going to visit relatives elsewhere on the island or were going to cabins and cottages in the country.

Sandra said, "Where are you going, Sadie?"

"Nowhere," Sadie said glumly. Already the euphoria of being Ariel was wearing off.

"Oh," Sandra said, then added kindly, "Maybe next year."

By the time Sadie had finished clearing out her desk, Flora was waiting for her by the front door. As soon as she saw her coming down the stairs, Flora rushed up to her. "You were good in the play, Sadie. You were the best."

Sadie smiled at her fondly. "Was I?"

"Yes, you were."

Outside, Sadie looked around for Teddy, though by now she was so late that she really didn't expect to see him. She would go down to the hotel after dinner and thank him for coming to see the play and apologize for her unfairness. Dinner was Sour Olive's fish cakes, which tasted better than Sadie expected. After they had done the dishes, Sadie and Flora went down to the Crosbie Hotel but they were too late. Teddy had gone.

"You just missed him," the new clerk said. "He and his parents left not more than twenty minutes ago." The news left Sadie so crestfallen that she thought she might cry.

"Are you all right, Sadie?" Flora said and took her hand.

"Of course I'm all right. Why wouldn't I be?" she snapped, then remembering her manners, she thanked the clerk and fled the hotel before she could make a total fool of herself. It was her own fault that she hadn't seen Teddy. If she hadn't been so stubborn and so angry, she could have seen him sooner instead of leaving it so late.

When they were back in their bedroom, Sadie took herself in hand and began making up a timetable for the Easter holidays. She wanted her little sister to know that during the holidays they would have something special to do every day. Flora's friend Peggy would be away in Halifax and she would need extra attention. Sadie had always been able to pull herself up by the boot straps—as her mother used to put it—and make the best of a situation. She could hear her mother's voice. "You can do it, Sadie, you're strong." Now the tears really did roll, coursing down her cheeks, making damp polka dots on the paper. Flora came over to the table and held Sadie's hand. She didn't say anything but waited quietly beside her sister until the tears stopped.

On Good Friday, the sisters went to a three-hour service at the cathedral. Their mother had died the day before Good Friday and Sadie prayed for her soul, wanting to believe that she was in heaven. She also prayed for her father, wherever he was. She tried to listen to the reverend's sermon, but her mind was occupied with thoughts of her father. It occurred to her that he may have wanted to go prospecting for gold in order to avoid being here with Flora and her on the day of their mother's death.

After a noon dinner of cold fish cakes, they climbed the hilly streets behind Willicott's Lane to the huge Roman Catholic Cathedral dominating the city. This was the first stop on Sadie's timetable. Though the building was only a five-minute walk from their boardinghouse and they often looked up to see its square towers, they had never been inside. Sadie opened a massive church door and she and Flora walked down the nave. Candles illuminated a small chapel on one side where worshippers prayed in front of a statue of the Virgin Mary. There was a golden halo around the Virgin's head. The girls slipped into a pew and looked at the stained-glass windows. Rays of afternoon sun slanted through the windows, transforming them into jewelled panes. The light fell on the head of an elderly woman, turning her white hair into an aureole of red, blue, green and yellow. She looked as if she was sitting at the end of a rainbow. The thought of a rainbow made Sadie think of leprechauns and pots of gold, and of course, her father. Her father would laugh if he knew she was thinking of leprechauns and gold. His idea of gold was far from being fairy gold. He thought of gold not in terms of fairy stories but in land formations: creek beds and valleys and rocky outcrops.

Sadie felt herself being elbowed by her sister. Flora was pointing toward the altar, where there were six golden candlesticks and above them, four golden lanterns hanging from a ceiling elaborately decorated in green and gold. Lining the walls of the nave were the stations of the cross gilded with gold. Sadie had never seen such gold. When her father attended the Church of England with its plain stone walls, did he miss the golden opulence and rich decorativeness of his former church?

When worshippers began coming into church for the three o'clock mass, the sisters went outside and stood on the cathedral steps, gazing through the archway at the harbour. There, beyond the Narrows, was an iceberg. "Look, Flora," Sadie said. "Look!" In the middle of the rocky V where the shoreline plunged into the sea was an enormous pyramid of gleaming ice. The peak of the iceberg was so high that it looked as tall as Signal Hill. "Did you ever see anything more perfect?" The iceberg was blindingly white, whiter than the statue of the Virgin Mary. Sunlight glanced off the pyramid and off the blue water that seemed to flicker and pulse with tiny gold fish. The sight of the iceberg lifted Sadie's spirits and she stood on the steps a while longer, a brisk wind lifting her hair.

"Why don't we go see Wanda?" Flora said.

"We'll have to go to her house," Sadie said. "The bar won't be open on Good Friday."

"But we don't know her house."

"We can ask, and I remember the way to Lime Street. Come on," Sadie said, though she wasn't entirely sure Wanda wanted them to visit her at her house.

They crossed the street, went down the steps and followed Queen's Road as far as the Presbyterian Church. Then they climbed uphill to Lime Street, following the route they had taken with their father on Christmas Day. Sadie remembered Lime Street as being rundown and bleak, but it was far from bleak today. With the sunny weather there were so many people outside that wherever she looked there were clumps and moving patches of colour as bare-armed grownups sat in doorways watching children playing on the dirt road. There were games of tag and swinging statues and a kind of soccer played with a bundle of rags tied into a ball. None of the children paid the sisters the slightest attention. Flora had a hungry look in her eye and Sadie knew that she longed to join the games.

"Let's walk along," Sadie said, "and see if Wanda is sitting outdoors." She took Flora's hand and they went down the road, looking to see if Wanda was among the grownups outside. A woman with reddish hair leaned out an upstairs window and waved, and for a brief moment Sadie thought she might be Wanda. When she realized that it wasn't, she stopped in front of a girl in a thin cotton dress who was sitting on a wooden step and asked if she knew Wanda Hatch. The girl shook her head, too shy to speak. Further along, Sadie asked a heavy-shouldered, white-haired woman who was sitting on a kitchen chair, a scrawny dog chained to its leg. The dog growled at Sadie and she backed away.

"Keep your distance," the woman said and cocked her head. "Who were you looking for?"

"Wanda Hatch."

"She's straight across the road in Mabel Mahoney's. You go over and tell Mabel you wants to see Wanda. She's as deaf as a post so you'll have to yell good and loud."

Sadie and Flora crossed the road and stood in front of Mabel Mahoney's. Both the front and back doors were open, which allowed them to see through the house to an outhouse in the backyard. She leaned into the open doorway and called out, "Mrs. Mahoney?" When no response came, she called again. Maybe Mrs. Mahoney was using the outhouse. Sadie stuck her head further inside the door and yelled, "Wanda? Wanda Hatch?"

She heard a thump upstairs, footsteps, then, "Sadie, Flora? Is that you?"

This was called through a second-floor window above the street. Wanda was in the window, wearing what looked like a nightgown, her red hair askew. "I'll be right down." Sadie heard her murmur to someone inside. She heard a man's grunted reply. He must be Wanda's boyfriend. Within minutes Wanda came downstairs wearing a Chinese red kimono. She was bare-foot and carrying a package of cigarettes. She said, "Let's have ourselves a seat." Except for the doorway, the only place to sit was the weatherworn bench outside. The three of them sat in a row, a sister on either side of Wanda, who lit a cigarette and blew out a practised ring of smoke.

Flora watched, entranced, as the ring uncurled and drifted away. Then she looked at Wanda and said, "Are you sick?"

"Sick? Me sick?" Wanda laughed. "Not me, I'm right as rain." She noticed Flora looking at her kimono and said, "Like I said, I works late on Saturdays and likes to spend Sundays in bed." She winked. "Except when I'm visiting you girls." She turned to Sadie. "You having trouble with Ma?"

"No trouble. We just wanted to visit you is all." *And see where you live,* she almost said before she changed her mind. She *was*

curious about seeing where Wanda lived and if it weren't for
her boyfriend, she would like to see upstairs. She felt Wanda's
arm hugging her.

"Well, aren't you sweet to want to visit me," she said in her
smoky voice. "How's your father? Is he still in Buchans?"

"He's looking for gold," Flora said. "But Sadie doesn't think
he'll find any."

"He was supposed to have come here for Easter," Sadie said
bitterly, "but he's gone to Sop's Arm to prospect for gold."

"Sop's Arm, where's that to?"

"On the other side of the island."

Wanda reached down and butted her cigarette in the dirt.
"That must be hard on you thinking of him way out there." She
was talking mostly to Sadie. "But maybe he will find gold. One
thing is sure; he won't find it unless he looks." She gave Sadie
another hug. "Will he?"

"No, I suppose not."

"You're brave girls, the pair of you." Wanda lit another cigarette and Flora told her about the iceberg. "The boys tell me
there's tons of them out there." She laughed. "That's what we
gets this time of year instead of flowers. Icebergs."

"I like them," Sadie said, and thinking of the blackened landscape that would reappear in Copper Cliff as soon as the snow
melted, she added, "They're so white and clean."

"They're a friggin' nuisance, if you want to know the truth,"
Wanda said. "Tearing up fishing nets the way they do."

Flora stood up and looked through the open doorway.
"Where's Mable Mahoney?" she said.

"Likely out back scratching in the dirt. She's got a bit of land
out there she likes to call her garden, though as far as I can tell
nothing grows in it except weeds."

"Wanda! Get back up here!" It was her boyfriend bellowing

from upstairs. Sadie wondered if he was the man who had beaten up Wanda or if he had been another man.

Wanda tipped her head back and shouted toward the open window, "Keep your shirt on! I'll be up in a while!"

Sadie stood up and said that she and Flora had to go. She wasn't in that big a hurry to leave, but it was awkward sitting out here with Wanda's boyfriend waiting upstairs. She thought they should go before Flora asked an embarrassing question about him. She might even ask if they could go upstairs, and as curious as Sadie was to see where Wanda lived, she didn't want to see it when her boyfriend was in the bed.

"I'll let you go if you promise you'll come see me again any time you're feeling blue," Wanda said. "Promise?"

"Promise."

At supper Mrs. Hatch asked them how they had spent the afternoon. Flora looked into the bowl of watery carrot soup and said piously, "We spent it in church."

"I didn't see you there."

"We were in the Roman Catholic Cathedral," Sadie said.

Mrs. Hatch's eyebrows shot up.

"It's part of our plan to become better acquainted with St. John's."

On Saturday morning after their chores were done, the sisters went down to the Royal Stores and bought themselves new stockings and underwear—their mother always bought them new underclothes for Easter. In the afternoon they went to a four-hour matinee at the Queen theatre. The feature movie was *The Texas Bearcat,* starring Bob Custer. Bob threw himself over cliffs, clung to a runaway horse and rescued a little girl by catching her around the waist with his lariat. The western was followed by three comedies featuring Will Rogers, a cowboy who, in spite of fumblings and mistakes, always managed to come out on top. Dazed after hours of watching the flickering screen, the sisters left the theatre and walked along Water Street, admiring the windows decorated with crepe-paper streamers of purple and yellow and cardboard pictures of bunnies and chicks. Back in their room they opened a package that had been mailed in Corner Brook. Inside the brown-paper wrapping was a box of chocolate fudge and a card wishing them Happy Easter and signed "Norah and Brian Leeson."

Flora helped herself to the first piece and said, "I wonder what Mrs. Leeson looks like." The corners of her mouth leaked watery chocolate.

"I saw a snapshot of her once but it wasn't very good. She was short with dark curly hair and a big smile," Sadie said. "I don't know what happened to the picture. I guess it got lost after Mum died." This was the first mention of their mother all day.

"I don't care what she looks like. She's nice," Flora said wistfully.

"She's kind to send us fudge," Sadie said. "She doesn't even know us."

That night Sadie wrote a note to her mother's friend, thanking her for her kindness. Out of politeness, she wrote, "I look forward to meeting you some day," though she didn't think it likely she would. Corner Brook was hundreds of miles away, on the other side of the island.

In the morning the girls went downstairs to an empty kitchen—Mrs. Hatch had left a half hour ago for church with freshly laundered linen for the communion table. Instead of fried bread there was a pot of sticky porridge on the stove and a glass of milk each on the table. Sadie served up the porridge sprinkling it with sugar from the bowl in the cupboard. The sisters ate in silence while Sadie stared out the window at the oak tree where last fall the injured crow had taken refuge.

After the girls had scrubbed the porridge pot and washed their bowls and glasses, they dutifully went to church and sat at the back so that they could slip out before communion service began. As they were leaving, Sadie caught sight of Miss Witherspoon and Miss Marsh sitting on the other side of the aisle. The sight of the headmistress and the teacher was oddly reassuring for Sadie—at least *they* hadn't gone away.

Back in Willicott's Lane, Flora agreed to stay inside the house and not look out the windows while Sadie hid Easter eggs outside. She had spent the last of their father's treat money on a dozen foil-wrapped eggs, which she hid in various parts of the garden, mossy and matted with clumps of soggy leaves. Sadie tucked the eggs inside a pile of stones at the bottom of the slope, in the crotches of trees, behind the shed and on the ledge of the Collinses' picket fence. She spent more time hiding the eggs than Flora did finding them. Though she claimed she hadn't peeked, Flora found all the eggs in less than five minutes.

"You can only eat one now. You have to save your appetite for dinner," Sadie said.

Dinner was boiled potatoes and carrots and a glass of tomato juice. When Sour Olive saw Sadie grimace at what was on her plate, she said, "No meat until I receive the board money from your father."

"I'm sure it will come in this week," Sadie said.

"We'll see," Mrs. Hatch said and went to sit in her rocker.

After the dishes were done, the sisters went out again and walked along Queen's Road, in the opposite direction from

Steer's Cove, until they came to Rawlin's Cross, near Bannerman Park. This outing wasn't on Sadie's timetable; she hadn't planned anything for Sunday after church because she'd thought that she would like to spend the time reading and perhaps writing to Millie. But the prospect of being shut up in the house with Mrs. Hatch drove her outside. Once she and Flora were in the park, Sadie was glad she had come. The Salvation Army Band was giving a concert in the middle of the park, where people stood listening, only a few of them wearing Easter hats. In fact, most of the people in the park were hatless and dressed in what looked like second-hand clothes. Though she hated to admit the truth of Mrs. Hatch's proclamation, looking at these people, Sadie couldn't help but feel that she and Flora were fortunate, probably more fortunate than most of the people in the park. Flora must have been feeling fortunate too, because when she was sitting on the bench after the concert eating the Easter eggs and throwing bits of chocolate to the birds strutting and cooing at her feet, she noticed a thin little boy, about four years old and wearing raggedy clothes, dart in and retrieve a bit of chocolate from the pigeons. "Would you like this?" Flora held out a chocolate Easter egg. Snatching it from her outstretched hand, the little boy ran to the far side of the park.

"You know what I think, Sadie?" Flora said and, without waiting, answered the question herself. "Even without Dad, we're having a pretty good Easter."

14

The Fall

O N TUESDAY MORNING WHEN THE SISTERS WERE
eating their porridge, Sadie asked their landlady if they
could please have some sugar.

"No, you may not," she said, bobbing her head up and down.
"I am out of sugar. You will have to go without until such time
as more can be bought. And I will thank you not to snoop in
the cupboard but eat what is on the table." As if that wasn't
enough she went on, "You girls have had the weekend to do as
you please and now must begin working for your room and
board. Since this month's rent is owing, starting today, you will
begin spring house cleaning. When I say spring house cleaning
I mean everything must be thoroughly turned out, the carpet,
the curtains and the bedding. As well, the walls, windows,
floors must be washed." Sour Olive's thin voice had been
steadily rising and was now close to a squeal. "Let it be known
that I won't tolerate shoddy work. Since we are forced to spend
this week together, we will make it count."

She's taking out having to spend the week here on us, Sadie thought. She's punishing us for being here instead of at the hotel with our father. She's bullying us because she knows we have no choice but to stay here. As Wanda says, she's pure mean.

Sour Olive wanted the downstairs windows done first: Flora was to clean the windows from inside, and Sadie from the outside. Once these orders were dispatched, their landlady left to do her errands. Carrying a bucket of water and vinegar, newspapers and rags outside, Sadie set to work. The front-room windows on the west side of the house were low and easily reached and at first the work wasn't unpleasant, especially with Flora making comical faces at her as she cleaned her side of the glass.

The work on the east side of the house was harder because here the land sloped away. When Sadie went to clean the kitchen window, she realized that it was well above her head and that she would need something to stand on. Sadie brought the kitchen stool outside and, positioning it on the stoney ground, climbed onto it. Holding the bucket, newspapers and rags, she began cleaning the window. On the other side of the glass, Flora tried to make her laugh by sticking out her tongue but Sadie ignored her. It took all her concentration to keep her balance as the stool wobbled dangerously. She had almost finished cleaning the window when one of the stool legs sank into the gravel and the stool toppled. Sadie was pitched off backwards. The next thing she knew Flora was kneeling beside her stroking her forehead.

"Wake up, Sadie, wake up. Please."

"I'm awake."

"You fell."

"Help me up."

Flora tugged on her arm and Sadie tried to sit up. But when she moved even the slightest bit, the pain in her back was so strong that she thought she would faint.

"I can't move. I've hurt myself."

"Sadie," Flora crooned. "Sadie."

"I think I'll just lie here a while. Get me something to cover me up." Strange how she could feel muzzy-headed and yet was able to think clearly. She was thinking that she should give Flora something to do.

Flora raced upstairs and was barrelling outside with the afghan just as Mrs. Hatch was coming in.

"Where do you think you're going with that?"

"To Sadie." Flora hurtled past. "She fell and hurt herself."

Reluctantly Mrs. Hatch followed Flora around the side of the house to where Sadie lay. "I might have known," she said as if it could have been predicted that as soon as she set the sisters to work, an accident would happen. Did she think Sadie had hurt herself on purpose, as a way of avoiding spring cleaning? "What's the matter with you?"

"I hurt something down here." Sadie tried to point to her spine, but of course she couldn't since she was lying on her back.

"We'd better get you inside. You can't stay out here," Mrs. Hatch said and looked furtively around, as if she feared the neighbours were watching. She bent over and taking hold of Sadie's elbow, dragged her roughly to her knees. Again, Sadie thought she would faint, but with Flora and Mrs. Hatch supporting her, she managed to get to her feet.

"Lean on me," Mrs. Hatch said. "I'll take you up to bed."

Taking one painful step after another, Sadie allowed her landlady to lead her along the side of the house, through the doorway to the stairs. "You can hold on to the railing," Mrs. Hatch said. "I'll stay behind in case you fall."

Sadie dragged herself up the stairs to the top and from there to the bed. Instinct told her to lie sideways, in which position the pain was slightly less. She began to shiver and Flora covered her with the afghan.

"You rest for a while," Mrs. Hatch said. "Your sister can do your work."

"She needs a doctor," Flora said. "She's badly hurt."

"Don't be foolish. She's taken a fall. What she needs now is rest. Come away now."

In a few minutes, Sadie was asleep. She slept most of the day, hardly moving from her sideways position, which had her facing the window. Her sleep was a delirium in which she saw her father scrambling over hills and outcrops, kneeling down every so often to pry something from a rock with his pick axe. In her dream she kept trying to call him, but no matter how hard she struggled to speak, her voice wouldn't work and he remained unaware that she could see him. It was as if she was watching an old silent movie, the kind they used to have when people on the screen didn't speak and moved jerkily like marionettes. Her father was like that. She could see him plainly but he seemed more of a puppet than a real person. It was a relief when she succeeded in willing herself awake. But wakefulness brought pain and the window light hurt her eyes. Whenever she tried to move, the end of her spine felt like it was being touched by a red hot poker. There was also a pain at the back of her head. She took her hand from beneath the covers and gingerly probed a lump above her neck at the bottom of her hairline where her head hit the ground. There was a swelling about the size of an egg. Although she'd had scrapes as a little girl, she'd never been hurt as badly as this.

She was intermittently aware of voices coming through the floor register from the kitchen, Mrs. Hatch's mainly. She was aware of Flora tiptoeing into the room, asking if she wanted anything. "Nothing," Sadie mumbled. She awoke briefly when Flora climbed onto her side of the bed and kissed her forehead. Sadie smelled tooth powder and smiled, knowing that Flora had remembered to brush her teeth.

In the morning Sadie awoke before Flora, who was sleeping quietly beside her, the edge of the blanket and her thumb jammed into her mouth. Sadie was feeling more alert and her head no longer felt quite so fuzzy. She heard a door open across the hall and knew that Mrs. Hatch was up.

Flora must have heard her too, for she stirred and opened her eyes. She took her thumb out of her mouth and looked at Sadie.

"Are you better?"

"My head is, but my back hurts if I move."

"You stay here and I'll bring you breakfast," Flora said.

"I don't want breakfast. Only a glass of water."

"Don't you worry," Flora said importantly. "I'll look after you."

Sadie smiled and closed her eyes. She was feeling drowsy again. She was aware of Flora getting dressed, then braiding her hair, something Sadie usually did for her. She was also aware of her opening the door and carrying the chamber pot downstairs. Later she heard voices coming from the kitchen, snatches of words, "breakfast," "sister," "doctor."

Mrs. Hatch herself brought up the glass of water and set it on the bedside table.

"How do you feel today?" she asked.

"A little better, but my back hurts."

"It's bound to get better if you lie still. I always say that there's nothing like bed rest to improve a body," Mrs. Hatch said and went downstairs. Sadie heard the outside door open and shut and knew that her landlady had gone out. She must have fallen asleep then because she didn't hear Flora tiptoe upstairs a few minutes later and stand by the bed. Nor did she hear the outside door open and shut again. Sadie heard nothing until she was awakened by the sound of a slow, steady footfall on the stairs, a man's, followed by her sister's quick, erratic steps. The man continued into the bedroom.

"What have we here?" a voice said, a gruff voice trying to be gentle.

Sadie opened her eyes and looked over her shoulder. Dr. MacDonald was standing by the bed in a black suit and bow tie. Beside him, looking pleased with herself, was Flora, holding the doctor's bag.

"Your sister tells me you had a bad fall," Dr. MacDonald said and went around to Flora's side of the bed so that Sadie could look at him without having to turn. He sat carefully on the edge of the bed. "Why don't you tell me what happened?"

Sadie told him, with Flora interrupting to fill in the parts she missed. "I will have to examine you," Dr. MacDonald said. His practised hands began exploring the length of her back, pausing at the base of her spine. She felt the heat of her body rising to his palm. His hands moved to her head and came to rest on the lump. "Nasty bump there," he said and shone a flashlight into her eyes, but not for long. Soon he dropped it into the leather bag which Flora still held.

"Well, Miss Morin"—surprisingly he remembered her name from the day Sadie had gone to see him about Flora's scalding—"you have a mild concussion and a bruised and possibly cracked tailbone. The concussion will ease in a day or two but the tailbone will take longer to mend."

"How long?"

"Two or three weeks. The first week you must lie in bed as

you are, on one side. You will have to get up from time to time
to use the chamber pot, because you are not to walk to the
bathroom. I don't want you going downstairs. It will be painful
enough getting in and out of bed. I could give you something
for the pain, but I prefer not to, since pain is an indicator of
how much you should move. The second week you may sit up
and walk around the house."

"But I'll miss school."

"Your sister can bring you your homework. By the way,
when you return to school you are not to take gymnastics or
whatever it is young ladies do for exercise in school these days."
The doctor stood up and picked up his bag. "I will look in on
you at the end of the week."

Flora accompanied Dr. MacDonald downstairs. Through
the register Sadie heard him talking to Mrs. Hatch. Had she
been listening from the kitchen, staying down there to avoid
being asked to pay the doctor? As soon as he had gone, Flora
bounded upstairs and, kneeling beside the bed, whispered, "He
told Sour Olive about you having to stay in bed. He said that
on no account must you be made to do housework."

Later that morning Mrs. Hatch came upstairs and asked
Sadie if there was something she wanted to eat. In nearly eight
months of living in Willicott's Lane this was the first time Sadie
had been asked this question. She wasn't hungry, but she said
she would like a piece of toast and a cup of tea.

Flora brought up the toast and tea, and fed Sadie bits of
toast. Then held her head while she sipped the tea.

"I feel like the injured crow," Sadie said.

"Sour Olive said I don't have to wash the walls but I have to
wash and wax the front-room floor and beat the carpet," Flora
said cheerfully. "I don't mind. It's something to do."

My little sister is growing up, Sadie thought, and although she had often wished Flora would be more grown up, it was sad to think that she might grow up too fast. When her mother died, Sadie was thirteen, which meant her childhood was over, but Flora had been seven and Sadie wondered about how much of her childhood she was missing.

For supper that evening, Flora carried a bowl of pea soup upstairs along with a buttered tea biscuit. Placing the food carefully beside Sadie, she said, "Sour Olive baked!"

Sadie told her she wasn't hungry and to eat the soup and biscuit herself. "Did Dad's money come?" she asked. She thought the baking might be a sign that Sour Olive had been paid.

"I don't think so. I was here both times when she came back from the post office and she was as grumpy as ever."

At the end of the week Dr. MacDonald came to see how Sadie was getting along, and after his examination eased her legs over the side of the bed and lifted her to her feet. He stood in front of her and, supporting her with his arms, encouraged her to walk to the table and sit in the chair. Her legs were shaky and her tailbone hurt when she sat, but she was clear-headed—the lump at the back of her head was almost gone.

"Good girl," Dr. MacDonald said. "I want you to do this every day and sit for a half hour at a time, then walk back to bed. Do you think you can do that?"

"I can."

"When you feel comfortable doing that, you can walk around the room."

Flora continued with the spring cleaning and by Saturday had washed and waxed all the floors including their bedroom, but not the two bedrooms across the hall.

Watching her work, Sadie teased, "You'll be glad to get back to school."

"Not to school," Flora said. "But I'll be glad to see Peggy."

On Sunday Sadie wrote a letter to Miss Witherspoon explaining her situation and asking if her homework could be given to Flora to bring home so she wouldn't fall behind in her schooling. Twice the following week Flora delivered assignments to Sadie as well as a note from Teddy saying he could hardly wait to see her.

Sadie's second week of recuperation was in some ways worse than the first. The stabbing pain was gone but her tailbone ached whenever she sat or walked, and with Flora in school, she missed her bouncy company. Also she received a short letter from her father written in a place called Howley, where he and Gutsy Pike were waiting for a horse and cart to take them to Hampden. From there they would travel by boat to Sop's Arm. The letter upset Sadie because it brought the anger back. Her father mentioned the magnificent scenery but he didn't write a single word about missing Flora and her. The letter was a description of how much distance he was putting between them and himself. There was nothing to suggest that he was aware that she and Flora might be lonely for him. He seemed to think everything was going on just fine without him. He seemed to have forgotten Flora's scalding or that anything could go wrong. Maybe he had to think everything was fine without him so that he could go off and do what he wanted.

Sadie was beginning to think that she understood why Aunt Rachel and Aunt Rose tried to prevent their father from looking after Flora and herself. After her mother's death, they had barraged him with letters and telegrams, insisting that they ought to be given the opportunity to look after their sister's daughters. They said that they would be able to provide them with the very best schooling and the advantages of a superior upbringing, which could not be had in Canada. Their father was scornful of their claims and stood up to them in a way he had not stood up to Miss Witherspoon.

Sitting at the wooden table on the bedroom's one chair, Sadie imagined the bedroom she would have if she and Flora were living with the Irish aunts. They would have canopied twin beds with curtains of flowered linen that they could close when they wanted to be alone. There would be proper desks and comfortably padded chairs, and a thick carpet on the floor. Also a fireplace, which the maid would light on winter mornings. Sadie would have a horse and Flora would have a pony—the aunts were keen on horseback riding. Sadie and Flora would dress in satin and ribbons and be invited to birthday parties. In summer they would be driven to the country and to the seaside, where they would picnic from a hamper packed with all sorts of delicious food prepared by the cook.

Sadie took a sheet of note paper and in her best hand began a letter to the aunts to whom she hadn't written since she'd thanked them for their Christmas gifts. She didn't mention Easter because the aunts did not celebrate it. Instead she told them about the kind of schooling she and Flora were receiving at Bishop Spencer. She told them that their father was prospecting in western Newfoundland but she didn't say that it was for gold—though she was angry at him, Sadie wasn't about to trade in her loyalty to her father. She mentioned that she was recovering from an injury, but she didn't say that it was the result of having to stand on a stool to clean windows. It was tempting to add this, since such an accident would never have happened if she and Flora were staying in Brighton with Aunt Rachel and Aunt Rose. The aunts had servants to do the kind of work she and Flora were required to do for Mrs. Hatch.

Next, Sadie wrote to her mother's friend in Corner Brook. She didn't mention the accident because she didn't know Mrs. Leeson well enough to complain. She merely asked if she would let her know if she heard anything from her father and to please tell him that Mrs. Hatch hadn't received his letter. She didn't include the fact that the letter contained the board money because she thought if she did, Mrs. Leeson, having been her mother's friend, might try to send money, and Sadie didn't want her to feel obligated. How had she come by pride so strong that it prevented her from asking for help? Though she resisted admitting it, she seemed to have inherited her father's pride. She remembered when the Irish aunts were trying to persuade him to let them bring up their nieces and her father telling them that he would never be beholden to anybody, that he was able to look after his family without anyone's help.

Sadie wrote a third letter, this one to Millie, explaining that she was recuperating from having fallen off the wobbly stool when she was cleaning windows. To Millie she confessed all her worry about the lost board money. She let it all pour out as she did the day Millie and she walked in the cold winter wind. "I hate being cooped up with Sour Olive. When she's in the house, all she does is sit in her rocking chair. Even with the bedroom door closed, I can hear her rocking."

Hour upon hour, day after day her landlady rocked, sometimes knitting, sometimes not. Why did she spend so much time this way? Wasn't she bored? Didn't she have work to do around the house? Of course not. She got Sadie and Flora to do her work. Sadie thought she would scream if she had to listen to another day's rocking. By now she was feeling better and could hardly wait to return to Bishop Spencer. The school wasn't her favourite place to be, but she would rather be there than stuck in Willicott's Lane with Mrs. Hatch.

15

Money

"COME IN, SADIE, COME IN," MISS WITHERSPOON SAID when she saw Sadie in her office doorway. "Welcome back to Spencer."

"Thank you, Miss Witherspoon. Dr. MacDonald asked me to give you this."

The headmistress put on her glasses and read the note while Sadie tried to read her face. Impossible—Spoony's face was as unreadable as stone. "I see the doctor recommends that you not participate in gymnastics or games. What a pity. Now that spring is warming up, the house teams will be playing field hockey, but you will miss all that."

What a relief, Sadie thought. Now she wouldn't have to stumble around the field, getting in the way of better players and letting down St. George's house. "Is there something else I could do?" she asked. After weeks of boredom in Willicott's Lane, she preferred to avoid being left in the classroom with nothing to do.

Miss Witherspoon gave her one of her bracketed smiles. "Now that you mention it, there is something you could do. While your classmates are occupied with sports, you could sort the new books for our school library."

Whenever she talked about Bishop Spencer, Spoony always made it sound more splendid than it was and "school library" was another one of her grandiose expressions. There wasn't, in fact, a school library, at least not a library in one room. There were hundreds of books in the school but they were shelved in various classrooms, most of them in the grade-ten-class cupboard because it was the largest.

That afternoon while the class went off to play field hockey, Sadie stayed behind and began the task of sorting and shelving ten boxes of books that Spoony's brother in England had donated to the school. As well as listing the books in a note-book kept in each room for that purpose, Sadie had to apply a sticker and a number inside each book before finding a place for it on shelves and inside crowded cupboards. Sadie didn't get much done that first afternoon, and it was two weeks, or six classes of field hockey, before she finished the job. The work might have been done more quickly, but the task required her to be more methodical than she was, and she had a habit of stopping every so often to read some of the books. One book in particular caught her attention, *The Mystery of Gold*. With its soiled blue cover and mouldy pages, it wasn't a book she would usually choose to read. What she preferred to read were stories of adventure and romance, and this water-stained old book, written by Martin Fairweather, wasn't a story at all. It was about gold, about how for centuries it had been used in churches and to decorate temples and castles, making it the Queen of worship and the King of money. By reading about gold, Sadie thought she might better understand her father and his fascination with gold. She knew she couldn't understand him completely, she couldn't understand anyone completely, not even herself, but she wanted to try. *Gold is the most highly valued metal in the world*, she read, *partly because it is one of the most difficult metals to find. Gold retains its lustre without polishing and can be stretched like no other metal. An ounce of gold can be pulled into a forty-mile-long wire without breaking, which means a little bit of it goes a long way. Gold casts a spell upon those who behold it in a way that defies logic and comprehension. Many a man as been struck with gold fever and sacrificed his health in the quest for gold.* Did her father have gold fever? Was it the fever that drove him to Sop's Arm with someone named Gutsy Pike? A fever meant you were ill, and Sadie worried that her father might fall so much under the spell of gold that, as Martin Fairweather wrote, he might sacrifice his health to obtain it.

Sadie asked Teddy what he knew about Sop's Arm. Since returning to Spencer, she had been meeting Teddy at the end of the lane every morning before school and they were now walking along Gower Street, Flora trailing at their heels. Teddy said, "As far as I know, Sop's Arm is just another outport, which means it's surrounded by rock and water." There was a yell from behind and Sadie turned to see Peggy, her bookbag bouncing against her hip, running to catch up. Flora doubled back to meet her. "Guess what!" Peggy said breathlessly. "There's a polar bear loose in Maddox Cove! My mother heard about it on the radio."

"Where's Maddox Cove?" Sadie asked

"About fifteen miles south of St. John's," Teddy said.

"There's to be no school until they shoot it. I wish we had a polar bear in the harbour so we wouldn't have to go to school."

Teddy laughed. "There's no chance of that, Peggy. Polar bears come ashore from the pack ice and the ice moved out weeks ago. And it's late in the spring for polar bears to be this far south. The one in Maddox Cove must have come ashore on a random ice pan."

Sadie waited until after Flora and Peggy had run on ahead before asking if there would be enough ice in Sop's Arm to bring a polar bear ashore.

"It's a bit farther north so there might be some ice at the bottom of the bay," Teddy said, "but your father would have a gun."

"My father doesn't have a gun."

"Then the man he's prospecting with, Gutsy, what was his last name?"

"Pike."

"Gutsy Pike probably has a gun. Between the two of them they would be able to look after themelves. When your father prospected in Ontario, didn't he encounter black bears?"

"Yes, and in Buchans too. When they were camping, a bear ate their food."

"And they survived all right. Your father will be fine, Sadie. Don't worry about him."

But Sadie did worry. She imagined her father being outrun by a polar bear and clinging to the top of a spindly tree while the bear shook him loose like an apple. She imagined Gutsy and him, wretched and starving, wandering over the rocky landscape after a bear had eaten their cache of food. And a few days later when a letter arrived from Mrs. Leeson telling Sadie that she hadn't heard from her father since he had written from Badger, Sadie worried that her father might be lost. It would be easy to become lost on an island as large as Newfoundland. Mrs. Leeson had included her telephone number in the letter and written, "Feel free to telephone any time you want." Sadie would have to write and explain that there wasn't a telephone in Willicott's Lane and ask that if she heard from her father, to leave a message for Sadie at the Crosbie Hotel. "Do you girls have any plans for the holidays?" Mrs. Leeson wrote. "It would be grand if you could visit us in Corner Brook this summer. I am longing to meet Mary's girls." The invitation cheered Sadie. It made her feel good to know that even though it was far away, on the other side of the island, that there was a place where she and Flora were wanted.

As the weeks passed without Mrs. Hatch being paid for room and board, her meals became increasingly sparse. Breakfast was still porridge, no sugar and a glass of milk, but dinner was, more often than not, nothing more than a plate of mashed potatoes or boiled carrots and cabbage. For supper there was a bowl of watery turnip soup and a slice of unbuttered bread, which meant the sisters often went to bed hungry. Using the dwindling expense money inside Madeleine's pantaloons, Sadie bought a package of biscuits and a bag of apples, which she and Flora wolfed down along with glasses of water carried up to their room. The sisters continued to do housework, mopping and sweeping floors, dusting and polishing furniture, washing and ironing, but now Flora emptied the chamber pot herself. They did not complain about the food, knowing that they would be lectured about how ungrateful they were. But the third Tuesday in May, when Sadie saw that supper that was nothing more of a slice of bread and a glass of water, she stormed into the front room and confronted Mrs. Hatch, who was sitting in the rocker but for once wasn't knitting. Instead, she was staring down at her cupped hands as if they held a small captured animal.

"Do you call bread and water supper?" Sadie said. She knew she was being saucy and belligerent, but she didn't care. Both

she and Flora had lost weight and if the meagre meals continued, they would become ill.

"It's supper for thieves," Sour Olive sneered and bared her
teeth. "When thieves are put in jail, bread and water is what
they are fed."

"We're not thieves."

"Yes, you are." Sour Olive stroked a thumb.

"What are you talking about?" Sadie said wildly. "We have
never taken a cent from you. It's you who has taken my father's
money."

"That's money I earned and it's been spent," Sour Olive said.
"He's owing two months' room and board."

"That doesn't make us thieves."

Mrs. Hatch clenched her fists, poked her head toward Sadie
and hissed, "Bring your sister in here!"

Flora appeared at once—she must have been listening from
the curtained doorway—and stood beside Sadie.

"There's a thief in the house. Five dollars is missing from the
money box."

"What money box?" Sadie said.

"Don't play innocent with me, girl. The box where I keep my
money."

"I don't know where you keep your money," Sadie protested.
She hadn't, in fact, even thought about where their landlady
kept her money.

"Then your sister does."

"I don't know either," Flora said.

"What makes you think we're thieves?" Sadie said. "Anyone
could walk in here and take five dollars. The door to the lane is
unlocked."

Sour Olive pounced on Sadie's words and a wily expression
crossed her face. "But who would know where to look for the

key to the money box? Or for that matter the key to the room?"

Sadie shrugged and said, "How should I know?" But she knew. Sour Olive must be referring to the smaller key on the ring she hung on the nail behind her dresser. The money box must be inside Thomas Hatch's room. "I didn't even know you had a money box."

"Well, one of you did, and there will be nothing for supper except bread and water until the one who took my money confesses to the crime."

Crime. Did Sour Olive think they were criminals? Sadie took her Flora's hand. "Let's go." She led her sister past the uneaten bread—let Sour Olive eat it herself, they'd starve before they'd eat it—and outside. It was chilly and they were wearing only sweaters, but they couldn't talk inside the house without their landlady hearing. They walked to the end of the lane, Sadie keeping her back straight, and didn't stop until they had turned the corner onto Victoria Street.

Sadie put her hands on her sister's shoulders. "Now, Flora, tell me the truth, did you take the five dollars?" As far as Sadie knew, Flora had never stolen anything, but when she was bored or had time on her hands, she was inclined to snoop and might have gone into Thomas Hatch's room to poke around and found the money box. Flora looked down and scuffed one shoe against the road. "No, I didn't."

"Then who did?"

"Maybe nobody did. Maybe Sour Olive made up a story about the money being stolen."

Sadie hadn't thought of that. "Why would she do that?"

"I don't know," Flora said and she began to cry.

Sadie held her close. "There, there," she said. "It will work itself out, you'll see." She wasn't sure that it would but she needed to reassure Flora, who if she became scared, might go back to wetting the bed. "Let's go up to our room and have apples and crackers for supper."

That night, after Flora was asleep, Sadie lay awake thinking about who could have taken the five dollars. The only other person who knew about Sour Olive's keys was Wanda. Could she have taken the money? Or had the money not been taken at all as Flora had suggested?

The next day after school, Sadie asked Mrs. Collins if she would keep an eye on Flora and she went off to visit Wanda at the Anchor and Chain. She walked down Queen's Road to the far end of Water Street until she saw a sign, Steers Cove → crudely painted on a rough board. Turning toward the harbour, she caught the smell of the salt water wafting in on the breeze. Riding the same breeze was the briny smell of spring fish drying on spindly wooden flakes. She caught a glimpse of masted schooners tied up at the finger wharves. She heard men's voices, rough unfamiliar voices coming from the direction of the harbour. The dirt-packed street was short and narrow, blocked on either side by sooty brick warehouses. At the end of the street, on the left, was an open doorway that had to be the Anchor and Chain because there was no other business in sight. In front of the door on the wooden step sat two elderly, harmless-looking men who smiled when Sadie asked if they knew Wanda Hatch.

"She's inside," the bearded man said. "Just you go inside. It's all right. It's early yet and there's not many about."

"Mind the step, girlie," said the one wearing a hat. "You wouldn't want to trip."

As she stepped into the gloomy interior, Sadie was framed by the daylight so that Wanda saw her immediately.

"Sadie!"

Blinded by the sudden dark, Sadie blinked and looked in the

direction of the voice. Wanda was behind a long counter that she was wiping with a rag with one hand while holding a cigarette in the other.

"Lonesome, are you?" Wanda grinned and stubbed out the cigarette. "Would you like a spot of tea? I just brewed myself a pot."

Sadie said she would and when her eyes had adjusted to the hazy gloom, looked around and saw a dozen or more tables inside the room along with an assortment of ill-matched chairs and stools. Fishing nets filled with cork floats were slung from the walls like hammocks. A large anchor hung over the bar where Wanda was pouring tea into mugs.

"Milk and sugar?"

"Milk."

"You came at the right time, before it gets busy. Most days I gets here early enough to have myself a mug-up. I likes to get myself composed before the boss shows up." When Wanda carried the mugs to the table nearest the bar, Sadie saw that she was wearing a low-cut white blouse, a black skirt and black laced boots. Wanda opened a cookie tin and put it on the table. "Help yourself to the shortbreads."

Noon dinner had been another bowl of turnip soup and Sadie was starving. She ate four cookies without stopping.

"Cookie. Cookie."

Sadie turned and looked in the corner beside the bar. To her astonishment she saw a green parrot inside a large cage hanging by a chain from a hook in the ceiling.

"Cookie."

"That's Sailor," Wanda said. She got up and gave the parrot a piece of shortbread. "That's all you're going to get. One more word out of you and I'll cover your cage."

Sailor cocked his head.

"I mean it."

Wanda sat down. "That bird is a frigging nuisance. The boss brought it back from Barbados but he leaves it to me to clean up after the thing. You'd think he'd show an interest in it but all he does is teach it to swear." Wanda took a drink of tea and lit a cigarette. She inhaled slowly and, when Sadie didn't speak, asked what was the matter.

Sadie blurted it out. "Your mother says five dollars has been stolen from her money box. She thinks Flora or I took it. She called us thieves and expects us to eat bread and water for supper until we confess." There, she'd said it. If Wanda had taken the money, this was her chance to admit it. "I don't even know where her money box is."

"If it's where it used to be, it's in the table drawer inside my brother's room." *She would never have told me that,* Sadie thought, *if she had taken the money.* She said, "Do you think she said the money was stolen when it wasn't?"

Wanda squinted at a fingernail through the haze of smoke, then bit off the end.

"Now why would she do that?"

"I don't know. Dad owes her two months' room and board money and she might be looking for an excuse to make us leave."

Wanda looked at Sadie through the spiralling smoke. "Listen, Sadie. No matter how mean she is, Ma wouldn't do that. If she didn't want you there, she'd find another way to throw you out. She didn't throw me out. I left of my own free will. You got to remember that Ma's bark is worse than her bite. The truth is that she can't afford to stay in the house, not with the pitiful amount my dad sends her."

"Your father's alive? I thought your mother was a widow."

"That's what she wants people to think. My father's a

longshoreman in Halifax. He sends Ma whatever money he doesn't drink up, which means she doesn't get much. He left her years ago for the same reason I cleared out. Neither of us could stand the way she wouldn't let go of my brother. After all these years, she worships Tom as if he was still alive. Cripes, Beaumont Hamel was eleven years ago." With her free hand, Wanda reached toward the ashtray, at the same time inhaling the last dregs of the cigarette. "But she always did favour him. Growing up it was always Tom this, Tom that. One day I asked her why he could do no wrong and she was always picking on me. Do you know what she said?" Wanda stubbed out the cigarette. "She said she didn't like girls!" Wanda looked around the room. "She'd like me even less if she knew where I works."

"I'm sorry, Wanda," Sadie said. She couldn't imagine a mother being so mean.

"Don't you be. I hardly thinks about it any more. I'm only telling you so you knows why she's bullying you. Growing up on Lime Street without a pot to pee in, she worries about money. She's afraid she'll end up living back there." Wanda made a barking sound that was too bitter for a laugh. "Kind of funny when you thinks that it's me that's ended up on Lime Street." She lit another cigarette. "But I'd rather live there than in a frigging shrine."

"She goes into your brother's room every day."

"Before I left, I tried her get her to sell the house and move into some place small but she won't live away from Tom's bloody room. She could've rented out his room dozens of times. It's the best room in the house. But she won't let go of the past. She'll be stuck in that house until the day she dies. She won't even sell the piano. She could get a lot of money for that piano but she refuses to sell it. My sainted brother used to play that piano, if you could call it playing. He had a tin ear."

Sadie heard loud voices outside and Wanda got to her feet. "Sorry, Sadie, but I got to get to work. There's last night's glasses to be washed before the crowd comes in." She picked up the teapot and the cookie tin and carried them to the bar. Sadie followed with the mugs. Wanda took the mugs and said, "Five dollars is a lot of money to Ma. That's why she raised such a stink. I hate to say this, Sadie, but maybe you should consider that your sister might've took it."

"But why would she do that?"

"Beats me." Wanda thrust a handful of cookies at Sadie. "Take these. Now you'd better scoot before the boys comes in here. Benny and Tinker are harmless but some of the fellas don't know how to treat a nice girl like you."

Walking back to Willicott's Lane, Sadie thought about the stolen money. Even though Wanda knew where her mother's money box was, Sadie was sure she hadn't taken the five dollars. If she had, she would have admitted it once she knew Sadie and Flora were in trouble. Wanda was right. Probably her sister had taken the money. Tomorrow she would have a long talk with Flora.

The next afternoon Sadie and Flora were sitting on a bench in Bannerman Park after school, one sister at one end of the bench, one sister at the other.

Sadie jumped right in. "I want to know if you took five dollars from Mrs. Hatch's money box. If you did, you should own up to it now and get it over with."

Hands tucked under her thighs, Flora leaned over, watching her feet swing back and forth as if they required her close attention in order to move.

Remembering the day Flora watched from the bottom of the stairs while Sadie returned the key ring to Mrs. Hatch's room, Sadie said, "Did you use the other key on the ring to open Mrs. Hatch's money box? Tell me."

In a small defiant voice, Flora said, "I don't have to tell you everything."

"Did you take the five dollars?"

Flora didn't answer, which Sadie thought was an admission of guilt. If she hadn't taken the money, she would have denied it.

Sadie waited, expecting her sister to confess, but Flora wouldn't speak. Forcing herself to speak gently, Sadie said, "That five dollars belonged to Mrs. Hatch and as much as we hate her, we have no right to steal from her."

Flora said nothing but continued swinging her legs in an irritating way. This was too much for Sadie. "You are so annoying," she said. "Can't you see the trouble you're causing? Things are bad enough without you making them worse. Why don't you grow up! Why do I have to do all the thinking and worrying and you get to do what you want!" This wasn't true, but Sadie was so angry at her little sister that this was all she could think of to say.

Flora's lower lip jutted out and she stopped swinging her legs. She got up from the bench and set off across the grass in the direction of Willicott's Lane, walking purposefully, her braids bobbing against her shoulder from the briskness of her stride.

Sadie followed, far enough behind her sister so that they weren't together, yet close enough to see that she got safely back to the lane.

That was how they passed the rest of the evening, at an unnatural distance from each other. The next day they barely spoke and were careful not to touch. Meal times were spent avoiding one another's gaze. Sadie fumed at her sister's silence. She hadn't known Flora could be so stubborn. Her sister had always been strong-willed but never so defiant and distant. Sadie wanted to bridge the gap between them, but until her sister admitted to taking the money, she didn't know how. For the first time since they began living in Willicott's Lane, the sisters slept without touching each other. They didn't put their arms around one another and each of them was careful to stay well over on her side of the bed.

16

Birthday Surprises

SADIE DIDN'T SAY A WORD TO TEDDY ABOUT THE skimpy meals at Willicott's Lane. She didn't tell him that for three days in a row noon dinner was turnip soup, and supper bread and water. She hadn't forgotten his response the day she told him that her father wouldn't be in St. John's for Easter, how apologetic he'd been for not being able to provide a place for Flora and her to stay. If she told him that she and Flora went to bed hungry every night, he would probably ask his parents if they could eat supper at the hotel and Sadie would have to say, "No, Teddy, I can't because I have no way of paying you back." She didn't want to hurt his feelings again, so it was better that she say nothing about Sour Olive's miserly meals. But Friday morning walking along Gower Street, out of the blue Teddy asked her to have supper with his family at the hotel the next day. He claimed that his parents had been asking about her and said it was high time he asked her in for a meal.

"I'd like that," Sadie said and didn't ask if the invitation included Flora. The sisters still weren't speaking to one another. This morning they had used the bathroom separately and neither of them said a word during breakfast or the washing-up. Now Flora was ahead, skipping along with Peggy, laughing as if she didn't have a care in the world, which she probably didn't, because she left them all to Sadie. Flora could stay at home tomorrow night with Sour Olive. It would serve her right for not admitting she had stolen the money.

"It will take my mind off my problems," Sadie said. She knew Teddy would assume she meant the missing room-and-board money, which she had told him about. But she hadn't told him about the missing five dollars or that her birthday was the day after tomorrow and that she was worried because there hadn't been one single thing in the mail from her father, not a birthday card or a note. Her father had never missed her birthday and she was convinced that something must be horribly wrong. She hadn't told Teddy about her birthday because she didn't want him to feel obligated to buy her a present, as he had done at Christmas. Not that she didn't want a present. She did, but she couldn't afford to give him a present in return. She didn't even know when his birthday was. Sadie had made up her mind to forget all about her birthday. What was the point? She couldn't afford to spend money on herself because every cent had to be saved for school expenses and for food to make up for Sour Olive's paltry meals. If she allowed herself to think of her birthday, she would start feeling sorry for herself and she couldn't afford that either.

On Saturday, the sisters did their chores separately without speaking, Flora mopping the floors and washing her soiled sheet and Sadie scouring sinks and ironing the week's laundry—Mrs. Hatch insisted that even the towels had to be

ironed. When Flora went outside to play, Sadie ironed her
summer dresses—the weather was warm enough for wearing
cotton. She had two summer dresses: a high-necked blue dress
with a wide sash, and a green and white dress tailored to look
like a suit. She chose the blue dress, which fit more loosely than
it did last summer—since she'd lost weight the bodice no
longer strained against her breasts. She pinned on the silver
note and brushed her hair.

At five-thirty Mrs. Hatch left to attend the potluck supper of
the Women's Missionary Association. Watching her carrying a
bowl of potato salad down the lane, Sadie couldn't help thinking that Sour Olive fed her church friends better than her
boarders. She looked up and down the lane and into the yard
for Flora but there was no sign of her anywhere. Maybe Mrs.
Collins had invited her for supper. Sadie wrote a note telling
her sister where she was going and propped it against the
spoon jar. Then she walked down Victoria Street to the hotel.

Teddy was waiting for her in the lobby. Sadie noticed his
cheeks redden slightly when she came up to him. Instead of
speaking, Teddy gestured toward the dining room. Sadie
walked ahead of him until they reached the doorway. At this
point Teddy took the lead, making his way between tables
where diners were eating. Every table in the room was occupied. When he reached what Sadie thought of as Teddy's
corner—it was the only place in the dining room where she
had seen him eat—Teddy stopped and pulled out a chair.
"Happy Birthday," he said.

On the other side of the table, crouched behind two balloons
tied to the salt and pepper shakers, was Flora. She popped up
like a grinning jack-in-the-box. "Surprise!" All the diners in the
room turned to look. Overwhelmed and confused, Sadie sat
down. Never once had it occurred to her that Flora would

arrange a birthday party. She was, after all, only nine years old and relied on Sadie to do the arranging. But there was no doubt in Sadie's mind that this surprise dinner was mostly her sister's doing. She must have told Teddy it was her birthday and asked for his help. The realization that Flora had done this was too much for Sadie and to her embarrassment, she began to cry. She couldn't help it. She wasn't prepared for the surprise or the mixture of love and regret she felt toward her little sister.

Flora reached for her hand. "Don't be sad, Sadie."

"I'm not sad. I'm happy." Sadie looked around for something to wipe the tears spilling down her cheeks. Teddy handed her a napkin.

"You did a good job surprising me," Sadie said.

The two of them sat there grinning like a pair of Cheshire cats.

"You didn't guess?" Flora said.

"No."

"I would have," Flora said solemnly, "because you've never let me down, Sadie."

The sisters sat smiling at each other and holding hands, both of them grateful that the wrenching impasse had been broken.

Now it was Teddy's turn to be embarrassed. Sadie knew that she and her sister were sometimes so close that they left out others, even someone like Teddy. She let go of Flora's hand and asked Teddy for a menu. Flora giggled but Teddy was unperturbed and waved the waitress over.

The girls studied the menu for a long time, though they knew what to expect from having seen it at Christmastime. They wanted to savour the selection of the food: riced potatoes with buttered peas, roast chicken with gravy and dressing, rhubarb pie with whipped cream. The sisters ordered roast chicken with all the trimmings. Teddy ordered his favourite

meal, lamb stew. When the food came, both girls began shovelling it in, until Sadie noticed the grin on Teddy's face and
slowed down.

After the waitress had removed their empty plates, Teddy
again asked for the menu. This turned out to be a ruse, because
dessert had already been decided and Teddy's parents were
parading through the dining room with the birthday cake.
They walked slowly so that everyone in the dining room could
join them singing, "Happy Birthday, Dear Sadie. Happy
Birthday to you!"

Mortification branded Sadie's face bright red. Her face was
so hot she thought if she was lying down, she could fry an egg
on her forehead. There was an outbreak of applause while she
blew out the candles. Mrs. Dodge handed Sadie a knife tied with
white ribbon and urged her to cut the chocolate layer cake iced
with two inches of thick white frosting. The waitress brought
both vanilla and chocolate ice cream, which made Flora roll her
eyes. She ate two pieces of cake and two helpings of ice cream.

When they were finished, Mr. Dodge stood up and said,
"Duty calls." Mrs. Dodge also asked to be excused. Sadie,
Flora and Teddy, who was carrying the cake, went to the
Dodges' apartment where Sadie opened two gifts, Flora's first.
Flora's gift was a medical kit, which she had wrapped in cray-
oned paper. It was a real nurse's kit of black leather with a
brass clasp and leather handles. Inside were rolls of bandages
and tape, wooden tongue depressors, a bottle of disinfectant
and a thermometer. So this was why she had taken Mrs.
Hatch's money. It was on the tip of Sadie's tongue to ask how
much it had cost—it had probably taken all of the five
dollars—but knowing how much trouble Flora had taken to
arrange her birthday, Sadie didn't have the heart to bring up
the subject of the stolen money.

"Thank you, Flora," she said.

"Teddy helped me pick it out but it was my idea," Flora said proudly. "It's for an emergency, in case we have any more accidents."

Teddy handed Sadie a heavy rectangular parcel wrapped in brown store paper.

"I'm not much good at wrapping."

Sadie untied the string and opened the paper. It was a book, *The Complete Works of Shakespeare*.

"Thank you, Teddy."

"The catch is that you have to read us something."

"Now?"

"Now."

Sadie leafed through the book looking for something to read. She wouldn't read anything sappy like what Juliet said to Romeo, and she wouldn't read the embarrassing bits Lady McBeth said about sex and breasts, which could set Flora and herself into a fit of giggling. The easiest part she could think of to read was Ariel's. Though she had memorized it, to please Teddy, she read from the book. When she finished, she turned to Flora, who had been unusually quiet all this time.

Flora was sitting on the chesterfield wearing a clown face: a white mustache, nose and chin. On the table in front of her was the destroyed cake—she had eaten the icing along with much of the cake, leaving what looked like a landslide of mud.

"Flora!" Sadie was horrified by her sister's bad manners. Then she burst out laughing. She couldn't help it. Flora looked so comical. Sadie looked at Teddy, who was laughing so hard he was hugging himself.

"You had better wash that off," Sadie said sternly, then giggled, more at Teddy's laughter than at her sister, who sat with her eyes cast down, a silly grin on her face. "We can't leave with you looking like that."

It was nearly dark when Teddy walked the sisters back to Willicott's Lane, Sadie carrying her gifts and Flora what remained of the ruined cake. Inside the house, the sisters used the bathroom and went upstairs, calling out "good night" as they went by the front room where, as usual, Sour Olive was sitting in her rocker. Flora got into bed and Sadie kissed her good night. She still didn't mention the stolen money, unwilling to change the closeness between them. The day of reckoning would come soon enough and the nurse's kit returned to the store and the money given to Mrs. Hatch. What she wanted now was for Flora and her to sleep with their arms around each other.

The next morning dawned balmy and warm. It was going to be another summery day and Sadie could feel the soft, silken air sliding through the window and across her face. She heard Mrs. Hatch making breakfast in the kitchen but she lay quietly, not wanting to waken Flora. But Flora was awake, having heard their landlady rattling the frying pan and filling the kettle. She rolled over to face Sadie. "Happy Birthday," she whispered. "Now you're fifteen." She got out of bed and padded across the floor to the dresser. She opened her drawer and took out a birthday card, which she gave Sadie. "I saw it on the kitchen table last week," she said, "and I put it away until today." The card from the Irish aunts showed a horse with a garland around its neck on which was written "Birthday Greetings."

"Girls!" Sour Olive screeched through the heat register. "Time for breakfast! Be quick about it!"

Sadie put on her bathrobe and slippers. Flora did the same and they went down to the kitchen and sat at the table.

"You're not dressed for church," Mrs. Hatch said and slammed down two plates of fried bread.

"We'll dress after we eat," Sadie said.

"It's her birthday," Flora said.

As if Sour Olive cared, Sadie thought, but she wasn't displeased with Flora, who she knew was trying to make the day special any way she could. When she was Flora's age and younger, Sadie would beg her mother to tell her about when she was born. Although she knew the story by heart, she couldn't hear it often enough. Her mother would obligingly explain that she had been born thirty minutes before midnight on the third of June on the brown velour chesterfield in Copper Cliff because there wasn't enough time for her father and the midwife to help her up to bed. While Sadie's father dashed upstairs for a clean sheet, the midwife covered the chesterfield with newspapers to keep the velour from being ruined. Her mother said that Sadie came out in a whoosh of water, and the moment she did, the cuckoo bird on the wall clock popped out and announced the half hour, which made everyone laugh except Sadie, who was screaming to beat the band. But she didn't scream for long and soon became a happy baby. Hearing this story every year always made Sadie feel special, not only because her mother laughed when she told it, but because Sadie knew that no baby in the world had been born exactly the same way.

Sour Olive did not respond to the news that it was Sadie's birthday. Angry about the stolen money, she seemed determined to ignore them both and went to the back door, put on her hat and coat and left for church without saying a word.

Because the sisters were late arriving at church, they were seated during the singing of the first hymn in a pew close to the front of the cathedral instead of their usual place at the back. Sadie dreaded the prospect of walking down the aisle in full view of the congregation and felt the urge to scoot outside, but

missed her chance because latecomers were already at her heels
and the man showing her to their seats was already halfway
down the aisle. As she followed him to the pew, Sadie was
aware of the reverend's piercing stare, and when she was seated,
felt grateful that she was obscured from his view by a thick
stone pillar. But she could see the head of his wife, a tall
woman, much taller than her husband, sitting in the front row
with the Eagles children in a diminishing row beside her. There
were seven of them, all girls. Sadie had counted them once
when the children were following their mother down the
aisle—sometimes they too were late for church. Except for her
swollen stomach, Mrs. Eagles was thin and bony with
porridge-colored skin.

During church services Sadie usually studied the congregation, which wasn't very interesting but helped pass the time,
which dragged, especially during the sermon. This morning's
sermon was entitled "The Pitfalls of Envy." The reverend was
well into his subject when Sadie felt her arm being tugged. She
looked down and saw Flora pointing at the woman sitting in
front of them. At a glance the woman seemed like the other
women in the row who were wearing dresses and straw hats.
What made her diffferent was the foot-long feather in her hat.
It looked like the tail feather of a wild bird and was attached to
a wide band of ribbon. As the reverend droned through the
sermon, her head nodded forward and the feather drooped
lower and lower. Soon she was fast asleep, and by the time the
sermon ended her snores were clearly heard. Flora giggled
outright. There was an answering giggle from someone sitting
further along the row. The woman awoke with a snort and
looked around, offended.

The reverend was now leading the congregation in prayer
and Sadie bowed her head and silently asked God to keep her

father safe and bring him back to Flora and herself. Sadie didn't really know if she believed in God—it was too big a subject for her to fully understand—but she wanted to try. Churches, cathedrals and temples had been built all over the world for the purpose of worshipping God, so why shouldn't she worship? It couldn't do any harm, could it? And it probably did some good. With this last thought it mind, she squinched her eyes and fervently prayed that her father was safe and well. The only way she knew how to take away the hurt of not hearing from him on her birthday was to pray, not for herself but for him.

The final hymn had been sung at last, and Sadie and Flora inched forward along with a tide of people heading toward the glut at the back door, where the reverend was enthusiastically shaking hands with members of the congregation. As they neared the doorway, Sadie tried to slip outside but the reverend reached out and caught her hand. "I would like a word with you, young lady. Please wait for me inside."

Sadie was seized by a dreadful fear. The minister never spoke to her except to say, "Good morning." What did he have to say to her now? Did he have some bad news about her father? Sadie took Flora's hand. "Come on. We'll wait in one of the pews." They sat near the front, both of them silent and bewildered, Flora swinging her feet, Sadie staring blankly ahead.

It was twenty minutes before the reverend, his robe flapping around his ankles, came up the aisle. "There you are," he said jovially as if they had been hiding and he had only now discovered their whereabouts. "I'll see you in my office. This way." The sisters began to follow and the reverend turned and said to Flora, "Not you." He didn't even use her name, probably because he didn't know it. He didn't know Sadie's either, because he said, "I want to speak to your older sister alone. It won't take long."

Anxious and trembling, fearful of what of what "it" was, Sadie followed the minister down the aisle to the front of the cathedral and down a corridor to a room with a thick wooden door. Inside the room was a large desk, bookshelves and several chairs—this was obviously the reverend's office. He closed the door and said, "You may sit down." He himself did not sit but stood near the desk, his fingers hooked on his surplice, his gaze directed at the picture of Jesus standing in a doorway holding a lantern. He said, "This is awkward, most awkward indeed." Sadie wasn't sure if he was addressing Jesus or herself, until he looked directly at her and said, "It is time to discuss your future."

"My future," Sadie said. "You mean this isn't about my father?"

"Not precisely, though you could say he is involved in a way."

Sadie let out a sigh of relief. At least he didn't have bad news about her father.

"The fact is that Mrs. Hatch, your landlady, is unable to keep you girls much longer and we will have to make other arrangements for you. Good Christian that she is, she has kindly agreed to allow you girls to stay with her until the end of the school term."

"She isn't kindly," Sadie said. "She's mean."

The reverend skewered Sadie with one of his fierce stares. "I suggest you watch what you say, young lady. Considering the fact that a sum of money was stolen from her by one of you girls, I would say that Mrs. Hatch has been most kind."

There was nothing Sadie could say to this without betraying her sister, and she could only sit and wait for what was coming next.

"I have daughters," the reverend said placatingly, "and I know this must be difficult for you. In fact I discussed the matter of your placement with my family, pointing out to my wife that she can always use another pair of hands about the house, but she reminded me that our little ones are already sleeping two to a bed and that the hired girl must make do on a cot in the pantry. I regret that there is no other recourse but for you and your sister to move into the Church of England Orphanage for Girls. As soon as school is over, you will leave Mrs. Hatch, who does not have the means to support you. I have taken the liberty of speaking to Mrs. Harris, the orphanage matron, and she has agreed that you can work in the kitchen. That means you and sister will be on the same premises, though of course she will sleep in the dormitory and you in a room off the kitchen. When school is over I will arrange for a driver to move you from Willicott's Lane."

Throughout this speech, Sadie sat stiff and wooden, so wooden that she might have been part of the chair. But she could think and had been while the reverend was speaking. Intuition told her not to resist, to say anything that would seem troublesome or uncooperative. For now she would appear to quietly accept the arrangements made on her behalf, though she had absolutely no intention of going to the orphanage. But there was one thing she was determined to say, which was, "I have a request."

"Speak up."

She hadn't realized she'd been whispering. "I have a request," she said more loudly.

"And what is that?"

"That these plans be kept secret. I don't want anyone in Bishop Spencer to know about them." Her voice faltered. "It would make it hard for Flora and me if it was known."

The reverend accepted these words as acquiescence and became jovial again. "Very well. Since you are a reasonable young woman, I will say nothing." He was almost bouncing with relief. "You may go now. It is time we had our dinners."

When Sadie didn't move—she wasn't entirely certain she could—he said it again and she got to her feet. The reverend held the door open and she went to collect her little sister.

Outside on the step, Flora looked at her questioningly, but Sadie said nothing. She couldn't tell her sister what the reverend had in mind, she just couldn't. She would be more terrified than Sadie if she knew his plans. And they couldn't return to Willicott's Lane where Mrs. Hatch would be waiting, wanting to know what the minister had said. She needed more time to think before facing Mrs. Hatch. In the meantime she would have to pretend everything was all right. She reached out and tweaked Flora's pigtail. "Come on, let's see if Teddy wants to go up Signal Hill," she said. "It's a lovely day for a walk."

"All right," Flora said and off they went to the Crosbie Hotel.

17

Silent Mirth

AN HOUR LATER SADIE AND FLORA WERE CLIMBING
Signal Hill, following Teddy past Dead Man's Pond. Here
he left the dirt road and walked along a path that crossed rocky
outcroppings and dipped into narrow valleys. The path
climbed steeply, then levelled off on a rocky mound called
Gibbet Hill, around which was a flat grassy field where Teddy
said soldiers practised their drills. He showed them the canon
that fired the noonday gun that boomed about the same time
the school prefect rang the bell. Then he followed the path to
the cliff edge, where vertical rocks were deeply scoured and
scarred from their prehistoric birth. Teddy indicated three
rocks that looked like chair backs, and when the sisters were
sitting beside him, pointed to the view.

The view was spectacular. Below them was the part of the
harbour that narrowed as it entered the sea. In a queer sort of
way the Narrows, together with the harbour, roughly dupli-
cated the shape of Newfoundland. On the other side of the

Narrows was Fort Amherst, where on foggy days the horn sounded. After a brief rest, they continued climbing the path that followed the cliff edge. Near the top Teddy took the path below the stone tower and followed the road up the back of the hill. When they reached the top, Sadie made an abrupt stop, not because she was winded or tired but to look again at the view. There, at her feet, was the wide expanse of the Atlantic Ocean, which she had crossed on *The Maid of Innisfree* when her mother had taken Flora and her to Ireland and back. Though it seemed so long ago, what Sadie remembered about the crossing was that the sea had been grey, the weather foggy and cold. It had also been grey and cold the day after Christmas when she had come up here with her father. Today the water shone with reflected light. There were brush marks on the blue that made the sea look as if it had been swept with an invisible broom. Above, the sky had the pale rinsed look of after rain, and far in the distance where sky met water a gleaming white mountain floated in a pinkish blue mist. Sadie pointed, "Is that an iceberg out there?"

"It's a straggler. You'll see the odd iceberg offshore until mid-summer," Teddy said and handed her a molasses cookie and a bottle of ginger beer he had brought from the hotel kitchen. For a time the three of them sat on a flat rounded rock to eat the cookies and drink the beer. It was much greener up here than it had been on Gibbet Hill. At their feet the land billowed out in skirtings of grass and clover that rustled like starched petticoats in the breeze. Although they were sitting near the grey stone of Cabot Tower, Teddy didn't say a word about it being named after the explorer, or that the hill itself was where Marconi received the first trans-Atlantic wireless signal from Wales. He seemed to know that Sadie's mind was elsewhere—she hadn't said a word in fifteen minutes. Even

Flora was silent but only, Sadie realized when she looked, because she was asleep. Her little sister was lying on one side, her thumb jammed into her mouth. Sadie stood up, put a finger to her lips and moved to another rock about twenty feet away. Teddy moved too and Sadie told him about the morning's meeting with the reverend and his intention of putting Flora and her in the Church of England orphanage as soon as school was finished. "He's already spoken to the orphanage matron about us."

"Can he do that without you agreeing to it?"

"I guess so. Without my father here . . ." In her determination not to blubber, Sadie's words trailed away, but she swallowed hard and pressed on. "Teddy, there's something wrong with my father. I know it. Otherwise I would have heard from him by now. He said he'd be gone six weeks and it's over two months. And he's never forgotten my birthday."

Teddy didn't offer his usual comforting words. He didn't say anything at all but sat listening, the beer bottle between his knees.

"I have twenty dollars hidden away that my father gave me for emergencies. For a while I thought of giving it to Mrs. Hatch to pay what's owing on our room and board, but since the reverend told me his plans this morning, I'm thinking of using the money to go to Corner Brook to stay with Mrs. Leeson, my mother's friend. She invited us for a visit. Do you know what the train fare would be?"

"It's a little more than a dollar to get to Avondale, so twenty dollars would probably get you both to Corner Brook."

"She gave me her telephone number and told me to call her if I ever needed to."

Teddy jumped at this. "Why don't you telephone her from the hotel?"

"Do you think I could tell from the telephone if she's nice? I'm pretty sure she is, but I'd want to be sure."

"She couldn't be worse than Sour Olive."

Sadie laughed, which made her feel slightly better. She stood up, impatient to leave. "Let's go," she said. She wanted to telephone right away, before she lost her nerve.

The telephone was answered on the first ring.

"Mrs. Leeson, is that you?"

"Pardon?"

There was static on the line and Sadie was keeping her voice low. She was using the hotel lobby telephone and didn't want anyone else to hear, especially Flora, who was sitting nearby with Teddy.

"It's Sadie Morin."

"Sadie! Is it really you?" There was an Irish lilt in her voice like there had been in her mother's.

"It's me."

"Have you heard from your father?"

"No." Sadie hesitated before plunging in. "I'm telephoning you to ask if Flora and I can come visit you this summer."

"Of course you can! Didn't I just invite you for a visit?"

The voice was so warm and welcoming that Sadie began to cry. There was a pause and Mrs. Leeson said, "Sadie . . . are you there?"

"I'm here," she said and, pulling herself together, went on, "We'll come by train."

There was a pause before Mrs. Leeson asked, "Is everything all right, Sadie?"

"Yes, except for worrying about Dad."

"How is Flora?"

"She's fine."

"Good. Have you decided when you'll come?"

"As soon as school is finished."

"Grand. That will be in three weeks, won't it?"

"Two weeks." Sadie was already thinking she would leave school early, as soon as exams were finished, before the reverend sent a driver to take Flora and her to the orphanage.

"Do you need help with the train fare?"

"No, but our landlady mustn't know about it," Sadie said. "She might not like it if we left."

"And why is that?" Mrs. Leeson asked.

"I'll explain when I see you."

"Well then, you just tell me when your train will be coming and Brian and I will be there with bells on to meet it."

"With bells on." Sadie hadn't heard the expression since her mother died. She knew she had to stop talking, a long-distance telephone call cost money, but she couldn't hear enough of Mrs. Leeson's voice with its Irish lilt.

Sadie said, "Do you think something bad's happened to Dad?"

There was another pause before Mrs. Leeson spoke. "I don't know your father, Sadie, but from what Mary told me, I expect he fancies that he'll find gold and has completely forgotten the time!"

Forgotten two whole months? Sadie nearly said, but she didn't because she knew that Mrs. Leeson was being kind. Instead she told her that as soon as she had the train tickets, she would let her know when she and Flora were due to arrive. Sadie hung up the telephone and smiled with relief. She had done the right thing calling Mrs. Leeson. It was settled. As soon as exams were finished, she and her sister were leaving St. John's.

By the time Sadie and Flora climbed the hill to Willicott's Lane, it was nearly seven o'clock and the house was empty. Mrs. Hatch had gone to evening service at the cathedral. She had left bread and water for them on the kitchen table. The sisters did not touch the bread but carried the water upstairs where they sat on the bed and ate the last of the ruined cake.

The next afternoon after school Sadie insisted Flora skip Brownies so that the nurse's kit could be returned. It had been bought at O'Mara's Pharmacy at the west end of Water Street, a forty-five-minute walk from school, counting the time it took to stop in Willicott's Lane to pick up the kit. Fortunately Mrs. Hatch was out. Because it had begun to rain, Sadie emptied her bookbag onto the bed and stowed the kit inside.

Flora sulked most of the way to the shop. She wanted Sadie to keep her birthday present and said Mrs. Hatch didn't need the five dollars because there was a whole bunch of bills inside the tin box. Flora no longer denied that she had used the smaller key on Mrs. Hatch's key ring to open the money box in Thomas's room. She admitted that she had gone into his room twice, the first time to poke around after she'd seen Sadie hanging up the key ring, and the second time to get some money to buy Sadie's birthday present. Sadie hadn't noticed the drawer, but Flora had noticed it the first time she'd gone into the room. She had known for months that it was where Sour Olive kept her money. The revelation startled Sadie. What else did Flora know that she wasn't telling?

The pharmacy was a high-ceilinged room containing shelves lined with giant-sized bottles and jars. The woman behind the counter smiled when the sisters entered the shop and asked what she could do for them. Sadie gave her the nurse's kit and told her she wanted to return it, explaining that her little sister had bought it as her birthday present but she couldn't afford to keep it. The woman remembered Flora and Teddy coming to the shop and after examining the kit said there would be no problem refunding the money. She took the kit to the back of the shop where Mr. O'Mara was working, probably mixing a prescription. Sadie saw him nod his head as the woman spoke and soon she was back, punching keys on the cash register. Sadie put twenty-five cents on the counter and the woman gave her a five-dollar bill.

As they walked along Water Street in the mizzling rain, Sadie said, "As soon as we get back, I want you to give Mrs. Hatch her money and say you're sorry."

"But I'm not sorry."

"It was her money and you were wrong to take it," Sadie said. "You have to learn that stealing is wrong."

"I'll do it, Sadie," Flora said mournfully. "I'll do it for you."

"Not for me," Sadie said. "Do it for yourself."

When they got back, Sour Olive was in the kitchen making what she called supper. Apparently they were to be given something to eat besides bread. Flora didn't even wait to take off her jacket and shoes but marched up to their landlady and gave her the five-dollar bill. She said, "I took the money to buy Sadie a birthday present, and I won't do it again."

Sour Olive's eyes glittered triumphantly. "I knew it was you." She didn't say "thank you" or "you did the right thing" or offer encouragement of any sort. Didn't she know how hard it was to confess a wrong? Or did she think she never did anything wrong herself? She looked at the muddy footprints Flora had tracked in and said, "You'd better mop the floor if you expect any supper."

Supper was boiled turnip greens, which Mrs. Hatch claimed they were lucky to get since they were the first greens of the season. The greens tasted bitter and without any butter the sisters had to smother them with salt in order to swallow them

After they had cleaned up the kitchen and were on their way upstairs, Mrs. Hatch called Sadie back. "I want a word with you in the kitchen."

"Sit down." Mrs. Hatch was sitting on one side of the table and Sadie sat on the other.

"Did the reverend speak to you yesterday about making other living arrangements for you girls?"

"You know he did," Sadie said. She didn't say, "You put him up to it, you weaselly witch," because if she said what she was thinking, Sour Olive might change her mind about letting them stay until school was finished.

"And what do you think of that?"

A stupid question. Did she expect Sadie to say that she was looking forward to living in the orphanage, that she could hardly wait to begin domestic work?

"The orphanage is the best place for your sister," Sour Olive said. "They'll teach her right from wrong. They don't tolerate stealing among the orphans."

"She's not an orphan and neither am I," Sadie said. "We have a father."

"But he's not here to look after his precious daughters, is he?" Mrs. Hatch sneered. This more than anything made Sadie want to scratch out her eyes. She wanted to lunge at her landlady and pull her hair. She wanted to scream that she was the meanest, vilest person she had ever met. She was fighting the urge to do all this when she heard Flora sobbing and raced upstairs. By the time she reached the bedroom, her sister was lying on the bed and sobbing so hard she was hiccupping. Sadie lay down and, holding her against her chest, stroked her hair.

After a while Flora whispered, "Will I have to go to the orphanage, Sadie?" She had heard every word through the heat register, as Mrs. Hatch had probably intended.

Sadie didn't answer. She was waiting for Sour Olive to leave the kitchen, which she took her time doing. No doubt she found pleasure in listening to Flora's sobs. Eventually Sadie heard the familiar sound of rocking and knew that their landlady had moved to the front room. Putting her mouth to her sister's ear, Sadie whispered, "Listen to me, Flora. We are *not* going to the orphanage. We're going to run away from Mrs. Hatch."

Flora lifted her head. "Truly?"

"Truly. We're going to run away to Corner Brook before school is over."

"To Mrs. Leeson?" Flora whispered back.

"Yes. She was the person I was telephoning yesterday from the hotel. I told you I was talking to Millie because I didn't want to tell you until I had figured out our plans. Yesterday the reverend told me that we would have to move to the orphanage as soon as school is over, so we'll have to leave school early, before he sends a driver to pick us up. No one must know that we're running away, not even Peggy. Promise me not to tell."

"I promise."

"If Sour Olive finds out we're leaving, she might try to prevent us from boarding the train so she can have the ticket money to settle up what she's owed. That's why we can't tell anyone our plans. Tomorrow after school we'll go to the train station and buy the tickets."

"But we don't have money for tickets."

"Yes we do." Sadie pushed her sister's snub nose. "You don't know everything, Miss Snoop."

Flora giggled.

"Shush! Sour Olive mustn't hear. She thinks we're going to the orphanage and we have to pretend to be sad."

But Flora couldn't stop giggling and soon Sadie was giggling, but it was a silent, desperate kind of mirth.

Flora eventually fell asleep but Sadie lay awake, exhausted but unable to sleep because she couldn't stop thinking. She was thinking not only about her father's whereabouts but how his absence was changing Flora and herself in ways she didn't like. Flora wasn't sorry that she had stolen money, and she had told Flora that they would have to pretend to Mrs. Hatch that they would be going to the orphanage when they weren't, which was another lie. Sadie had already told Sour Olive lies and she would have to tell her more. She would also have to lie to Miss Witherspoon and to her other teachers. She would have to pretend she was doing one thing while she was doing another. To carry out their plans she would have to be dishonest and sneaky. For the first time in her life Sadie knew what it was like to be trapped in a situation she couldn't escape without practising deceit. She thought of the ragged children she had seen playing on Lime Street and wondered if, like Flora and herself, their situation was affecting them in the same kind of way.

18

Playing with Fire

Tuesday after school the sisters went to the train station and Sadie bought two second-class tickets to Corner Brook for eighteen dollars. It was fifteen minutes past five when they returned to Willicott's Lane, which meant they had to put up with a tirade about shirking housework and being late for supper, which was a potage of turnip greens heaped onto watery potato. Sadie gulped the mess down quickly, but Flora played with her food as if it would taste better if she moved it around the plate. Sadie washed the dishes and the kitchen floor. Then she went upstairs and wrote to Mrs. Leeson, telling her that she and Flora would be arriving in Corner Brook on June 19th. She sealed the letter and she and Flora walked down Victoria Street to the hotel. Sadie wanted to mail the letter right away, knowing she and Flora would feel better once it was done.

Later that evening when Flora was asleep, Sadie unscrewed the handle of the silver brush, rolled up the tickets and tucked them inside. She knew she was taking a chance leaving the brush on the dresser where Mrs. Hatch could easily take it if she had it in mind to pawn something of Sadie's to make up for the unpaid room and board. This thought had come to Sadie when she and Flora passed a pawn shop on their way back from the train station, but she had dismissed it right away. If Mrs. Hatch intended to get her room and board money back by stealing something of Sadie's, she would have done it weeks ago. In any case, after the fuss about Flora stealing five dollars, their landlady wasn't likely to steal something of theirs. With the train tickets bought and the letter written, Sadie fell asleep soon after she got into bed. Some details for getting away still remained to be worked out, but the big decisions had been made and she could now buckle down to school work. Flora didn't have to write exams but Sadie did, and because of all the worries about her father and the missing room and board money, she had fallen behind in her studies.

The next morning during assembly, Spoony lectured the students of Bishop Spencer on the dangers of fire. "It has been brought to my attention by Mr. Buckle and Mrs. Collins that there has been smoking in the washroom," she said. "Under no circumstances can this be tolerated and any girl reported smoking inside Bishop Spencer will be suspended."

The students gave no outward sign of being dismayed or even surprised by this news but sat as still and silent as the Sphinx, not one of them daring to whisper or turn.

"You will recall when the fire chief visited our school last September, he was at pains to explain that in a building such as ours, every possible precaution must be taken against the outbreak of fire. That is why we maintain regular fire drills and why there are fire extinguishers in every classroom. It is also why prefects supervise the corridors as you move from room to room. By taking these measures, we have so far been able to protect ourselves against fire. It has also been brought to my attention that Bishop Spencer students have been seen attempting to purchase cigarettes at the Bull's Eye Shop. Let it be clearly understood that any girl caught smoking on school premises does not have the welfare of Bishop Spencer in mind and, as I have said, will be suspended.

Chastened and docile, at least outwardly, the girls filed out of the hall after assembly and went to their classes. For the grade-ten and -eleven girls, classroom time was given over to review and study. With exams only a week away, senior girls were expected to spend all their time in exam preparation. Sadie tried to concentrate on the answers to old exam questions the teachers wrote on the blackboard and mostly she succeeded. She read her notes and wrote out answers, but every so often her mind veered off as she tried to figure out exactly how she and Flora would be able to get away to the train station without Mrs. Hatch interfering.

On Thursday Sadie was going into the washroom after school when the door opened and Eunice and Tina came out. Both of them looked startled to see her, and for an instant Sadie thought she saw fear in Eunice's eyes. But the moment passed and Eunice shouldered roughly past as if Sadie wasn't there. Nelly wasn't with them—several times lately Sadie had seen her with a Feildan student and guessed that now that she had a boyfriend, Nelly was no longer interested in going around with the girls.

As soon as she opened the washroom door, Sadie smelled smoke. There wasn't much of it but the smell was unmistakable and seemed to be coming from inside one of the cubicles. She opened the cubicle door and saw a thread of smoke spiralling from the waste can beside the toilet. She picked up the can and saw tissue burning. There wasn't any flame but one of the tissues had a blackened corner that was curling upwards. "Foolish girls," she muttered as she took the can to the sink and tipping it beneath the spout, turned on the tap so that water flooded the tissues. She put the can on the floor, deliberately leaving it beside the sink where Mrs. Collins would see it when she came in to clean.

During next morning's assembly, the headmistress again brought up the matter of smoking in the washrooms, and Sadie knew that the evidence she had left behind had been found. Miss Witherspoon said that if one more incidence of smoking occurred in Bishop Spencer, she would undertake a thorough search of every girl's belongings and that someone from the fire department would be called in to examine what she referred to as "telltale signs." As before, none of the girls indicated that the headmistress's warning had the remotest connection with them. But after school, when Sadie stayed behind to straighen the book cupboard (Spoony still expected her to look after the library), Eunice stayed behind as well. Sadie ignored her, hoping she would leave, but even after everyone else in the class had gone home, Eunice was still there. She sidled up behind Sadie, who continued pretending she wasn't there. If she was expecting Sadie to say anything, she was mistaken. Apparently the thought finally occurred to her and she spoke. "Thanks for not telling on me and Tina yesterday," she said. "I took you for a Miss Goody-Two-Shoes but I guess I was wrong."

Without bothering to turn around, Sadie said, "If I smell smoke again I will tell on you." She shoved a book to the back of the cupboard, hard, so that it gave a loud knock. "I don't want the school to burn down and it'll be your own fault if you get expelled." Eunice stomped out the door and Sadie called after her, "By the way I know you fouled my mug for no good reason but I don't care about that any more. I have more important things on my mind." She was surprised how good it felt to tell Eunice exactly what she thought. She should have told her months ago before Eunice's bullying became a habit. Sadie continued straightening the cupboard, and when she was finished, picked up her bookbag and left the room. By now Flora would be waiting for her downstairs in the entryway. Sadie had started down the stairs when she heard her name being called. She looked up and saw Spoony standing in the doorway of her office.

"Would you come up here for a moment, Sadie." Though this was phrased as a question, it was a command, and Sadie went back upstairs. She knew this was about smoking in the washroom, she just knew it. The question was how much or how little she would say. She had just told Eunice that if she smelled smoke again, she would tell on her. Having said that, she resolved to say nothing about finding a tissue burning inside the waste can. Sadie stood in the office doorway.

"Please come in."

Sadie went into the office and waited until she was told to sit down. Spoony sat back in the chair and crossed her hands beneath her chest.

"I know it has been a challenging year for you, Sadie. Being a new girl is never easy. Having a younger sister to look after cannot be easy either, particularly with your father away so much."

How did she know this? Had Mrs. Hatch told her, or the reverend? Had he told her about moving Flora and her to the orphanage after telling Sadie that he wouldn't?

Spoony went on, "In spite of these responsibilities, you have managed to achieve high marks and to be pleasant and cooperative about whatever you are asked to do. I am particularly pleased with the effort you have put into our library. I am telling you this now, since with exams coming up next week there may not another opportunity to do so before the summer break." Spoony seemed to be letting down her guard, for she sighed regretfully and said, "One of the disadvantages of my position is that I spend most of my time interviewing my weaker students about their results and seldom have time to speak to my better girls. I regret that we have not spent more time together, but I want you to know that I am recommending you for a blue deportment belt, which is awarded only to those students who demonstrate outstanding qualities of character."

"Me?" Sadie squeaked and immediately felt silly.

"Yes, you. You have character, Sadie Morin. All my teachers have noticed." With the briefest of smiles, Spoony added, "Your spirited defense of Jane Miller was most impressive and gave me pause for thought."

Sadie felt an unexpected rush of gratitude for this formidable woman who in her own way was admitting that she had been unkind.

"Deportment belts will not be awarded until December's prize-giving, but I wanted you to know that you are in line for the highest honour Bishop Spencer can give."

"Oh," said Sadie with perhaps a whiff of disappointment. Would she be here in December?

"That is not such a long wait," Miss Witherspoon said.

"Oh no," Sadie said. "It's only that I'm surprised." It was all she could do not to burst out with the news that she had to leave school early and might not be able to attend Bishop Spencer next year.

"That is all. Flora will be waiting for you, I am sure."

So she knew about that too, all the waiting and fetching.

Flora was at the bottom of the stairs. "I thought you forgot me, Sadie, and I was worried."

"Have I ever forgotten you?"

"No."

"I had to sort some books before the weekend." Sadie didn't mention the meeting with Spoony or the blue belt. She didn't know why exactly but instinct told her to keep what Spoony said to herself. It was the kind of hopeful flame that would burn more brightly inside if no one else knew about it. In any case, if she didn't return to Bishop Spencer next year, there wouldn't be a blue belt. Until she heard from their father, nothing at all was certain.

Sadie had two more details to work out before she and Flora could board the train for Corner Brook a week Sunday. She needed someone to prevent Sour Olive from spoiling their departure and she needed help getting their suitcases to the train station. Teddy had offered to help carry the suitcases, but he couldn't do that and at the same time prevent Mrs. Hatch from ruining their plans. There was only one person who could stop Sour Olive from interfering and that was her daughter.

Late the following afternoon when the sisters had finished the Saturday chores—Sour Olive had given them twice the work, insisting that the stove be blackened and polished and the carpets beaten again—Sadie and Flora walked to Steer's Cove to visit Wanda. Sadie found the Anchor and Chain much the same as it had been on her previous visit. The same pair of elderly men were sitting on the step in front of the open door, and the bar was empty except for Wanda, who was behind the counter. She was even wearing the same clothes. She looked up as the sisters came inside and paused, waiting for their eyes to adjust to the darkness. "Sadie! Flora! How are you girls?"

"Cookie!" screamed Sailor. "Cookie!"

Flora immediately went to the parrot.

"Don't put your finger in the cage. He'll bite it off, the vicious little bugger," Wanda said. Then putting her elbows on the counter, she leaned forward and whispered, "Did she take the five bucks?"

"Yes, to buy me a birthday present."

"Aw, that was sweet of her." Wanda lit a cigarette and looked at Flora, who was watching the bird. Then she looked back at Sadie. "Happy Birthday."

"Wanda," Sadie blurted out, "we're taking the train to Corner Brook right after I finish my exams. I used Dad's emergency money to buy the tickets."

Wanda gave a long whistle and to Flora's delight, Sailor whistled back.

"We're going to stay with my mother's friend," Sadie went on, "before the reverend puts us in the orphanage. Last Sunday he told me that your mother couldn't keep us any more and that as soon as school was over, we'd have to move to the Church of England Orphanage for Girls. Flora would sleep in the dormitory and I'd sleep in a room off the kitchen."

"So Ma got him to do her dirty work," Wanda said. "I warned you about her, didn't I."

"If she got the chance I'm sure she'd try to stop us from going to Corner Brook."

"You're right. Ma would do that. She wouldn't be above using the constabulary to stop you so she could get her hands on your train tickets. When exactly do you plan to leave?"

"A week Sunday at one o'clock."

Again Wanda whistled and Sailor whistled back.

"That soon. You're moving fast."

"I've got to," Sadie said grimly. "And I need your help getting away. My friend Teddy will help carry our suitcases to the train station but . . ."

"You needs someone to keep Ma busy," Wanda finished. "She'll be home from church long before one o'clock and you wants someone to keep her from noticing that you're gone."

"Could you do it?"

"I sure can." Wanda grinned. "Nothing would give me more pleasure." She winked. "Well, that's not entirely true. I can think of one or two things that would, but sure, I'll look after Ma for you." She blew out another ring of bluish smoke and picked a shred of tobacco from her tongue. "I don't know how but I'll think of something to keep her occupied until I hear the train whistle. Don't you worry your head about that."

Sadie said, "I knew I could count on you."

Her words seemed to embarrass Wanda, who said, "Enough of that," with unaccustomed roughness and slammed three mugs on the counter. "Time for a mug up. Sadie, you pour the tea."

Wanda opened the tin of shortbreads and gave half a cookie to Flora to feed Sailor. As soon as they had finished their tea, Wanda said, again speaking roughly, "Now you two better skedaddle before the fellas gets here. They always comes in earlier on Saturday."

Flora said, "Are they hangashores?"

Wanda grinned. "Some are, some aren't."

When Sadie reached the doorway, Wanda called, "Send me a note from Corner Brook, you hear?"

"I hear."

"Be sure to print it."

"I will." Sadie looked through the smoky haze and saw Wanda with her head bent furiously scrubbing the countertop.

"Why did she say that?" Flora whispered.

Sadie didn't answer until they had left Steer's Cove and were walking along Water Street. "I don't think Wanda can read, at least, not handwriting. She can probably read printing."

Flora thought this over and then asked another of her penetrating questions: "Can Mrs. Hatch read?"

"I don't know," Sadie said. She had never seen her reading. Then remembering the underlined passages of scripture in Thomas Hatch's room, she added, "I think she can read parts of the Bible."

19

The Picnic

EXAM WEEK BEGAN ON MONDAY MORNING WITH MISS Bugle instructing the grade-ten girls about how to rearrange desks so that they were far enough apart to prevent students from looking at one another's papers. "Not that any of you girls would do such a thing," Miss Bugle said, wanting to think the best of everyone. "But that is the rule at Spencer and we will abide by it." When the desks were in place, she instructed the students to put their ink bottles in the wells and the pens in the wooden hollows of the desks—pencils were not permitted. Nor were any of them permitted to use the washroom or to have as much as a scrap of paper on a desk. But new ink blotters were passed out to each of them by the prefects.

When all this had been done and each desk was checked, Miss Bugle handed out the geography exam face down. Only when she was seated at the desk where a large alarm clock ticked away the anxious minutes were the students allowed to turn their papers over and begin writing. Every fifteen minutes

Miss Bugle or Miss Beamish or Miss Witherspoon or Miss Marsh or Miss Fraser—during the next few days each exam was supervised by a different teacher—would get up and pace the rows between the desks, careful to avoid looking at the students with their worried faces and puzzled frowns. Glancing from one side to the other, the teacher appeared not to notice the inked thumbs, the drumming fingers, the exaggerated sighs.

On Tuesday the grade tens wrote history; on Wednesday literature and grammar, and so on throughout the week. Sadie didn't find the exams particularly difficult. The teachers had told the class what to study and there were no surprise questions—Miss Bugle had come right out and told the class exactly what questions would be on her exam.

Apparently it was different at Bishop Feild. When they were talking about the exams, Teddy told Sadie that one of the masters had deliberately misled students into thinking this or that question would be asked so he could sneak in surprise questions that were meant, the master said, to separate the sheep from the goats. Teddy wrote his exams the same week as Sadie wrote hers but he didn't finish until Friday afternoon, whereas she was finished by Friday noon and like the rest of the class had the afternoon off to do as she pleased. Not Flora—classes continued as usual for elementary girls. Sadie spent the afternoon avoiding Mrs. Hatch so she wouldn't be given extra chores. When her landlady went out to collect the mail and do her errands, Sadie pulled the suitcases from beneath the bed and began to pack. The packing had to be done while her landlady was out, since the sound of suitcases being dragged across the floor and dresser drawers being opened and shut would arouse suspicion. Because their winter clothing was already folded away in a suitcase, it didn't take long for Sadie to finish packing and she was done before Mrs. Hatch returned. She even had time to buy apples and biscuits, postage stamps, a colouring book and crayons before fetching Flora from school.

On the way back to Willicott's Lane, Flora said, "I'm sad because I couldn't say goodbye to my friends or my teachers."

"I couldn't say goodbye either," Sadie said. She meant to her teachers, since with Millie gone, she didn't have any friends at school.

"But I don't mind too much because I'm excited that we have only one day left before we get on the train."

"I'm excited too," Sadie said, "but we mustn't show it when Mrs. Hatch is around. We should make a pact not to talk when she's near. It would be easy to give ourselves away."

"Maybe she'll go out tonight," Flora said hopefully.

But Mrs. Hatch did not go out. After supper she went into the front room and began knitting a sweater that she announced in her pious way was for the Women's Missionary Association sale. After the dishes were put away, Sadie mopped the floors upstairs and down and Flora scoured the sinks. By eight o'clock the sisters were in their bedroom. Flora went to bed but Sadie stayed up and wrote a letter to Miss Witherspoon explaining why she and Flora would be missing the last week of school and giving her the Leesons' address. Then she wrote a letter to Millie telling her she would write to her again from Corner Brook. She stamped the envelopes and put them in her school bag with the apples and crackers—she and Flora were using their school bags to carry what they wanted to use on the train. At nine o'clock Sadie heard their landlady come upstairs to bed. When the bedroom door was closed, Sadie pulled out a suitcase, put their school uniforms inside and shoved it back beneath the bed. The dresser drawers had been emptied but the clutter on top remained. As far as Sadie knew, Mrs. Hatch

seldom looked in their room but she didn't want it too tidy-
looking in case she did.

In the morning the sisters wiped the furniture and base-
boards, and while Sadie emptied the icebox and wiped the
shelves, Flora cleaned the bathroom. The only chore left
undone was sponging their uniforms and washing their underwear. If she had been there, Mrs. Hatch might have noticed
this, but after assigning them work, she went out and didn't
return until dinner time. Dinner was a plate of cold boiled
potatoes to which the girls could help themselves. Mrs. Hatch
wouldn't be eating because she was "saving" her appetite for
the reverend and Mrs. Eagles's garden party that afternoon. It
hardly mattered to the sisters what they ate because Flora was
going on a picnic with the Collinses at Hogan's Pond and Sadie
and Teddy were having a picnic in Bowring Park, where Teddy
promised to show her the monument to Beaumont Hamel he
had talked about last fall.

The afternoon seemed to have been made for picnics. The
sky was cloudless, the air warm and windless. The sun poured
down on Sadie's head—it hadn't occurred to her to bring a hat.
She was wearing a blouse, a cotton skirt and sturdy school
shoes. Teddy was wearing what were obviously old clothes, and
carrying the picnic basket. They walked along Water Street as
far as the train station, where they waited for the Speeder-
Reider, the electric car that would take them to the park. A
family of six were also waiting for the electric car and, like
Teddy, the father carried a picnic basket. Soon the Speedy-
Reider was skimming toward them along the tracks, and the
eight of them got on and the car zipped ahead on tracks that
ran parallel to a river where stately old houses stood behind
yards of grass. With their wide verandas and roofs trimmed
with wooden lace, the houses made Sadie think of well-dressed

wealthy women in long fancy gowns taking their leisure. It made her think of the Irish aunts drinking tea on a veranda in Brighton, eating cakes and pastries from a silver tray.

The electric car let them off at the entrance of the park, where there was a pond around which dogwood and laburnum trees were about to flower. There were ducks and gulls in the pond waiting to be fed. Teddy had brought a bag of breadcrusts for this purpose and held out the bag so that Sadie could take a handful. They stood side by side throwing bread on the water for the birds. "The greedy gulls are getting it all," Sadie said. Though she aimed the crusts so they would land in front of the ducks, a gull always swooped in to get the food. Behind Sadie on top of a rock was a statue of Peter Pan, who with his flute looked like a youthful Pied Piper piping angels, rabbits, birds and mice into the rock. "Flora would enjoy seeing this," she said.

"I'm sure Flora is enjoying herself where she is," Teddy said. "Right now she's probably eating the icing off the cake." Taking her hand, he led Sadie along a gravelled path beneath the trees leafed out in virginal green. The grass and shrubs were also green and smelled of recent mowing. Golden daffodils bloomed on either side of the path. Sadie inhaled their strong waxy scent. They followed the path until they reached another bronze statue, this was of a soldier with a rifle in one hand and a hand grenade in the other. "That's the Fighting Newfoundlander," Teddy said, "not the monument for Beaumont Hamel. Come on, I'll show you where it'll be built."

Teddy led her off the main path toward the river where, abruptly, the landscape changed from parkland to wilderness. Here the land was rocky and steeply cliffed with spruce and birch growing alongside the river, which was wide and fast flowing, churning over rocks and around islands and uprooted trees. There were shadowy pools in which brown trout hovered above the stony bottom. Ahead was the thundering music of falls. Sadie and Teddy walked in silence, their ears full of the sounds of the pummelling, pounding stream.

Before they reached the falls, Teddy led her away from the river along a narrow path that led to a knoll, a huge craggy rock with a flattened top.

"This is it," Teddy said. "This is where the monument will be built. It will be a large bronze caribou identical to the one in France."

Sadie had never seen a caribou, only pictures of one.

"Why choose a caribou for a war memorial to the dead?"

"Well, it's on Newfoundland's coat-of-arms." Teddy paused. "It's a wild animal and most of Newfoundland is wild."

As they stood there on the path, a train whistle shattered the solitude. Soon they heard the train shuddering along the tracks running through the park. The train was so close they could feel the shaking air, the pulsing ground. They made no attempt to speak but waited out the clattering noise. By the time the train had passed and the park was quiet, tears were rolling down Sadie's cheeks. Teddy asked what was the matter, but Sadie couldn't speak. The train reminded her that if all went according to plan, this time tomorrow she would be on the train heading for Corner Brook and that as relieved as she would be to escape from Mrs. Hatch and the dreaded orphanage, she was sorry to be leaving Bishop Spencer and St. John's. She was sorry to be leaving Wanda. Sorry to be leaving Teddy, who was a true and trusted friend.

"Come on," Teddy said. He took her hand. "I'll show you a hideaway."

Below the proposed site of the monument, on the other side, was a grass clearing beside a pool of brown water on which green lily pads floated. Frog rafts, Flora called them.

Here the river sounds were subdued, muted to a faint rushing noise that could have been wind. Teddy spread the blanket he had used to cover the picnic basket. On top of this he laid a linen tablecloth he had "swiped" from the hotel dining room. He had also swiped china, silverware and glasses. Sadie helped him lay out the food. There was potato salad, cold chicken and ham, devilled eggs, dill pickles, buttered brown bread, chocolate cake and ginger beer.

They sat on the blanket beside the pool, their backs to the craggy rock. They ate without speaking, listening to a junco singing from its perch in a flowering crabapple tree, watching small fish making plops on the still water. No one entered the clearing. Once they heard people passing the crag overhead but that was all. They were alone in the peaceful glade.

"This is what those young men at Beaumont Hamel believed they were fighting for." Teddy grinned. "Between trains, that is."

Eventually they picked up the leftover food, the china and silver and folded the linen. When the basket was packed, Teddy leaned forward and kissed Sadie on the lips. It was a long slow kiss that might have gone on had Teddy not broken it off. "Just one," he said, "maybe two . . ." His voice trailed off. Sadie noticed the flush on his cheeks. Neither of them made any effort to leave. They kissed again and afterwards sat a little while longer watching the jumping fish. Later they rode the Speedy-Reider back to town and walked to Willicott's Lane. Before she went inside, Sadie told Teddy that it had been a perfect afternoon, which it was. Even with the sadness, it had been perfect. Maybe, she thought, the sadness had made it possible to feel the happiness more. "See you tomorrow," Teddy said before ambling down the lane, the picnic basket bumping and clinking against his leg.

20

Carpe Diem

WITH UNCERTAINTY AND EXCITEMENT BALLOONING inside her head, Sadie hadn't expected to sleep a wink on Saturday night, but she did. It was a sound sleep and Sunday morning she awoke feeling refreshed. She might have slept longer if she hadn't been wakened by the scrape of the key as her landlady let herself into Thomas's room, just as she had so many mornings. When the monument to Beaumont Hamel was built, would she take the Speedy-Reider to Bowring Park and worship him there? She probably wouldn't, Sadie thought. The monument in the park was to be in memory of all the soldiers who had died at Beaumont Hamel. Mrs. Hatch was only interested in keeping the memory of one soldier alive and wanted to do it in the privacy of his bedroom.

Sadie thought of her own mother, her wise, practical mother, who until she became ill, was light-hearted and lively. Her mother would have been horrified at the thought of maintaining a shrine to a dead person inside a house. A house was a place intended for the use of the living, not the dead. How many times had Sadie heard her say, *"Carpe diem"*? When her mother was in grade school in Ireland, her Latin teacher used to write *carpe diem*—which meant "seize the day"—on the chalkboard every single morning. Whenever Sadie moped about the house complaining that she had nothing to do, her mother would say, *"Carpe diem!"* which was another way of saying, "Take hold of your life!"

Sadie heard Mrs. Hatch locking the door and going downstairs. *"Carpe diem,"* she said to herself, as if it were a talisman or a spell, and put her feet on the floor. She went to the other side of the bed where Flora was balanced precariously on the edge. "This is the day!" she whispered. She groped beneath the covers. Miraculously the bottom sheet was dry. "I'm going down to the bathroom. Remember we don't say a word to each other." A few minutes later when Flora was on her way to the bathroom, they passed each other in the hallway in silence. Upstairs Sadie began to dress. She and Flora had decided to wear good summer dresses so that Mrs. Hatch would think they were going to church. When they were ready the sisters went down to the kitchen and ate their fried bread without looking at each other, afraid they would betray their excitement if they did.

Mrs. Hatch noticed the silence. "You girls have another falling-out?"

"No."

"It's not like you to be so quiet."

When neither of them replied, Sour Olive went on, poking her head toward them as she spoke. "That's girls for you, always on the outs with each other, always sulking and pouting. If it isn't one thing it's another."

Sadie carried her bowl to the sink and began running the

water for dishes, turning the tap on full to drown out Mrs. Hatch, who was shrieking, "Turn it back! You're wasting water!"

"There's lots of water. You're just being stingy," Sadie said. After vowing not to say a word, here she was, rising to Sour Olive's bullying. "You're stingy and you're mean."

"You're the meanest person we know," Flora said from the table.

Sadie didn't look at Mrs. Hatch, but she knew she was right behind her. "The reverend will hear about this," she hissed in Sadie's ear. "Just you wait. When you get to the orphanage, they'll knock the sauce out of you."

"Let them try," Sadie said grimly. She heard footsteps pattering across the floor and without looking knew that Sour Olive was at the door pinning on her hat before leaving for church. It was all Sadie could do to remain at the sink pretending to wash the dishes in case Mrs. Hatch should return. It was part of the plan that they would wait five minutes to be on the safe side. The minutes dragged by and when it was apparent that their landlady wouldn't return (she seldom did), the sisters hugged each other and danced around the kitchen. Abruptly, Sadie stopped. "Come on, let's bring the suitcases down."

Teddy was meeting them on Duckworth Street with one of the hotel's loading carts, a wooden box mounted on wheels that was mainly used to carry supplies to the hotel kitchen. Sadie and Flora carried their suitcases and bags down to the cart, and while Teddy stowed them, Sadie ran back to Willicott's Lane and raced upstairs to the bedroom to make sure nothing had been forgotten and that the printed note she had left on the dresser for Mrs. Hatch would be seen. The note consisted of thirteen words: We have moved to Corner Brook and will send you the money owed. Sadie didn't know when or how Sour Olive would be paid, but she thought she was less

likely to come after them if she knew they would. Until Flora
had disclosed the fact that there was a lot of money inside the
tin box, Sadie had briefly considered pawning the silver brush
to pay for the room and board because even though Sour
Olive was stingy, she was entitled to be paid what she was
owed. But Sadie wasn't about to sacrifice her mother's silver
brush to someone who had money locked away. She was
certain that when Sour Olive found the note she had left, she
would rush into Thomas's room, open the drawer and take
out the tin box and count her money to make sure none of it
had been stolen.

Downstairs, Sadie passed the unwashed dishes without a
glance and went outside. As she sped down the lane, she saw
a face appear in a window. (There were two or three people
who could, and later did, verify the fact that the Morin sisters
had left Willicott's Lane while their landlady was in church.)
By the time Sadie reached Duckworth Street, Flora had
climbed in with the luggage. They set off, the cart groaning
beneath the weight. Farther along Duckworth Street they had
to unload the cart and carry it down a set of steps to Water
Street. When the cart was reloaded, they set off again. It took
half an hour to reach the train station. Partway there Flora
asked Teddy to stop the cart and beckoned Sadie over.

"I forgot to empty the chamber pot," she whispered.

"Never mind," Sadie whispered back. "Sour Olive will empty
it in the toilet."

The thought of Sour Olive emptying the hated chamber pot
sent the sisters into a fit of hilarious giggling that went on until
Teddy asked what was the joke.

"Nothing. Flora forgot to do one of the chores."

It was twelve noon when they reached the train station. By
now the congregation, under the reverend's fierce stare, would

be singing the last hymn and soon Mrs. Hatch would join the line of people waiting at the door to shake the minister's hand.

After the suitcases were ticketed for the baggage car, there was nothing to do but wait. Sadie and Teddy waited on the platform and Flora in the cart with their school bags and the winter coats that wouldn't fit into their luggage. It was awkward waiting. Sadie didn't know how to say goodbye to Teddy, at least not in a way that would express how she felt. Teddy filled the silence by describing how he expected to spend the summer on Gander Lake working as a handyman for his Uncle Norman, who owed a fishing and boating camp. Teddy had told her weeks ago about the job, but now he was describing the chores he would have to do: repairing the dock, scraping and painting the boats, cleaning the cabins. At last a porter appeared with a wooden step he placed on the platform beneath the train steps and it was time to go aboard. The porter helped Flora and Sadie up into the train, and Teddy followed carrying a bag of sandwiches from the hotel kitchen. Their seats, in the first row on the train's north side, were wooden with narrow armrests on either side; a paper bag hung from a metal clasp below the square window. Teddy put their coats on the rack above and sat on the seat on the other side of the aisle. So far they were the only ones in the car and Sadie kept peering out the window to see if other passengers were coming. She fidgeted with the strap of her Christmas watch and looked at the time, 12:15. By now Mrs. Hatch would have left the church and was probably walking along Gower Street.

Finally, at 12:30 passengers began boarding the train. The first passenger, a young woman wearing a rose-coloured suit and hat, came aboard and claimed the seat Teddy was using. He got up and stood in the aisle. "I wish people would hurry up," Sadie said. "Mrs. Hatch will be home by now."

"Right," Teddy said. "It's time for me to keep an eye out for the constabulary in case they come after you." He said this jokingly to make it obvious he didn't think the police would come. But Sadie could imagine one of Mrs. Hatch's neighbours turning up on her doorstep with the news that her boarders had been seen going down the lane carrying their luggage. She could imagine Mrs. Hatch using the neighbour's telephone to call the police. It all depended on Wanda. If Wanda was there she would do everything possible to prevent her mother from coming after Sadie and Flora.

Sadie said, "You'd better go, Teddy."

"I'm on my way." Fortunately he didn't try to kiss her but dropped the bag of sandwiches in her lap and told her to be sure to write—they had already exchanged addresses. He squeezed past passengers wrestling packages and bags down the aisle. It was a relief when he was finally posted himself outside on the platform. Through the window Sadie watched him looking toward the road in case anyone unwanted should come along.

It was 12:45. By now Mrs. Hatch would be in the kitchen or the front room. Usually by this time on Sundays she had finished making dinner and was sitting in the rocker. Today of course was different. Wanda would be in the kitchen trying to prevent her mother from going upstairs. She might be telling her mother that there was no point calling her boarders downstairs because she'd seen them going off for a picnic so they wouldn't be eating the boiled turnip greens. She would eat them instead. It had been a long time since she'd eaten turnip greens. Where was the butter? She liked them with butter. The greens were so fresh, did her mother buy the greens from a farmer's cart? It was early in the season for greens, wasn't it? But the first greens always tasted best. Sadie's imagination galloped on until she saw Wanda and her mother sitting at a table eating greens and laughing, having a good time together. This was the way she wanted to imagine them. She hated the thought of Mrs. Hatch not liking her daughter.

At one o'clock the train whistle blew, jolting Sadie out of her reverie. The whistle was Wanda's signal that she had done her job, that she no longer needed to keep her mother from going upstairs. Sadie looked out the window and saw more passengers boarding and Teddy still watching the road. Another ten minutes dragged past during which Sadie imagined Mrs. Hatch upstairs reading the note on the dresser and saying, "I always knew those girls were a sneaky pair!"

The whistle blew again and at 1:20 Sadie felt the train lurch. She heard a squeal of metal as the wheels beneath her feet began to move. She looked out the window and saw Teddy grinning and giving the victory sign. She and Flora waved back. *"Carpe diem,"* Sadie said softly. She had seized the day.

21

Crossing Newfoundland

SADIE SPENT THE FIRST HALF HOUR OF THE TRIP alternately watching the city slide away from her and turning to Flora, who couldn't stop talking about escaping from Sour Olive. "We did it!" she crowed. "We ran away."

"Shush!" Sadie whispered. "Don't say running away. We don't want anyone reporting us to the police."

"There's no police aboard."

"You never know. There might be."

Their car was half full. Besides the woman who sat across the aisle, three rows ahead were two nuns. Across from the nuns were two elderly women who looked so much alike that Sadie thought they must be twins. Scattered about on other seats were half a dozen men, some neatly dressed in trousers and others in baggy pants.

The conductor came into the car and asked for their tickets. Granite-faced and taciturn, he glanced at their tickets and remarked, "You girls have a long way to go."

"Yes."

"Someone meeting you in Humbermouth?"

Humbermouth was where the Leesons would meet them. Corner Brook, she said, was only a mile or two from there.

"My mother's friend."

Fortunately he didn't ask about their mother but punched their tickets and turned his attention to the woman across the aisle. When he had moved further down the car, Sadie whispered in Flora's ear, "There goes someone who looks like he would report us to the police if he heard you say we were running away." Chastened, her sister took out the colouring book and crayons and, balancing the book on her knees, began to colour. Frustrated by the absence of a surface flat enough to enable her to colour within the lines, she soon gave up and announced that she was hungry. Sadie took out a cheese sandwich for each of them. When these were finished, she dug two apples out of her bookbag. The porter opened the door and entered the car. Unlike the conductor, he was friendly and good-natured, never far from a smile. He grinned at the sisters.

"You young ladies all right?"

"We're fine, thank you," Sadie said.

"Anything I can help you with, you just let me know," he said and loped down the aisle.

Flora picked up her colouring book again and Sadie unfolded the map of Newfoundland she had sketched from the school map and stared out the window at the passing country-side, which was either boggy or forested except in places where small farms had been cleared. The train passed a sign saying Upper Gullies and she located the place on the map. Then she

located Holyrood, which was at the bottom of Conception Bay.
She waited for the bright band of clear blue water she remembered seeing last year when they moved to Newfoundland. The
memory of that trip reminded her that their family had slipped
into major difficulties since then. Last year, with her father
beside her, Sadie had been full of excitement about moving to
St. John's, travelling to a new place in a first-class car with plush
sleeping berths. Now she and Flora were sitting on hard
wooden seats with no padded headrest or cloth slings for
holding their possessions, no table for colouring, no metal
trash container, only a paper bag. Worst of all was the absence
of her father. Now that the excitement had ebbed away, Sadie
was left with worry, worry about arriving in Humbermouth
and about what the Leesons would be like. The sight of
Conception Bay did nothing to cheer her up, for when it came
into view, it wasn't the blue of last summer but a dull, bleary
grey.

The train motion was making Sadie drowsy and she
exchanged seats with Flora, who wasn't the least bit sleepy.
Bunching her winter coat into the window corner, Sadie leaned
against it and gave herself up to the rhythm of the train. As she
drifted into sleep, she heard Flora say something to the woman
across the aisle and a faint smile flickered across her lips—it
was just like her little sister to strike up a conversation. While
Sadie slept, the train chugged past Brigus Junction. Mahers.
Whitbourne.

When she awoke, she saw Flora sitting across the aisle,
beside the woman. It took a few moments for Sadie to realize
that the woman was asking her if she wanted a drink of
orangeade. "Your sister is having a bottle," she said. "I bought
three from a vendor when we stopped in Whitbourne. I
thought you might like one when you woke up."

"Thanks," Sadie said and reached into the bookbag for the green change purse. After buying the train tickets, she had two dollars left, one to buy food during the trip, the other to pay for transportation if for some reason the Leesons didn't meet the train.

"Let me pay, please," the woman said. "It's my treat." Sadie was uncomfortable with a stranger buying Flora and her drinks, but it was too late to do anything about it now. Reaching across the aisle to accept the orangeade, Sadie noticed that the young woman had soft brown eyes and, beneath her hat, unruly brown hair.

Sadie said bluntly, "Do you mind my sister sitting there?"

"Not at all." The woman smiled at Flora. "I'm enjoying her company."

Flora smiled and nonchalantly swung her legs.

While she drank the orangeade, Sadie looked out the window. The train was now crossing the narrow saddle of land between Placentia and Trinity bays, but because of the mauzy weather, she could see very little water. Finishing her drink, she folded the coat on the seat, lay down sideways on the seat and was soon asleep. The train rumbled past Arnold's Cove. Goobies. Northern Bight. Flora shook her awake as they were coming into Clarenville. By now it was five o'clock. Sadie heard the train whistle. She sat up.

"Let's get off," Flora said. She was still sitting with the woman on the other side of the aisle.

"There's half an hour's stop," the woman said pleasantly, "which is plenty of time to stretch our legs."

Through the train window houses came into view, then slid past. There was the screech of steel upon steel, a lurch, and the train jerked to a halt. Below the window Sadie saw a woman in a striped apron walking along the station platform selling

baked potatoes from a tray. Flora and the woman got off the
train and grumpily Sadie followed, annoyed that her sister
would go off with a stranger and assume she would follow.
Sadie bought three potatoes at five cents apiece, paying quickly
before the woman could. When Sadie gave her the potato with
its dollop of melted butter leaking through its paper wrap, the
woman put out her hand and said, "My name is Marcella
Sullivan." She smiled. "And you, I know, are Sadie Morin."

The three of them strolled along the platform, eating and
talking.

Marcella said, "Your sister tells me you are going all the way
to Corner Brook."

"Yes."

What else had Flora told her?

"Where are you going?"

"Bishop's Falls."

"Have you been there before?"

"Never."

"She's getting married," Flora said.

"I might not get married," Marcella said. "I won't decide for
sure until I get to know the man." She hesitated. "You see, we
haven't met, we've only exchanged letters." She looked embarrassed confiding this to strangers and lowered her eyes. "Six
months ago I answered his ad in the newspaper and we've been
corresponding since."

Flora wanted to know if she was scared and Marcella
admitted that she was. It occurred to Sadie that Marcella had
encouraged Flora to sit with her because she needed company
to keep herself from thinking about the man who might, or
might not, turn out to be a suitable husband. When they got
back on the train, Flora curled up in their seats and Sadie sat
beside Marcella. Marcella told her that she came from a family

of eleven, all of whom lived in the village of Calvert, south of St. John's. "All my sisters are married," she said, "but I've never even had a boyfriend. I figured if I didn't leave home, I would never get married." Marcella said she wasn't fussy. She wasn't looking for a man who was handsome or rich. She wanted to marry a kind man who would be good to her and their young-sters. That was the main reason she wanted to marry, so she could have youngsters.

While she talked, the train lumbered through Port Blandford. Terra Nova. Maccles. It didn't stop in any of these places, though in each place there was a small building pretending to be a train station. At Gambo the train stopped and cargo was loaded. Two untidy-looking passengers got on one car back.

"First-class passengers are two cars ahead," Marcella said. "The dining car is between us and them." She said she wouldn't be using the dining car. "The food's too dear. Besides, I'm too nervous to eat much." Sadie and Flora wouldn't be using the dining car either—they didn't have the money to spend on expensive meals.

It was past eight o'clock when the train reached Gander Lake, where the railway ran parallel to the water. The long finger of the lake shone like blue satin in the early evening light. Now that they were inland, well away from the sea, the air was clear. A flaming coral ball hung over darkly wooded hills, laying down a shining ladder of golden light than ran the length of the lake. Lucky Teddy, Sadie thought, to be spending his summer in a place as beautiful as Gander Lake.

There was a half hour's stop in Notre Dame Junction, where Marcella got off the train but Sadie stayed on. Her tailbone ached from sitting but she couldn't leave Flora sleeping by herself. Instead, through the darkening light she watched passengers either stepping onto the platform into the arms of loved ones or leaving those arms in order to board the train. Watching the loving way these people either greeted each other or said goodbye filled Sadie with a longing that made her think again of her father.

Marcella climbed aboard and the train began moving. The motion made Sadie sleepy but she forced herself to stay awake to keep Marcella company. By the time they reached Bishop's Falls, it was completely dark. Marcella stood up and picked up her bag. "This is it, Sadie. It's time for me to get off." Her voice was shaky. "For better or worse, here I go."

Sadie got up and impulsively gave her a hug. "Good luck," she said.

"I'll need it," Marcella said. She looked down at the sleeping Flora. "Say goodbye to her for me," she said and went down the steps.

Sadie leaned forward and peered out the window, hoping to get a glimpse of her and the stranger she was meeting, but the platform was poorly lit and all she could see were dark shapes moving slowly like fish through murky water.

More minutes dragged by as the train shunted back and forth, changing engines, but finally it was moving west again, and Sadie curled up sideways on Marcella's double seat, this time her head pillowed on her school bag, and went to sleep. Though the train made a long stop in Windsor, no one except the porter passed through the car where passengers, including the sisters, dozed as best they could. The train set out again. Red Cliff. Badger—Sadie didn't even hear the Badger stop called—Millertown Junction, Mary March, Gaff Topsail—these were whistle stops she absorbed in her sleep. At six o'clock she awoke with a start. Flora was prodding her shoulder. "I'm hungry, Sadie, and you're sleeping on the food."

Sadie sat up, looked out the window and saw that they were passing another large lake, this one sunken in dawn shadows. Then she looked at the changed landscape inside the car—while she'd been sleeping, passengers had got off the train and new ones had boarded. There was now an elderly gentleman sleeping one seat ahead and a priest sitting halfway down the car. She reached in her bag and gave Flora the last cheese sandwich, and took out an apple and some biscuits for herself. She told Flora that Marcella said to tell her goodbye.

"Did you see the man?"

Sadie shook her head. "I wouldn't want to be in her shoes, marrying a man I'd never met."

Between mouthfuls of sandwich Flora said, "I'm never getting married. I'm going to live with you, Sadie. We'll live in a little white house with shutters. We'll have kittens and puppies and a big yard with a fence around it."

"What if I get married? Will you live with me then?" Sadie was joking—the prospect of marrying was so far away that she could afford to tease.

Flora said, "Then I'll live with you and your husband."

The porter loped down the aisle. His legs were so long that he could cover the length of the car in a dozen strides.

"Next stop, Howley!" He paused beside the girls and said, "Rise and shine. It's a grand day out there, just grand," and continued down the aisle.

Howley! Howley was where her father had written his last letter to her on April 20th. Sadie leapt to her feet and rushed after the porter before he could leave the car. When she caught up with him she said, "How long do we stop in Howley?"

"Ten minutes, maybe fifteen. You want to get off?"

"Yes."

"There's not much to see and you'll have to be quick."

Sadie went back to her seat and grabbed Flora's hand. "Come on, we're getting off."

The porter was right; there wasn't much to see, only a scattering of houses along the track. The station was a house with a freight shed beside it. The sisters passed a burly-shouldered man in a cloth cap boarding the train and a young man in a railway uniform pulling a cart toward the baggage car. Sadie ran to catch up. "Have you seen a man named Russ Morin?" she asked. "He and another prospector left here for Sop's Arm two months ago."

The man continued hauling, but he called over his shoulder, "Couldn't say. Prospectors come through here all the time." He jerked his head toward a woman standing in the station doorway, holding a baby. "Ask the missus."

Pulling Flora behind, Sadie ran toward the woman, who was so large that she almost filled the doorway. "I'm looking for my father, Russ Morin," Sadie said. "Do you remember him? He passed through here two months ago with another prospector."

The woman jiggled the whimpering baby and shook her head shyly. "If you see him," Sadie said desperately, "could you tell him that his daughters are on their way to Corner Brook?" The woman nodded but still didn't speak, which convinced Sadie the message wouldn't be passed on even if by some miracle her father should come this way.

"All aboard!" The porter was on the platform gesturing for the sisters. They got back on the train and it lurched forward. Sadie looked out the window and thought, *Dad could be anywhere out there. Will he ever come back?* She felt desolate and abandoned.

They passed another lake, this one with a yellow sandy shore, and Flora asked how much longer it would be before they arrived in Corner Brook.

"About two hours. We have to go through Deer Lake and then we come to Humbermouth, where Mrs. Leeson said they would be waiting."

"I can hardly wait," Flora said.

But Sadie could. Now that they were almost there, she half wanted to delay their arrival, and the closer they came to Corner Brook, the more anxious she became. She worried about whether or not the Leesons would remember to meet the train and if she would recognize them if they did. What if she and Flora didn't like the Leesons? She knew she would like Mrs. Leeson who, after all, had been her mother's best friend. As soon as she'd heard her voice on the telephone, she'd known that she would like her. But what about Mr. Leeson? What would he be like? What if it turned out to be worse staying with the Leesons than it had been with Mrs. Hatch? Sadie shook off the idea. Nothing could be worse than staying with Mrs. Hatch.

They had passed another lake and were following a fast-flowing river through a rocky wooded canyon that Sadie knew from the map was part of the Long Range Mountains. In a few minutes they would be in Humbermouth.

The Leesons were waiting on the station platform. Sadie knew who they were at once. Both of them were waving, wide smiles on their faces, a short stocky couple, one of them with a balding head, the other with dark greying curls. They looked plump and happy and older than Sadie had expected. The train screeched to a stop, and Sadie and Flora stood up and picked up their belongings. Sadie held back, letting Flora get off first while she checked to make sure that they were leaving nothing behind. She gathered up her courage and opened the door, went down the steps and immediately fell into Norah Leeson's arms. That was what it felt like, falling. Falling into someone who smelled of baking and soap, of warm kitchens and warmer beds, someone who was loving and kind, who reached out to hold you, who would care for you forever if you asked. Sadie was laughing and crying, letting go, letting relief flood through her, carrying away the anxiety and fear, letting her know that she had been right to trust her instinct to come all the way across Newfoundland and deliver Flora and herself into the welcoming arms of her mother's friend.

22

Dream

Mr. Leeson had borrowed a truck with Newfoundland Pulp and Paper painted on the sides. The suitcases and bags were put in the back and all four of them piled into the front, the sisters squeezed between the Leesons. 'Never mind," Norah Leeson said, "we don't have far to go." They drove alongside the Humber River through a gap in the mountains, the road winding steadily downward until suddenly there it was, Corner Brook, a town tucked into a space between mountains and a deep blue bay. As they entered the valley, Sadie saw that the town had been carved from a forest and that there were huge stands of spruce on all sides except where the town had the helter-skelter look of being half finished. There was a tall smokestack coming from the paper mill by the water and thick clouds of yellowish smoke belched from it into the sky. The smokestack was a familiar and ominous sight. In Copper Cliff the stacks poisoned the air with their venomous smoke. Did that happen here? Sadie strained to see but there was no sign of the roasting yards whose smoke blackened the rocks and treeless yards of Copper Cliff.

As they drove through the townsite, Mr. Leeson pointed out the school and recreation hall, the churches and stores. "We're the fastest-growing town in Newfoundland," he said proudly. The truck began climbing a hill divided into streets where there were houses in various stages of completion.

When they reached the last house on a street at the top of the hill, the truck stopped and the four of them got out, and Sadie and Flora stood together, both of them needing time to convince themselves that they were actually here. In front of them was a white house with a pitched red roof and window shutters. There were red hearts painted on the shutters. When they finished looking, the sisters followed the Leesons inside and up the stairs. "This is your bedroom," Norah Leeson said in her lilting voice. "There's lots of room in the closet and dresser for your clothes. Our bedroom is across the stairway and the bathroom is in between."

The sisters' bedroom had twin beds snugged under the eaves on either side of a dormer window. Between the beds was a window seat that was home to a clutch of dolls. The walls were papered with a picture of a little girl wearing a sunhat and holding a watering can. Hanging on the walls were framed pictures of hand-stitched flowers. All the furniture in the room was painted white: the beds, the dresser, the rocking chair and the wooden chests where Mr. Leeson had put the suitcases. On one bed was a blue nightgown and on the other a yellow one Sadie knew at once that Mrs. Leeson had made them, probably especially for their arrival today. In fact the entire room seemed to have been decorated with them in mind.

"Are you hungry?" Norah Leeson asked, her husband hovering beside her. "I made a batch of sticky buns in case you were.

"Sticky buns!" Flora said. "I haven't had them since . . ." She went to Sadie and, burying her head in her waist, began to sob.

"Poor wee maid," Norah Leeson said. "She's worn out." She patted Flora's shoulder. "Brian and I will go and make the tea. When you girls are ready you come down. Take your time. There's no hurry."

Sadie knew Flora was crying because Norah Leeson had brought back memories of their mother, memories they had often pushed aside when they were living with Sour Olive but which now flooded in on the tide of Norah Leeson's kindness. She sat in the chair and pulled Flora onto her lap and held her. From downstairs Sadie heard the comforting murmur of voices, steady and low like the buzz of summer bees. Flora heard it too and stopped crying. Sadie said, "Are you ready for some sticky buns?"

Downstairs they went along the hall to the kitchen, where geraniums bloomed on the windowsills and there was the smell of recent baking. Sadie heard voices outside and looked through the screen door and saw the Leesons sitting on lawn chairs on a wooden deck at the bottom of the steps. In front of them on a table was a tea tray and a plate of sticky buns.

Norah Leeson looked up and said, "There you are!"

The sisters sat themselves on lawn chairs and Norah Leeson poured them tea. "Milk and sugar?"

"Mostly milk," Flora said. Mr. Leeson passed her the plate of buns, which had been slathered with butter and were full of raisins and brown sugar. Flora ate three without stopping. Sadie tried not to eat quickly but within ten minutes she had eaten four buns. She was aware that the Leesons were exchanging looks, but she couldn't help it, she was starving. When she was finished, she said, "Thank you for the buns. I've never tasted anything so delicious."

"Look!" Flora said.

Sadie looked across the wide swath of grass where there were several lawn ornaments made of brightly painted wood: Snow White and the Seven Dwarfs, two rabbits, a lamb and a puppy. Sitting beside the puppy was a taffy-coloured cat who was eyeing the sisters balefully, trying to decide whether or not they were the kind of people he wanted for company. Apparently he decided they were, at least Flora was, for he crossed the lawn and rubbed against her legs.

"That's Gobble," Norah Leeson said. "You can pick him up. He adores being petted." The cat settled in Flora's lap and much to her delight turned on his purring engine. "You're a friend for life," Norah said.

After a while, Flora said blissfully, "I'm so glad we ran away."

Brian Leeson frowned. "What do you mean, ran away?"

Sadie said, "Mrs. Hatch didn't want us to stay with her any more and the Reverend Mr. Eagles was going to put us in the orphanage after school was over. That's why we left right after my exams were finished."

"Put you in the orphanage!" Brian Leeson spluttered. "But you're not orphans." He got up and paced the deck, his manner becoming increasingly agitated with every step.

"That's what I told Mrs. Hatch," Sadie said. "But without Dad I couldn't stand up to her or the reverend. They had decided everything between themselves."

"That's outrageous," Brian Leeson said. "I think I'll telephone the reverend and give him a piece of my mind."

"Maybe later, dear," Norah Leeson said. "For now I think you should show Flora your workshop. The workshop was where he made all this." She swept an arm in the direction of the lawn, and Sadie looked at the swinging chair, the birdhouses hanging in the trees and the picket fence enclosing a patch of dark earth where green shoots poked through. There were thick woods on two sides of the garden. "Until recently this was all woods," Mrs. Leeson said, "before the land was cleared to make way for the house."

Mr. Leeson asked if Flora would like to see the dollhouse he was making.

"Can I bring Gobble?"

"Sure. He thinks I'm making the house for him. That's where he often takes a nap."

As soon as they were out of earshot, Sadie said, "Mrs. Leeson, have you heard from Dad?"

"No, but Brian has alerted everyone who works for the mill to be on the lookout for him. There's a boat that ships lumber to White Bay and there are company men logging on the east side of Deer Lake, which isn't that far from Howley. I know it's hard, but do try not to worry. We'll hear from your dad one of these days."

"Mrs. Leeson," Sadie blurted out, wanting to get it out before Flora came back. "Can Flora and I stay with you until he comes back? We don't have any money but we can do house-work to earn our keep. We did all of Mrs. Hatch's housework."

"Sadie, Sadie. There is something you must understand." Norah Leeson sat on the arm of Sadie's chair, sitting so close that Sadie caught the scent of mint mixed with a floury warmth. "We love having you here and want you to stay as long as you like. Brian and I longed to have children but we never had any luck, so for us your being here is a blessing. But . . ." Norah Leeson wagged a finger. "No more of this Mr. and Mrs. Leeson. From now on I insist that you and Flora call us Norah and Brian."

"Norah," Sadie said and grinned. "Do you think I could have a bath? I haven't had one since Christmas when we were staying in the hotel with Dad. Mrs. Hatch thought baths were a waste of water."

"How did you bathe and wash your hair?"

"In a basin. Flora and I had to use the same water."

"Well, we have plenty of water. Come on, while you unpack, I'll run your bath."

Norah sprinkled lavender bath salts in the tub and put a bottle of shampoo on the soap rack, then went downstairs. Sadie lay in the deep scented water watching the summer sun shining through the curtains and making lace patterns on the wall. She looked at the shells lined up on the sill, the stool with its frilled cushion, the basket of purple flowers on the corner plant stand and thought that being here was like living inside a pleasant dream, a dream that if her father were here, she wanted to go on forever.

After a long soak Sadie washed her hair, combed it out and when she was dressed, finished unpacking. While she sorted clothes and put them away, she heard Flora chattering to Norah and Brian in the kitchen. She couldn't hear exactly what she was saying—there was no heat register in the floor—but she was sure her sister was telling them about the difficulties of living with Mrs. Hatch. Every so often Sadie heard the clang of a pot and the bang of a cupboard door and knew that Norah must be making supper. After a while the smell of roasting meat drifted upstairs, but Sadie was in no hurry to go down. Up here in the coziness of her room, she felt the exhaustion and worry draining away. Not all of it—there was still the worry about her father—but now she was with people who were willing to share the burden.

Supper that night was roast beef with Yorkshire pudding and potatoes with gravy and minted peas; for dessert there was fresh rhubarb pie with whipped cream. When they finished eating Sadie cleared the table and ran water for washing the dishes. "Let them soak," Norah said in her lilting voice, "and come with us for a walk. It's a lovely night for a stroll." The four of them put on sweaters—the evening air was cool—and they walked down the street lined with houses similar to the Leesons. "Company houses," Brian explained.

Partway down the hill they followed a path through spruce woods where they were swarmed by blackflies. "Pests," Norah grumbled, scratching her neck. "They are always worse in the evening."

When they got back to the house, Sadie made Flora help her with the dishes before she went upstairs. After Flora had a bath, she put on the yellow nightgown and Sadie put on the blue. For the first time since coming to Newfoundland, the sisters slept in separate beds. Sadie offered to push the beds together but Flora said she liked having a bed of her own.

During the next few weeks, the Leesons couldn't do enough for the sisters. Every morning Sadie awoke to the smell of baking. When she came into the kitchen, muffins or sticky buns or rounded loaves of bread would be cooling on the counter, their tops a shiny golden brown. Norah made date squares, gingerbread, poppyseed cake and strawberry apple pie. She roasted chickens, which she served with savoury dressing and gravy. She baked a ham decorated with pineapple and cherries. On the dinner table there was always a pitcher of milk and a bowl of potatoes whipped with butter and cream. For breakfast there were scrambled eggs or pancakes or waffles served with partridgeberry syrup or clear apple jelly. Norah claimed that the sisters were nothing but skin and bones and that it was her job to fatten them up.

Norah seemed determined to keep Sadie busy. (But not Flora, who had made friends with Johnny who lived two doors

down the street and preferred to be with him. Though he was
two years younger, he liked skipping and playing marbles and
was still willing to be bossed around.) Norah taught Sadie how
to make lemon sponge and apple pandowdy and how to use
the Singer sewing machine. She had a chest filled with all kinds
of fabric and a box of patterns. She helped Sadie pin a skirt
pattern onto the material Sadie had chosen and how to cut it
out for basting and sewing. In the evenings after supper, Sadie
helped Brian work on the Victorian dollhouse, which had an
upstairs and downstairs, nine rooms altogether. The walls and
windows had been built, and Sadie was given the job of wall-
papering the tiny rooms while Brian painted the trim. She liked
working on the house better than sewing. She liked the smallness of the house, the fact that everything about it was miniature and therefore of manageable size. There was something
magical about its tininess and she enjoyed imagining the
family that would live inside. Two boys and two girls, she
decided, and two parents—with an imaginary house you could
have two parents.

On Saturdays Brian took the sisters trouting in a nearby
pond. They didn't catch anything and felt they were being
eaten alive by blackflies but they didn't care. On Sundays, if the
flies weren't too bad, they ate a cold supper outdoors. Sadie
also wrote letters. She wrote a formal letter to the Irish aunts
telling them that she and Flora were on holiday in Corner
Brook. This wasn't a lie because it was the school holidays and
it seemed that every day was a vacation. Sadie wrote to Wanda
and Millie. Wanda didn't write back but Millie wrote a short
letter in which she reported that she was as big as a house and
was certain the baby was a boy. Twice a week Sadie wrote
Teddy. Since coming to Corner Brook, she had received five
letters from him. He was working hard getting the camp ready

for the fishermen who were expected any day soon. He had painted his uncle's boats and helped repair the dock and was learning how to handle a canoe. Every morning he ate fish he caught off the dock before breakfast and hadn't read a single book. By the time he ate supper, he was so tired he fell asleep soon after he hit the sack. But he wasn't too tired to write Sadie letters or to add "I miss you" across the bottom.

Sadie tried not to think about her father, because to think of him was to worry herself into the helpless state of believing that he was lost and that she might never see him again. Most of the time during the day she was able to push worrying thoughts away, but at night the power to choose her thoughts deserted her and she was sometimes wakened from sleep by a dream. It was always the same dream: a thin bearded man in a battered hat was walking along a road bent under the weight of an enormous dead bird. The man looked at her, his eyes glittering feverishly, a pleading expression on his face. He seemed to expect something from her but she didn't know what it was. She tried to walk toward him but was frozen to the spot. She couldn't move an arm or a leg and was forced to lie there useless and immobile while the man stood there, waiting for her help.

23

The Man on the Road

NORAH KNEW HOW TO MAKE HOMEMADE ICE CREAM and every summer before the berry season was over, made strawberry ice cream. Yesterday she had picked the berries and bought the cream and this morning bought the ice and salt on the way home from swimming—Norah, Brian, Sadie and Flora swam in the same pond where they went trouting. By noon the cream had been whipped and folded into the crushed berries and three hours later Sadie was sitting on the front step turning the handle of the wooden bucket. Although she was in the shade it was stiflingly hot even for late July. The sun beat down and there was no breeze to relieve the still air.

Sadie and Flora were supposed to be taking turns, but as usual Sadie was doing most of the work. She had been churning steadily for over an hour and her arm ached from the effort. Flora was to have been here half an hour ago to take over but was playing with Johnny somewhere and had likely forgotten the time. When it came to eating the ice cream, Sadie thought grumpily, Flora wouldn't forget. She would be first to dip in her spoon. Sadie pushed back the damp hair stuck to her forehead and looked idly down the empty street, which was a glare of white gravel burning beneath the sun. Sometimes kids played in the street but it was too hot for that today. Sadie stopped churning and added coarse salt to the ice to keep it from melting and began turning the handle, this time with her left hand, to give her right arm a rest. She heard a slight crunching sound coming from the road and looked up.

A man was climbing the hill but so slowly that all she could see was his hat and his shoulders heavily stooped beneath a pack. As she watched, the rest of him appeared and she saw a thin bearded man with long dishevelled hair and dirty clothing. He wasn't wearing a jacket but a torn shirt and trousers with holes in the knees. He reminded her of the scarecrow prospector she had seen in Copper Cliff. Though he seemed to find it difficult to walk, the man kept coming along the road, probably, Sadie thought, to ask for a glass of water. Since the Leesons' house was the last on the road, that must be his intention. She wasn't afraid of him exactly, but if he came much closer it was reassuring to know that Norah and Brian were just inside. When he reached the front of the house, the man took off his pack and with a groan swung it to the ground. For a full minute he stood staring at her while she pretended not to notice. Then he took a step toward her and in a hoarse voice called, "Sadie?"

"Dad?" She stood up and peered at the man. "Is that you, Dad?" Surely this couldn't be her fastidious, well-groomed father. This wasn't her father but someone else.

"It's me."

When she realized it really was him, she could scarcely breathe. She felt as if she had been punched in the chest. But then he said, "I'm here at last," and lifted his arms and she ran into them and held on tightly. "My darling daughter," he said over and over.

She stepped back and looked at him. "I can't believe it's you."

He laughed, a wild crazy laugh. "It's me all right."

She caught the odour of dirty clothes and matted hair. He didn't smell like her father. He didn't look like him or sound like him either. She didn't know what to make of him. But what did that matter? He wasn't lost or missing. He wasn't dead. He was her father and he was here at last. That was the main thing. He didn't say any of the normal things like "How are you" or "It's good to see you," and Sadie didn't say them either. She didn't know what to say. He said, "Where is Flora?"

"Playing with Johnny, but she's supposed to be here helping me churn the ice cream." Gathering her wits, Sadie suggested they go inside. She opened the door and called, "Norah? Brian? Dad's here!"

"You don't mean it!" Norah said from the kitchen. She came into the hall. "My stars!" she said and clapped her hand over her mouth. But she recovered quickly and, wiping her hands on her apron, shook his hand. "We meet at last. I'm so glad you're here."

Sadie heard the screen door slam in the kitchen and Flora came in followed by Brian. What would Flora think when she saw their father? Her sister didn't take the time to think but raced to their father and flung hers arms around him. "Dad! Oh, Dad!" She had recognized him immediately. "I knew you'd come!"

Sadie's father picked her up and as he had with Sadie said over and over, "My darling daughter."

The Leesons didn't seem to know what to do with themselves until Norah remembered the ice cream. She went outside and soon Sadie heard her churning. Brian followed her, but he returned right away carrying the heavy pack. With a grunt he lowered it to the floor. Sadie's father put Flora down and Brian said, "What's inside the pack, the whole world?"

Flora said hopefully, "Are there presents?"

"Nothing but rocks seamed with gold." Sadie's father looked around. "Would you mind if I sat down?" Brian pointed to a gingham rocker in the living room but Sadie's father shook his head. "I'd rather sit in the kitchen. I'm too dirty to sit in the living room."

Sadie noticed tiny red spots that looked like pricks of blood all over his face. She said, "Would you like a glass of water, Dad?"

"Thank you, I would."

That sounded more like her father.

They went into the kitchen, where her father and Brian sat at the table and Flora climbed onto her father's knee. Sadie went to the sink and poured him water. When he lifted his hand to take the glass, she noticed that it shook. Even so, he lifted it to his lips and drank it down. Sadie carried the glass to the sink and poured him another.

Brian said, "How did you get here, Russ?"

"Today, you mean?"

"Today."

"By train. I boarded it at Howley."

"It's too bad we didn't know when you were coming," Brian said. "I could've borrowed the company truck and picked you up."

"I didn't know exactly when I'd arrive," her father explained. "But I knew you were here because I sent a telegram to the

Dodges at the Crosbie Hotel and they telegraphed me back, telling me that you girls had left St. John's a month ago. Later I spoke to the station master's wife and she remembered seeing you at the Howley station." He looked at Sadie. "She gave me your message."

"How did you get to Howley?" Brian asked. He was asking the questions Sadie might have posed if she had been thinking clearly, which she wasn't, because her thoughts were scrambled. All she could do was lean against the counter and stare at her father.

"Gutsy and I took a horse and cart from Hampton."

"Who is Gutsy?"

"My prospecting partner. He's staying overnight with the station master in Howley and will take the train to St. John's the day after tomorrow. He has to get to a hospital and see to his leg."

"What happened to his leg?"

"He broke it. I tried to set the bones but I didn't do a very good job." Sadie's father laughed.

Why was he laughing about a broken leg? There was something unsettling about him. It wasn't just the dirty clothes. His manner was all wrong. There was a feverish glint in his eye.

"But I had no choice. We were deep in the bush, hundreds of miles from a doctor or anyone else."

"Is that why you took so long?" Flora said.

"Yes. With Gutsy's broken leg, we couldn't walk very fast."

"Sadie was worried, and so was I."

"I'm here now," their father said and lapsed into silence, his eyes unfocused, as if he couldn't quite believe where he was.

The front door opened and Norah called, "Brian, could you spell me off? Another half hour and the ice cream should be ready."

"Sure." Brian got up and went outside and Norah came into the kitchen and looked at Sadie's father. "Would you like something to eat?"

"No thanks, but I would appreciate a bath and a pair of scissors."

"Sadie, why don't you run your father a bath and set out the scissors and towels. When you come down, bring some sheets and a pillow from the linen closet and we'll make up the bed for him in the den. I'll see if I can find something of Brian's for your father to wear."

Sadie went upstairs to run the bath and fetch the linen, glad to have something useful to do. Her father climbed the stairs, Flora beside him.

"You can't go into the bathroom with him," Sadie said.

"I know. I'm just keeping him company as far as the door."

Their father went into the bathroom and Flora went into their bedroom. Sadie brought the sheets downstairs and made up the davenport in the den. Then she went into the kitchen to help Norah with supper, peeling potatoes for a scallop while Norah readied the salmon. While the food was baking, Sadie set the table and Norah made coleslaw, and as usual when they worked together, they chatted.

"I doubt your father will eat much of this food," Norah said. "I recall from my nursing days that after someone has gone a long while without food, the digestive system doesn't work very well. You mustn't be disappointed if he doesn't eat the ice cream."

"I won't be," Sadie said, though she knew that Norah had put her finger on something she would rather not admit, which was that her feelings for her father were muddled and confused. Of course she was relieved that he was here, that he was alive when she thought he might be dead, but she was also disappointed that he wasn't himself. After so long a wait she'd expected that when she saw him he'd be his usual energetic and jaunty self. It was a shock to see that in the seven months since she'd seen him he'd become a feeble old man.

Later when her father came downstairs wearing Brian's clothes, Sadie's father looked a little more like himself. For one thing he was clean and for another he had cut off the matted hair—hacked off was a better word because in some places the hair had been cut close to the scalp whereas in other places it was as long as an inch. He'd done a better job with his beard, which was neatly cut and had more grey in it than brown. Brian's clothes were too big for him and hung on his bony frame like a scarecrow's. "Now I feel I'm more presentable," he said. He didn't seem to know how odd he looked.

"You're just in time for supper," Norah said and led the way to the kitchen.

For a while Sadie's father simply stood looking at the food on the table: the potato scallop and salmon, the coleslaw and pickled beets, the homemade rolls and bread. "What a feast," he said and sat between his daughters.

Sadie dug into her food but she noticed that although her father went through the motions, stabbing bits of food and putting them into his mouth, he didn't eat much. When it came time to dish out the ice cream, he waved away his portion. "I won't have any, thanks. It's a bit too rich for me."

"But you like ice cream," Flora said. "And we made it ourselves."

When they had finished the meal and were sitting in the living room, which was cooler than the kitchen, Brian urged Sadie's father to tell them about his adventure.

"You mean my misadventure," Sadie's father said.

"Tell us about it."

And so he began his tale.

"Last April Gutsy and I left Buchans, heading for Sop's Arm. We caught the train in Badger and got off at Howley. From there we hired a horse and cart to take us to Hampton, where we boarded a fishing smack headed for Sop's Arm. At first we made good progress, arriving in Sop's Arm a week ahead of schedule with most of our grub. We'd packed enough food for six weeks and had over a month's supply left, which we thought was plenty. Gutsy had prospected most of the area before and estimated that we could finish prospecting it in a month. He was right about that and after four weeks we had collected enough rock samples to satisfy ourselves and were on our way out when things took a turn for the worse."

"Did you get lost?" Flora asked. She snuggled against one side of their father while Sadie sat upright on the other.

Her father shook his head. "Yes. I don't know how we could've made such a bad mistake, but for two days we followed the wrong river without realizing it, a river that took us where we didn't want to go." He laughed crazily. "We didn't even know the name of it, but we should have been suspicious because now that I think of it, it was more of a stream than a river." He stopped and stared out the window at nothing in particular.

"Go on," Sadie said and gave her father a nudge, which startled him. He looked at her with unfocused eyes.

"What did you say?"

"I said go on. I meant with your story."

"Oh yes, with my tale. Where was I?"

"You were following a stream."

"Yes, the wrong one. We were lost. We were thoroughly lost, but we figured out how we went wrong and began backtracking. Trouble was we didn't go very far when Gutsy slid down an embankment and broke his leg. Usually he was good on his feet, but it had been raining and he lost his footing and didn't stop rolling until he knocked himself out at the bottom of the embankment."

Sadie's father shook his head and stopped talking but he started again without being prodded. "It was a bad break and I had never before made a splint, but I cut straight branches and used them to make a splint for his leg and a pair of crutches. We hobbled along, staying close to the river—this time it was a river—where most days I managed to hook a few fish. By then our provisions were nothing more than a quarter of a sack of flour and a few handfuls of tea. We were going so slow that there were times . . ." Her father's voice broke. "There were times when I found it difficult to stick with Gutsy. He was holding me back and I knew that if I struck out on my own I could make better time. After a while I became convinced that if I stayed with him I might never again see my girls." Sadie's father made a choking noise. "I thought I'd go mad trying to decide." He looked at Sadie. "You see, I couldn't leave him there alone, yet the thought of being far away from you was driving me wild." He put his hands to his head as if he had to keep his thoughts from exploding. Then abruptly he laughed, not his normal laugh but a short barking sound. "It wasn't helped by blackflies that were at me day and night. Gutsy, too. But he never complained. We kept going but we made poor time. I don't know if we'd have made it out if a fisherman hadn't found us. He led us out and took us to Hampton, where we managed to hire a horse and cart to take us to Howley, where I caught the train." Sadie's father spread his hands. "And here I am, a sadder and wiser man."

Brian asked, "Did you find much gold?"

"We did."

"You don't seem happy about it," Flora said.

"I'm not." He stared bleakly at the wall.

"Why don't you go to bed?" Norah said. "You're exhausted and need to rest. Sadie's made up a bed for you in the den."

"You're right," Sadie's father said, "I need to rest." But he didn't move. He didn't seem to have the energy to stand.

"Come on, Dad." Sadie stood up and pulled him to his feet, and he allowed her to lead him into the den, where he lay on the davenport in Brian's clothes. Sadie covered him with a sheet. It was the first time in her life she had put her father to bed.

He was much better in the morning, and when Sadie and Flora came downstairs, they heard him outside on the deck talking to Norah—Brian had left for work two hours ago. "Here come my lovelies," he said when they came down the steps. He stood up and spread his arms and the sisters stepped into them.

There was a pot of tea and a basket of muffins on the table and the sisters helped themselves to breakfast. Sadie said, "Did you eat anything, Dad?" She was worried about his thinness.

"I did."

"He ate a piece of toast and honey," Norah said, getting out of her chair. "Don't you worry, we'll fatten him up in time. I'll leave you Morins to yourselves. I have a few errands to do." Sadie usually went along when Norah did errands but she didn't today. Today was for her father. The three of them sat on the shady deck in the soft morning air, watching Gobble hunkered down between Snow White and Dopey, trying to decide what the odds were of catching one of the sparrows dipping into the garden from its house in the trees. Apparently he decided the odds were poor and that he was better off napping in Flora's lap. "He's my friend for life, Dad," she said, stroking the cat.

Their father poured himself a cup of tea and settled back in his chair. "Now," he said, "tell me your news. I want to hear all about you girls."

"We ran away from Mrs. Hatch," Flora said. "And Sadie has a boyfriend."

Sadie's cheeks reddened. She felt like slapping her sister.

"The young man at the hotel?" There was a silly grin on her father's face.

"Yes." That was all Sadie would say.

"Why did you run away?"

Sadie said, "Mrs. Hatch didn't want us to stay with her any more. She wanted to send us the orphanage. She and the reverend had it all planned."

The grin slid from their father's face. "How dare they! You're not orphans."

"The room and board money didn't come and Mrs. Hatch said she couldn't afford to keep us any more."

"But I mailed her a cheque from Buchans."

"It never arrived."

"When we didn't hear from you for two whole months," Sadie went on, "I thought something awful had happened to you. I was worried sick. I thought you might have been eaten by a polar bear."

Her father laughed, an explosion of surprise and alarm that rankled Sadie. It was easier to believe he was making fun of her than it was to believe he was crazy.

"Sadie didn't get a birthday card from you either, but Teddy and I had a birthday party for her at the hotel, so it turned out all right," Flora said. She didn't mention the nurse's kit or the stolen money and for now Sadie decided to leave it that way. Flora went on at length telling their father how Sadie had fallen from the stool while cleaning the windows and couldn't go to school for three whole weeks.

"You've had a tough time," Sadie's father said.

"Flora's only told you half of it," Sadie almost said, but changed her mind. Her father had been through worse and was so fragile that she thought he might break down if she told him how much they missed him and how hard living with Sour Olive had been. And she noticed that he was having trouble staying awake. As Flora prattled on, Sadie saw his eyelids flutter and then close. She tapped her sister on the shoulder and pointed to their father, whose head was slowly slumping forward. For a long time the sisters sat beside him, content to listen to his muffled snore and Gobble's satisfied purr.

24

The Word for Home

SADIE'S FATHER MADE A SWIFT RECOVERY. THREE DAYS after his arrival in Corner Brook, he walked downtown accompanied by his daughters—a shadow on either side—and went to the barber for a haircut and shave. When he emerged from the barber's chair half an hour later, his chin was pale and his cheeks were hollow but the overall change was a noticeable improvement. From the barber's he went to a dry goods store where he bought himself work pants, plaid shirts and a pair of boots. These weren't the kind of clothes he usually wore but they fit and made him look less like the man on the road. Then he went to the post office and mailed Mrs. Hatch a cheque.

That night after Flora had been tucked into bed, he telephoned the Reverend Mr. Eagles from the Leesons kitchen and asked him to tell Mrs. Hatch the money owing to her was in the mail. Sadie, who was listening nearby (the Leesons had tactfully removed themselves to the deck), heard her father say, "I strongly object to you trying to force my daughters into the orphanage. As a man of the cloth, you should have tried to come up with another solution." For a few moments her father was silent listening to the reverend's response, but then he jumped in for the last word. "Why don't you try the golden rule, you know, the one about doing unto others as you would have them do unto you." He hung up the phone muttering, "the blustering fool," and Sadie thought, *Dad's getting better*.

Each day her father grew stronger and within a week had lost the wild haunted look. He smiled more often and no longer burst into crazy laughter. He stopped taking a nap in the afternoons and at mealtimes ate as much as Sadie. Sometimes he would wiggle his ears for Flora and make a nickel disappear up his sleeve. The sisters became used to their father's gradual reclamation of his former self and were less inclined to shadow him everywhere he went.

In the afternoons Flora went off to play with Johnny and Sadie worked with Norah, who was helping her piece together a quilt for Millie's baby. Because it was hot upstairs, they usually took their sewing outside to the shady deck, where Sadie's father sat, either reading or gazing around the yard.

In the evenings after Flora was in bed Sadie worked on the dollhouse with Brian; he was now making furniture and she was making curtains. It was finicky work and neither of them said much—they seldom did when they worked together. The workshop door was left open to let in the cooler evening air and Sadie could hear her father talking to Norah on the deck. She often heard Mary's name and knew they were talking about her mother. Sometimes her father would come into the workshop to watch Brian and her working, but he never offered to help.

Neither did he offer to help when Sadie and Brian weeded the garden, but sat on a lawn chair beside Norah and watched. When the weeding or the dollhouse work was finished, Sadie and Brian would join the others on the deck for iced tea and they would sit drinking and chatting until blackflies drove them inside. (Not Sadie's father, who claimed to have had so many bites on his body that the Corner Brook blackflies left him alone.) One night when they were drinking their iced tea, Brian asked him if he intended on staying in Corner Brook.

"I don't know," her father said vaguely.

"Because if you're interested," Brian went on, "we're looking for a book keeper at the mill."

Sadie's father looked at her and said, "What do you think? Should I take it?"

"How should I know?" she said. She knew she was being saucy, but how could her father do this to her? After all their family had been through, why was he expecting her to make the important decisions just as he had a year ago about repeating a grade at Bishop Spencer? There was an awkward silence. Sadie stood up and in a stiff voice announced that she was going to bed.

Upstairs she brushed her teeth, put on the blue nightgown and got into bed. It was too early for her to be in bed and she couldn't sleep. She lay in the dark listening to Flora's soft breathing and thinking. It had been ten days since her father had found Flora and her living with the Leesons, and in all that time, he hadn't said one word about their future. Sadie hadn't mentioned it either because she was waiting until he was well enough to take charge. She wanted him to take charge of their family. She wanted him to be a father. She was tired of being the one to shoulder responsibilities and make decisions. Didn't he know how hard it had been for her? Didn't he realize the difficulties he had caused Flora and her by going off searching for gold? And what about the gold? What about the rocks in the pack on the floor of the den? Why had he lugged them all the way here as if they were precious jewels? And why hadn't he said he was sorry for abandoning them to Mrs. Hatch when he knew they didn't like her? Was her father too weak to be a good father? Would he ever be strong enough to be the father she needed? When Sadie eventually fell asleep, she dreamed, not of the man walking on a road bent under the weight of a huge dead bird, but of a magician, a thin man wearing a top hat and carrying a globe, who with a wave of his wand made the hat and the globe and finally himself disappear.

She awoke in the morning feeling heavy-headed and wooden. As before, the woodenness came from impotent rage, from not knowing what to say or do. When she glanced at the robin clock she saw that it was mid-morning. Flora must have gotten up hours ago. Her bed was made; she hadn't wet the bed since they'd come to Corner Brook. When Sadie went downstairs, she was relieved to see that no one was home and that she wouldn't be required to talk. She made herself toast and took it outside to the deck.

Later, when she heard footsteps on the front walk, she ducked inside and went up to her bedroom. A few minutes later, Flora appeared in the doorway with two envelopes. "These are for you," she said. "One of them is your report card. I got mine too. Dad wants to know if you want to go swimming this afternoon."

"Tell him no thanks," Sadie said. "I want to finish the quilt for Millie's baby."

The Bishop Spencer envelope contained her report card, which showed that she had again led the class. There was also a note from Miss Witherspoon asking Sadie to confirm her and

Flora's attendance at Bishop Spencer. "We very much look forward to your return and will require a cheque or money order to ensure your positions. Kind personal regards, Miss M. Witherspoon." The *M*, Sadie knew, was for Margaret. The other envelope contained a letter from Teddy, who asked when Sadie would be returning to St. John's. He said he'd be home by September 3rd, which was three weeks from now. Sadie took the envelope from Bishop Spencer with her downstairs and when she was setting the table for noon dinner, put it in her father's place. Norah had everything ready: cold chicken, potato salad and rice pudding.

As soon as they were seated, Norah looked at her husband and said, "The girls received their report cards today."

"And how did you do?" Brian asked, looking at Flora.

"Good," she said. "But my writing's messy and I have to be neater about my uniform."

"How was your report card, Sadie?" Brian said.

Sadie shrugged. "It was good." She didn't say that she had led the class or that Miss Witherspoon had written *excellent work* across the bottom. She knew Brian was trying to draw her into the conversation but she didn't help him. Later when her father asked how she had spent the morning, she answered with a shrug and continued eating in unhappy silence, noticing how the Leesons exchanged looks. They were probably wondering what had got into her. It wasn't like her to be rude and hardhearted but she certainly was now. She was so hard-hearted that she didn't know if she would ever forgive her father.

Brian returned to work and after the kitchen was cleaned up, Flora and their father went swimming, leaving Sadie and Norah to work on the quilt, which they spread on the kitchen table. The piecework was finished and the lining cut and hemmed. Now all that needed to be done was to put the cotton batting between the two sides and sew them together. They worked in silence, which was unusual for them. Sadie was aware that Norah was looking at her from time to time, but it wasn't until they were finished that Norah spoke. "You'll have to look after supper tonight, Sadie. Brian and I are going to the mill supper dance. Do you think you can manage?"

"Sure." Sadie folded the quilt, which had alternating squares of pink, turquoise, yellow and blue. It was plain, what Norah called a starter quilt, but she was proud of it. "Thank you, Norah, for all your help."

Norah didn't give her the usual hug but looked at her sombrely. There were bluish smudges beneath her eyes that Sadie hadn't noticed before. Norah said, "I think I'll go upstairs for a nap before I bathe and dress. I didn't sleep very well last night."

Sadie went out to the workshop. She wanted to finish making the tiny curtains and she always felt better when she was working on the house. It was comforting to be able to make a home, even a miniature home that you could arrange the way you liked and where nothing bad ever happened. It wasn't the home in Copper Cliff. That was gone and would never come back. It wasn't the Leesons' home either. Tiny as it was, this little house meant a lot to Sadie. It was a way of imagining a home of her own.

Sadie heard her father and Flora return with Brian, but no one bothered her and she stayed in the workshop until it was time to get supper ready. She went into the kitchen and sliced tomatoes, cucumbers and ham and arranged them on a platter of lettuce. She sliced a loaf of Norah's bread and put it on the table, along with a dish of mustard pickles.

Norah came downstairs wearing a yellow dress and high-heeled shoes. The dress had a dropped waist and a bow at the hips.

"You look pretty," Sadie said and smiled. "I like your dress."

"I made it myself," Norah said. "But I don't often get to wear it."

Brian came downstairs dressed in a black suit and tie. He grumbled about the tie and before they left the house, took it off and hung it on the doorknob.

During supper Flora did most of the talking. That was one thing you could count on with Flora, Sadie thought, she could always talk. When they finished eating, Sadie's father said, "Sadie, we have to have a conversation."

"I know." She turned to Flora. "I got supper ready so you can do the dishes."

Flora didn't object and Sadie opened the screen door and went down to the deck, knowing her father would follow and that she would have to talk to him. She didn't want to talk to him, but she couldn't keep her feelings about him bottled up forever. It was too difficult. Her father came down the steps and sat in the chair opposite Sadie, his back to the lawn. He took the envelope out of his shirt pocket where he had put it during dinner and said, "You did extremely well at Bishop Spencer. Do you want to go back?"

"That depends." She had been anticipating his question.

"Depends on what?"

"On you."

"I would have thought that it depended on you and Flora, on whether you liked the school and want to go back."

"We liked it," Sadie said. "Well, I didn't at first but I got to like it. Flora liked it too. It's a good school."

"Norah tells me the school here is good."

"Are you saying you want us to stay here?"

Her father shrugged. "It's up to you to decide what you want."

Sadie said, "If it's up to me to decide, I'll tell you what I want. I want a father who doesn't hand his responsibilities to his daughter, a father who acts like a father and doesn't abandon his daughters to a mean, stingy woman so he can go off prospecting for gold. That's what I want."

Her father flinched as if he'd been slapped. "I didn't abandon you," he said.

"Yes, you did. You promised you'd come to St. John's for Easter and you didn't. Instead you went off with Gutsy Pike, leaving us to look after ourselves. Maybe you thought Mrs. Hatch would look after us but she didn't. She didn't like us and she kept complaining about not being paid. She wouldn't feed us properly and she expected us to do all her work. I fell off a stool when I was cleaning her windows and injured my tailbone and had a concussion. When you didn't remember my birthday, Flora stole five dollars from Mrs. Hatch to buy me a present, which we returned." Sadie was saying more than she'd intended but she was fed up with keeping so much inside. "And, as you already know, Mrs. Hatch went to the reverend, who cornered me after church and told me that after exams were finished he would send someone to move us to the orphanage, where Flora would sleep in a dormitory and I would work in the kitchen. We had to run away to the train station when Mrs. Hatch was in church because if she found out we were taking the train, she'd try to stop us so she could get her hands on the ticket money. Flora and I had to pretend that we were staying in school until it was over and I had to lie to Miss Witherspoon and pretend that I would be there in December to accept the blue belt, even though I didn't know if I would be. Flora couldn't tell her best friend that we were leaving. Both of us had to lie and sneak around and pretend and it was hard." By now Sadie was crying and fidgeting with a corner of her blouse. "It was so hard. I know being lost in the wilderness was hard. I know it was worse. But it was hard for us too."

"Sadie."

She looked up and saw tears streaming down her father's cheeks. He said, "You're right, I did abandon you. I'm sorry, I didn't know it was so hard for you." He reached across the table for her hand and for a while she held it because in spite of everything, he was her father. "It was selfish and shortsighted of me to leave you girls so I could pursue my dream of finding gold."

"You found it," Sadie said bitterly. "Now what will you do with all those rocks?"

"Give them to Gutsy."

"Don't you want them?"

"No." The tears kept streaming down his cheeks. "I paid too high a price. They're only gold-veined samples. If he's crazy enough, Gutsy can go back to Sop's Arm and mine the gold."

The screen door slammed and Flora came down the steps, but she didn't hang around. She walked across the lawn calling for Gobble. The interesting thing about Flora, Sadie thought, was that in spite of being a chatterbox, she knew when to say nothing. She could be so annoying, but most of the time she was exactly the sister Sadie wanted.

"So what will you do?" she asked her father.

"I'll find other work either here or in St. John's. I'll do whatever it takes to pay the bills. If we return to St. John's, I'd look for a job as a surveyor. I worked as a surveyor for a couple of years when I was younger. The main thing is being with my girls—if you'll have me. The last few days I've been thinking that you might want to stay with the Leesons and go to school here. I can see how close you are to Norah and Brian. They'd like you to stay, Norah told me as much. If you do want to stay, I'll take the bookkeeping job at the mill and find myself a room nearby. I wouldn't want to impose myself on the Leesons who've already been more than kind." Sadie's father wiped his cheeks with the back of his hand. "I know it's important for a girl, especially a girl your age, to have the influence of a woman like Norah, a woman who was close to your mother. I wouldn't want . . ."

"Stop it, Dad!"

Sadie's father looked at her, bewildered, and she thought, *He really doesn't understand what he's saying but I do. At last I have him figured out. I understand why he keeps saying "whatever you want" and "it's up to you to decide." He knows he can never replace Mum and knowing that, he's afraid he'll let me down.*

She began to explain. "When Mum was alive, before she got sick, you were away a lot of the time prospecting and Flora and I were left with her."

"Yes."

"So it was natural that when we thought of home, we thought of it as her. She was home."

"Yes."

"Then she died and we moved to Newfoundland and you went away again, so we had no home."

"No."

"You see, Dad, because we don't live with Mum any more, the word for home has changed."

"It has?"

Sadie felt a flash of impatience, but it vanished as quickly as it came because she realized with sudden clarity that she understood home better than her father and that she had to help him understand what it meant. She also realized that his not being able to understand had something to do with the loss of her mother, that without her he didn't have the confidence to believe that he was as important to Sadie and Flora as he was.

"Home isn't a place, Dad. It's you. The word for home is you."

Once again he reached across the table for her hand and this time she held on to it.

Flora appeared with Gobble from behind the swing where she had been avoiding bed and listening. She came up to their father and kissed his cheek. "And it's Sadie and me."

Sadie's father stood up and moved three chairs together and sat down again, a daughter on either side. For a while the three of them sat looking at the garden, at the way the sun spilled the last of its golden light onto the grass and transformed the tips of the spruce trees into golden spires. When their father finally broke the silence, he sounded stronger and more decisive. "I think we should find ourselves a place to live in St. John's," he said, "not too far from Bishop Spencer."

"Or Teddy Dodge," Flora said.

Why not? Sadie thought. She wouldn't mind living close to Teddy.

"Could we come back here next summer?" Flora said.

"I think so."

Pressing the advantage, Flora said, "Can I have a kitten?"

"Sure, and maybe a dog."

"I don't want a dog," Flora said. "I want a parrot."

"Could we live in a house with a bathtub and good beds?" asked Sadie.

"I don't see why not."

"And you won't leave us again?"

"No, I won't leave you again."

Should she make him promise? Sadie knew that her father was feeling so badly that he would promise her anything, but she didn't want to make him promise. It was better, she thought, watching the sun releasing its hold on the day, to rely on trust.

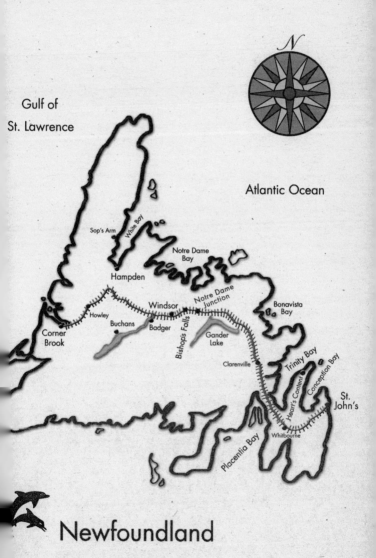

Gulf of
St. Lawrence

Atlantic Ocean

Sop's Arm
White Bay

Notre Dame
Bay

Hampden

Windsor
Notre Dame
Junction

Bonavista
Bay

Howley
Buchans
Badger
Bishop's Falls

Corner
Brook

Gander Lake

Clarenville

Trinity Bay

Hear's Content
Conception Bay

St.
John's

Placentia Bay

Whitbourne

Newfoundland

Acknowledgements

I WOULD LIKE TO THANK ST. JOHN'S HISTORIAN PAUL
O'Neill, Anglican Synod archivist, Julia Matheson, the city of
St. John's archivist Helen Miller, and Memorial University
Newfoundland Studies archivist Bert Riggs for help in providing information about the city in 1926-7. Thanks also to Penny
Hansen for "lending" me her house on Willicott's Lane. I am
indebted to Bishop Spencer graduates Helen Whiteway, Sonia
May and especially Elizabeth Reynolds, who read the manu-
script and was in all ways generous with her time. Two other
graduates, Jane Crosbie and Jean Murray, also provided information pertinent to the story. Thanks to Anne Hart and Norah
Lester for reading an early draft, Rachel Dragland for reading a
later draft, Mary Adachi for a vigorous copyedit and Cynthia
Good for her ongoing editorial help and enthusiasm. As well, I
am indebted to the Canada Council for its financial assistance
during the writing of the first draft.

Although I have used the name Bishop Spencer and have
tried to be true to the spirit of the school, all the characters and
incidents in the story, including those who attended or taught
in the school, are fictitious. Once a landmark of old St. John's,
the building that once housed Bishop Spencer was destroyed

by fire in November 1999 and was subsequently razed to the ground. Plans are underway to erect a statue at Rawlin's Cross to mark the importance of the school in the lives of the people of Newfoundland. The statue will depict a girl in a Bishop Spencer uniform.

Joan Clark
St. John's

Joan Clark

ISBN 0140249508

Eiriksdottir
A Tale of Dreams and Luck

Nearly one thousand years ago, the Greenlanders and the Icelanders left their homes to seek Vinland, a land both mythical and real. Leading the Greenlanders to their new found land was Thorvard and his enigmatic wife, Freydis, daughter of the notorious Eirik the Red and sister of Leif the Lucky. Was Freydis a manipulator who incited a bloody massacre, or a bold-spirited and resourceful leader?

"Clark blends fact and fantasy to create a novel reinventing the history we thought we knew so well." —The Newfoundland Herald

ISBN 0140386297

The Dream Carvers

Winner of the Geoffrey Bilson Award and the Mr. Christie's Book Award, *The Dream Carvers* is the story of Thrand, a Norse boy in the eleventh century who is captured by the Beothuk, the red ochre people of the new found land. At first his thoughts are only of his home in Greenland, and he struggles with his sense of identity as he lives among people so different from him. But slowly he adjusts to the world of Beothuk, learning their language and their ways.

"The Dream Carvers creates a compelling world to itself. Clark's style is straightforward and deceptively simple, directing all her efforts toward telling a story that has its own inner momentum." —The Globe and Mail